Insatiable

Insatiable

Sherri L. King

Elizabeth Jewell

S. L. Carpenter

Pocket Books

New York London Toronto Sydney

This book is a work of fiction. Names, characters, places, and incidents either are products of the author's imagination or are used fictitiously. Any resemblance to actual events or locales or persons, living or dead, is entirely coincidental.

Published by arrangement with Ellora's Cave Publishing, Inc.

First Pocket Books trade paperback edition August 2007

POCKET and colophon are registered trademarks of Simon & Schuster, Inc.

Designed by Carla Jayne Little

Manufactured in the United States of America

10 9 8 7 6 5 4 3 2 1

For information about special discounts for bulk purchases, please contact Simon & Schuster Special Sales at 1-800-456-6798 or business@simonandschuster.com

ISBN-13: 978-1-4165-3617-8
ISBN-10: 1-4165-3617-5

Contents

Prologue

It had been seven days since she'd seen another living soul. Seeing the new faces staring at her now from out of the shadows of the church, she was almost afraid, even knowing that the stares belonged to humans and not zombies. But it couldn't be helped—there was no way she was going back out tonight.

"We don't want you here," said one of the women in a shaky, frightened voice. "This is *our* hiding place."

"I don't give a rat's ass what you want," Anna gritted out as she squatted down to tighten the laces on her calf-length boots. "I'm staying here for the night. Suck it up and deal with it and we'll all be happier, okay?"

"How did you get in here anyway?"

Anna drolly eyed the man who'd asked the question. "Through the window in the bathroom."

"Shit, now they'll get in here, you stupid—"

"Hey! Listen to yourself. You have to know by now that they can't cross onto consecrated ground. A broken window into this place isn't going to endanger anyone," Anna pointed out.

"If that's true then why aren't there more survivors?" The woman's eyes were wide with a traumatized look of shock.

Anna sighed and gentled her approach. It wasn't these people's fault that the world had suddenly turned topsy-turvy. "Look, I don't have all the answers. I just kill the bastards. I stayed out too late tonight gathering supplies to get back to the graveyard where I've been hiding, so here I am. Deal with it already."

"It's fine, really," said the man. "Calm down, Liz, we're still safe."

"What's your name?" Anna asked him.

"I'm Ray, this is my wife, Liz." He turned to look at the others huddled behind him. "That's Tawny, Frank and Doug. We've been here almost a week, pretty much since this whole nightmare began. Who are you?"

"My name's Anna. And you're lucky you found a hiding place here. I haven't seen anyone in almost seven days. Well, anyone living, that is."

"How do you know so much about them?" Ray frowned questioningly.

"Who, the zombies? I don't know. Just lucky, I guess."

"You go out around them in the daylight?"

"Well, they're a lot slower in the sunshine, haven't you noticed? Much easier to kill that way."

"You kill them?" Ray asked incredulously.

"What else would you do with them?"

"But . . . they're human."

"No, they're not," Anna snorted. "They're nothing *close* to human anymore."

"How do you know?" This from Doug who was huddled nervously in the background.

"Haven't you ever read any zombie novels? Watched any horror movies? It's all pretty easy. I don't know why fiction has suddenly turned to reality, but I know enough to stay alive while the world turns on its axis. You should too."

Tawny sighed heavily. "We haven't left this place since it started. Back then there were twelve of us. Those who leave never come back. We're stuck here until help comes . . ." Her words faded into an uncertain silence.

"Help isn't coming. And you're not stuck here. But you are safer here than most anywhere else," Anna told her gently. "The zombies burn on consecrated ground. I've been staying in a graveyard since this started, only going out by day to get food and supplies for when I make a break for the marina."

"You're thinking to sail away from this?" Ray asked.

"Yeah." She smiled. "I've got a simple little sailboat out there waiting. You're all welcome to come with me, but you'll have to carry your own weight. I don't have time to play babysitter."

"You're crazy," Liz spat.

"Maybe so, but I'll be out of here and off to freedom in a few days. Where will you be?" Anna responded hotly, looking up at Liz from behind the heavy fall of her long auburn hair.

Liz only growled in response.

"Look, Anna . . . was it?" Ray tried to play diplomat between the two of them. "I can see you look like you know what you're doing. But we've been here for so long, seeing no one, you have to understand that we're a little paranoid. It's hard to trust you so soon."

"Desperate times call for desperate measures, but I understand. I do. Just let me camp out here tonight and whoever wants to come with me tomorrow is more than welcome to."

"I don't want to die here," Doug said suddenly.

"Then you won't die here if I can help it," Anna promised him, not knowing exactly where her selfless words had come from. She was used to fending for herself, even before this hell on earth, but here she was inviting strangers along in her escape. She was even vowing to look out for them, much as she could. She didn't understand herself, but there it was. Perhaps the end of the world had changed her. Hopefully it was for the better, or they'd all end up dead.

"What's happening out there?" Tawny asked.

"A lot of bad shit." Anna shook her head. "Those zombies are all over the place. I don't know what happened, but in less than seven days everyone out there is either dead or undead. Like I said, you're the first people I've seen in a while. There might be more survivors in the other churches throughout the city, but for some reason I doubt it. Anyway, I haven't gone to look. I've been too busy."

"How do you know that help isn't coming?"

"I *don't* know. The radio's nothing but static and I can't check the television because there's no power. After seven days of this, though, I seriously doubt that help is coming. I'm thinking it's more likely that there'll be an air strike or something to obliterate this city. That is, if the plague hasn't spread outside the city limits."

"You really have watched too many horror movies," Liz said, but her tone was growing friendlier.

"Hey, I calls 'em like I sees 'em," she quipped. "And it was those horror movies and scary novels that have gotten me this far."

"What did you do before all of this?" Ray asked curiously.

"I was a yoga instructor." Anna smiled slightly and wondered if she'd ever see her little dojo again.

"So all the practice in meditative peace and serenity has trained you to be a zombie killer?" Liz laughed.

"Hey, I'm not about to die without putting up a fight," Anna answered. "I'm fit and full of endurance because of my practice, and if this is how I was meant to put it to use then that's what I'll do. There's no way in hell that I want to end up like those things out there." She sighed and went to sit on one of the many benches. "So what did all of you do? Before?"

"I was a mechanic," Ray answered. "My wife was an administrative assistant."

"I was a dentist," Tawny supplied.

"I was a security guard," Frank piped in.

"And I was an unemployed screenwriter," Doug answered with a wan smile.

"Well, hopefully, once we get out of this city, we can all return to our daily lives."

"But you don't think so," Ray observed.

"I don't know what to think," Anna admitted. "But I'm not going to get my hopes up too high. What I want to do now is get enough food and fuel to get my boat out on the water and find a nice deserted island to lay low on for a year or so."

"How did this happen?" Tawny sobbed softly.

"I don't know for certain, but I'll bet it has something to do with the disease control center in the middle of the city." Anna sighed and leaned back in the pew. "Now if you don't mind—I'm beat. At dawn I'll go out again and those of you that want to come help can. Otherwise I'll say my goodbyes with the first rays of the sun."

She settled back and closed her eyes, not opening them again until the sun shone through the stained glass windows of the small church.

Chapter One

The time has *come again to defend the Earth, for Pestilence has been unleashed.*

Enigma opened his eyes and looked around. "Is this why have you awakened me from my slumber?"

You have been in a warrior's stasis for nearly a hundred years. It is time once again for you to fight. The Earth is in danger and all of its peoples with it. You must save those you can and destroy those you cannot.

"I will do my duty for my people and the people of Earth."

There is someone near, a human woman, who can help you keep our peace accord assured. Find her and Gift her with Sanctuary and you shall once again know glory.

"I shall find her."

Then go. And do not fail. The future of all worlds is at stake.

"*Is that the* last of the canned goods?"

"Only one more box to go, Anna," Frank answered as he shoved a flat of canned corn into the back of the SUV.

"Ray, do you see anything?"

"Just a few stragglers wandering around a ways down the street, no one really aggressive."

"See, I told you—they're weaker in the daylight. They don't even notice us—just keep the gun pointed at them in case they actually come toward us."

"I only wish I'd known this two days ago when we started running low on food," he answered with a grin.

"Yeah, those vending machines at the church could only go so far with all of us," Liz supplied as she dropped off several boxes of dried cereal.

"Well, I wish that I'd had all of you to help me this past week. I didn't know just how much more work could be done," Anna laughed. "Come on, there's only an hour of daylight left. Let's get a move on." She hopped into the cab of the vehicle. "Everyone hang on tight and we'll get to the graveyard in a few minutes."

"At least we don't have to worry about stoplights," Frank chuckled.

"Yeah, but the traffic will be hell," Tawny quipped back.

And the traffic *was* hell. The roadway was full of wrecked and abandoned vehicles. Debris and litter dotted the ground like confetti, and a few bodies here and there slowed their progress considerably. That so much chaos and damage had been done in such a short time was a shock to all of them, but Anna managed to maneuver the vehicle through the maze of debris with relative ease, hopping curbs and sidewalks whenever she could.

None of them dared to look at the dead and fallen victims too closely. No one wanted to chance seeing someone they had once known and cared for. It was an unspoken agreement amongst all of them that they not mention those they had lost. In desperate times such losses were felt keenly and it would do them no good to mourn just yet.

As they arrived at the graveyard where Anna had been staying they were so frazzled and nerve-racked from the drive, it was no surprise that they almost hit him. "Holy shit!" Anna swerved the SUV and hit several grave markers before coming to a skidding halt. "What *was* that?"

For a moment she was sure she'd seen a man—but how could that be possible? Anna looked out her window in disbelief.

Indeed it was a man. And he was naked. Gloriously so.

Was he a zombie?

No, he looked whole and alive. The zombies looked like any Hollywood horror, with dead gray flesh and bloody wounds. This man . . . looked good enough to eat.

Anna stamped down on her libido with gritted teeth. No way was the sight of a naked man going to get her all hot and bothered like some giddy schoolgirl. She jumped down from the cab and approached him cautiously. "Hey, mister. Are you all right?"

"I am well. I am here to save the world."

His voice sounded like the ringing of a hundred iron bells.

It was difficult, but Anna managed to hold back her bark of laughter. "Were you planning on saving the world in your skivvies?"

He looked at her strangely.

"We have some extra clothes that might fit you, if you like."

"You are she," he said at last. He walked toward her so that she had to back up or be touched by him.

"Yeah, I'm she," she said sarcastically. "Look, as much as I hate to tell you to get dressed, you're going to have to or catch cold tonight. We'll be staying down in the crypt so we don't have to hear the zombies, and it's nearly freezing down there."

"I have no time for sleep," he said, cocking his head curiously, as if he thought she should know this. "And neither do you."

"Frank, will you bring me some pants and a shirt for this guy? Oh, and maybe a jacket, too. He seems a little dazed," Anna called out, never taking her eyes off the stranger.

"Maybe he's infected," Liz said.

"No," Anna answered. "If he were, he wouldn't be able to set foot on this blessed soil."

Frank brought her the clothes, while warily avoiding getting too close to the nude man. "I hope you're right about that, Anna."

"Oh, I am. You can count on that." She'd seen too many of the bastards go up in smoke when they dared to try and set foot inside the graveyard fence.

Dusk was swiftly approaching, the orange glow of the setting sun catching like fire in the stranger's shoulder-length, whitish-blond hair.

Anna eyed him curiously. He looked normal enough—nothing like the zombies. But . . . different somehow from any man she'd ever seen. She couldn't put her finger on it, but there was something truly alien about the man. Perhaps it was in the way he stood, so unashamed in his nudity. Or in the incredible width of his heavily muscled shoulders. Or perhaps it had to do with his height—he was well over six feet tall, long of limb and torso and graceful in his height, which had to be a feat unto itself.

Or maybe it was in his sex. Long and thick and full, it was a sight that might have sent her swooning with lust in any other situation. Even unaroused, he was a stallion of a man. She wondered where he had come from. He looked capable enough to have survived the plague, but where had he been hiding all this time? Why had he come to the graveyard now, after hiding such a long time elsewhere?

"You are she," he reiterated. "I will need your help."

Anna frowned. "I'll help you, just put these on, okay?"

He took the clothes and looked at them as if they were foreign objects. "We have no time to waste," he told her after a few moments.

"What's your name?" she asked.

"I am Enigma."

Anna laughed, then choked her mirth back again. "Are you injured anywhere? Like your head, maybe?"

"I am not jesting with you, woman."

"Okay, *Enigma*. My name is Anna, not woman, and these are my friends. Get dressed and we'll talk about where you came from and how you managed to get here unhurt, all right?"

"An-na." He said the name softly, liltingly in that bell-toned voice of his. A soft shiver traced its way down her back, as if he'd trailed his finger down her naked flesh.

He put the clothes on, awkward in his movements where he had been nothing but graceful before. He didn't seem at all used to wearing clothing.

Maybe he was a nudist. Anna almost laughed out loud at the thought and she wasn't even sure why. Lots of odd things had seemed funny to her lately.

"We need to make up a shift, to take turns keeping an eye out for anything," she told her comrades.

"I thought the zombies couldn't come in here," Liz said in a high, frightened voice.

"We aren't looking out for the zombies. We looking out for other survivors," she clarified. "People like Enigma here."

"I hope we see some more," Tawny said.

"I don't. I'm not willing to capsize my little sailboat for the sake of goodwill," Anna said testily, not really meaning it, but liking how tough and capable it made her sound. A lot had changed in the past week, her perhaps most of all.

The plague had struck without warning, taking almost everyone with it in a matter of days. Before, Anna had been a peace-loving yoga nut. Now she was a survivor, and she meant to keep it that way no matter what. If that made her soulless, then so be it. She wasn't ready to die, and she sure as hell wasn't ready to become one of the living dead.

She'd seen her best friend and business partner become one of the zombies. Johanna had been bitten that first day and within hours she'd died. Anna had sat back and watched it all, not knowing what to do, racked with guilt and sorrow because she hadn't been able to save her friend. When Johanna rose from the dead, Anna had almost been too late to pull the trigger of her gun. If she'd waited half a second longer she, too, would have met the same fate as her friend.

Everyone Anna had known and loved was now dead. She almost hated herself for surviving, but she would do what she must to make it out of this living hell with her wits and her health intact. She would think of her many losses later, at her leisure.

As far as she was concerned it was every man and woman for themselves. But she'd still do her best to make sure her new acquaintances survived long enough to make it out to sea. How she could manage it was a conundrum, but then she'd never been one to back down from a challenge and she wasn't about to start now.

The marina was an hour's drive away. How they'd make it there without encountering some zombies, she wasn't willing to hazard a guess.

Better to face that inevitability when they came to it.

Chapter Two

His mouth played havoc over her breasts. Anna arched up into his kiss, wanting—no, needing—him to devour her completely. She felt as if she were dying on the inside, wanting him to take her so badly she could have expired from the force of her desire.

"This is a dream," she gasped. "I don't even know you, how can I want you this badly?"

"Dreams are sometimes far more real than our waking hours," he said against the full swell of her nipple. "You want me inside of you," he whispered. "Don't you?"

Anna gasped as he nipped her skin, twisting her nipple delicately between his teeth. "Yes, I want you inside of me," she gasped. "Now."

"Patience, my lovely. Let me learn you more."

His hands skittered down her body, pausing to investigate her curves and hollows with great and thorough interest. Anna moaned as his palm pressed into her pussy, kneading the moist, heated flesh of her arousal until she was mindless to all else.

"Taste me," she begged shamelessly.

He moved down her body, his skin rasping over hers as he shifted. He pushed her thighs wide apart with his hands. Anna arched up, seeking him. His mouth—oh god!—his mouth came down, open over her sex. His tongue speared her. His lips suckled her. His teeth . . .

Anna screamed as he found her clit. "Yes, yes, yes."

Enigma moaned into her flesh, vibrating it. Her body flooded with desire and her pussy became drenched with her passionate juices. His fingers came up to play with her back entrance. He traced the seam of her buttocks and delved even deeper within. His fingertip pressed into the dark, forbidden opening of her anus and she bucked in response, driving her pussy deeper into his mouth.

"I'm going to fuck you dry," he promised.

"Oh please," she begged, wanting everything he had to offer her.

His dark wings came forward and covered them both like a blanket that blocked out all sight and sound of the world beyond, and the dream was gone from her.

Anna awoke with a gasp, startled to find herself inside the crypt where she'd waited on the dawn for the past week. Her body felt as though it were still aflame from Enigma's touch and she tamped down on her desire.

With a sigh she tried once more to sleep, but it was a long time in coming.

"I must speak with you." Enigma approached Anna a few hours later while she stood just outside the crypt door, taking her shift as lookout. He'd put on the jogging suit, though it barely fit him with all his bulging muscles underneath.

"Are you feeling better now?" she asked, knowing Liz had made him some warm noodle soup. She did her best not to look at him too closely, still wrapped up in the forbidden memory of her dream.

He sat down next to her in the grass. The dark made his hair look like a bright halo around his head and shoulders. "Yes. I am not so disoriented as I was. It happens sometimes, when we fold space from our world to this one."

Anna rolled her eyes. "So you're not okay. Here, let me see if you have any head injuries."

"I have no injuries and you know it. You had Tawny check me." He smiled at her, ultra-white teeth blazing. "You think me mad?"

"I think you're overstressed. Hell, we all are. It's a wonder we're not all acting kooky like you," she sighed.

"You are gifted, it is easier for you than the others."

"Gifted? Oh yeah, I feel really gifted," she scoffed. "It's the end of the world and here I am caught in the middle of it. It's a real fuckin' field trip."

"It is not the end. It is merely a transition."

"How would you know?"

"I know many things. For instance, I know that this plague has not yet reached beyond the borders of this city. But Pestilence will see that it does, if you do not help me to stop it."

Anna looked at him incredulously. "You are totally crazy, do you know that? You're telling me it's been a whole fucking week and this plague hasn't spread beyond the city? I don't believe that—if the government knew enough to quarantine us they would have sent in troops to help or something."

"I know not how your government conducts its business, but I would hazard a guess that they have been busy keeping this plague contained. Sending in reinforcements would have only fed the plague, not controlled it, and they must have known this."

"So they're just going to cut their losses, is that what you're trying to say?"

"That is correct. And you are being given a chance to ensure that this plague does not spread beyond the borders of this city. You can keep many lives safe if you but try."

"What the hell can I do to stop this?"

He smiled at her gently. "You've been chosen by my people to fight this battle."

She shook her head and looked away. "You are totally nuts."

"I am not, and if you look deep inside of yourself you will know I am telling you the truth."

"That I'm chosen, whatever that means?"

"You are chosen. I am a Fae, ancient and endless. My people watch over these lands of Earth to protect them from evil. Now is the time of evil, and I have been sent to stop its curse from spreading over all the land. You have already killed many of these abominations on your own, rising to the fray like any seasoned warrior, and I am come to gift you with an even greater power, one that will keep you immune from their taint."

"You're a Fae? As in fairy? Right. How do you expect me to believe something like that?" she exclaimed.

"You believe in zombies now, do you not, where a few days ago you would have scoffed at the very idea."

"That's not fair and you know it."

"Then hear me out. I will prove to you that I am what I say. And you must agree to help me, else the whole world might be lost."

"How can you prove something like that to me, Enigma?" She spat out his name like a curse.

"Like this," he said, pulling off his shirt. He gave her his back and she gasped at the sight.

His spine was covered in crimson fur.

His flesh rippled and the fur expanded into wings that shot straight out at her. Anna screamed her surprise and he turned to quickly silence her with his hand over her mouth. She couldn't tear her eyes away from his furred wings, which now fanned out behind him like a cape.

It was just like her dream.

"Do not let the others know. This knowledge is only for you," he warned her with a steely look in his pale blue eyes. He lowered his hand, and she gasped for air.

"*Ohmygod, ohmygod, ohmygod,*" she chanted.

"Anna, why does this shock you so after all you have seen?"

She couldn't think of an answer, so surprised was she still.

A loud noise at the edge of the graveyard drew her attention. It was one of the zombies from the crowd that had permanently gathered outside the gates. He'd strayed too close and had caught fire. And even though Anna knew she was safe enough from them where she was, she still waited and watched to be sure that the zombie died before he made any further progress into the boundary of the fence and gate. When she looked back at Enigma the wings were gone again, retracted underneath the red fur that traced down the middle of his back.

"Why in the hell didn't I see that before, when you were buck naked?"

"I used a glamour to hide it. See." He turned to let her see his back again, but the crimson fur had disappeared completely from view.

"I think I'm going to pass out," Anna groaned.

Enigma ignored her. "We must stop the plague from escaping the city. Your people have quarantined the area, but humans cannot control this plague for long. It took your government three days to respond to this threat, but luckily none of the undying who escaped the borders were allowed to live. The military and disease control groups have seen to it that no more infected can escape and no outsiders are allowed in. But the efforts of your government only delay the spread of the disease; they do not completely prevent it. You and I, we must be the ones to fight and destroy these abominations and ensure that the plague does not spread."

She looked at him incredulously. "I'm leaving the day after tomorrow with them." She gestured to the crypt behind her. "I'm setting sail for some deserted island and I'm never coming back here."

"There isn't any time left. An air strike is already being

planned by your military. If you and your friends are to leave then you would have to do so tonight."

"What? Why didn't you say something sooner?" she screeched.

"You needed your rest." He eyed her devilishly.

Did he know about her dream?

Anna brushed her suspicions aside. "I am *not* going to help you fight some battle."

"Then you have doomed mankind."

"Oh fuck you, buddy. Like I need that extra guilt on my conscience after the past week of killing people with faces I remember from better days," she spat.

"You have killed monsters—there is no shame or guilt to be had in that. But you must do more. Bond with me and I will give you Sanctuary from their taint. Fight with me and you will win immortality and the right to dwell with my people."

"Oh, good grief. I can't believe this is happening," she wailed, looking toward the crowd of waiting zombies. "It's like some kind of sick, twisted nightmare."

"Believe it. And know that you must rise in your duty to save your people from this horrible curse. For if you do not help me, no one else will."

"I don't believe that."

"Will you bond with me?"

Damn it. Did she really have a choice? "How do I bond with you—and if you don't tell me it's through sex or anything kinky, I *might* do it."

He smiled a devilishly wicked smile and she felt her belly do a thousand flip-flops in its wake. "A kiss. A willing kiss is all I ask to gift you with Sanctuary."

"Sanctuary, eh? And after this kiss I'll be immune from the zombies?"

"Yes."

Anna swallowed hard and thought about it. To be free of the plague would be an incredible boon. But why her, why no one else? Why hadn't he found someone better prepared for such a thing? Why couldn't he give this Sanctuary to all of them?

Searching for answers to all the whys would drive her insane if she let it. "Fine. One kiss," she agreed at last. "But only if you promise to help me get my new friends out of here safely. Then I'll help you all you want."

"Done." He smiled again and leaned into her.

Damn, how did she get herself into this mess? She closed her eyes and prepared for the kiss. But nothing, absolutely nothing, could have prepared her for the press of his lips on hers.

A bolt of sheer electricity washed through her, making her nearly black out with its intensity. His lips pressed onto hers like a fire that burned straight down into her soul. She gasped and his tongue found entrance into her mouth, moving at once to stroke alongside hers. He tasted of sunlight and trees and crisp, clean waters, making her head swim with overwhelming sensation.

He caught her wrists in his hands and brought her arms up around his neck. He sank deeper into her, lowering them to the ground, catching each of her panting breaths within his mouth. His arms went around her, pulling her close and tight against his hard, muscular body.

Bright lights danced behind her closed lids, mesmerizing her. Her heart thundered and her nipples tightened against his well-muscled chest. One of his hands trailed down over her neck and chest, moving to cup a pebble-peaked breast, and the kiss changed dramatically.

Something warm and effervescent seemed to flow from his mouth into hers. She opened her eyes and saw that a golden glow had enveloped them both. His fingers pinched and pulled at her nipples and the glow brightened, blinding her.

With a cry she pushed free of him and rolled away, jumping to her feet as the glow subsided. "You perv! I should have known the kiss was just an excuse to get your paws on me."

"You are quite beautiful. I could not resist," he teased, a grin playing around the corners of his lips.

"What just happened?"

"I have given you the power to be free of the plague's taint."

"It glowed."

"Such is the power of Fae. And now you have some of that power within you."

She frowned thoughtfully for a moment, wondering at the possibilities. "I'm going to go get the others. We'll leave here in the next thirty minutes if I have to drag everyone out. And you—" she pointed at him angrily, "you stay right there until I come back out. You can take the watch. Who knows, maybe your *Fae* magic can help you weed out some more survivors or something," she said sarcastically.

He laughed as she turned to go, and it was all she could do to keep from screaming her frustration out into the night.

Chapter Three

She was a warrior princess, this he could clearly see. It was no wonder she'd been chosen by his people. Not only did she have everyone ready and in the vehicle before the thirty minutes were out, but she'd also loaded up all the extra supplies she'd stockpiled herself over the past few days.

She was a fighter and a survivor, but she was also a vixen. A beautiful goddess of form and grace. With her rich auburn hair and green eyes, delicate skin and lithe form she had almost a Fae look about her, though she was definitely human. He'd never seen a human so lovely, and his people were well known for their love of humans. Especially human women.

"C'mon, let's get a move on here, Enigma," she called to him as she climbed back into the SUV. He joined her in the front seat and tried not to stare at her incredibly long legs as she pressed her foot to the gas and started the vehicle on its journey.

"How do you know they're going to bomb the city?" Tawny asked curiously.

"Uh, he's in the military," Anna answered for him when he refused to respond to the question.

"Is he a deserter? Is that why he was in the graveyard with no clothes on?" Liz demanded.

"I already told you that's classified," Anna pointed out. "Just be glad he happened to be here tonight or else we would have all been fried come morning."

"And you're not coming with us—I just don't understand it."

"Neither do I, Liz. But it's the way things have to be. I'll be fine and so will our Enigma here. Just wait and see."

Enigma merely smiled and let her work her way through the explanations with her comrades. While he did so, he watched her maneuver the vehicle with deft efficiency through the throng of zombies outside the cemetery gates.

It had been centuries since he'd ventured into the human world and much had changed. No longer did the world move on the backs of horses or camels. Now it moved on technology, on fossil-burning machines and computers. Enigma wondered if any of his brothers-in-arms had been here in recent times to see the wonders for themselves.

It was too bad that the fate of those wonders rested on his shoulders and those of a human woman.

He knew that if they failed in their mission, all would eventually perish and the world would become a hotbed of undead minions wandering about the lands. This he must never let happen, even if it meant his death. It was his duty and it would be done. And he would do everything in his power to keep the lovely Anna safe.

It wasn't odd that a Fae and a human should join forces together. It was well-known among his people that humans were strong and valiant allies. Sometimes, when necessity called, a Fae would bond with a human such as he had done with Anna. And Anna was truly a gifted human. She was strong and fit and full of endless courage. That she had survived this long in such dire circumstances was a testament to her abilities, and one that very much impressed him.

She'd taken these human stragglers under her wing as well, though he well knew she would deny it if he pointed it out. Her leadership abilities had ensured the survival of not only herself but now these new friends of hers, and soon she would be put to the test in a mission to save the world from a similar fate as this poor, lost city.

And this wasn't the first time Pestilence had plagued the Earth. It had happened in Roanoke, Virginia, once and another time in Atlantis. Both times the Fae, despite their love of humans, had been forced to obliterate the area to keep the plague from spreading. This time though, the humans would obliterate the city themselves and save the Fae the trouble.

It was up to Enigma to find this Pestilence, secreted away in an underground laboratory in the heart of Willoughby Bay, and destroy it before it was released in the blast. If he failed, the plague would become airborne and destroy the world and everyone in it in a matter of weeks. If Anna helped him, he would make sure that she was rewarded mightily.

Already he was growing enamored of her. His kind could rarely resist the great lure of a human female, and he was no exception. He wondered if the elders who had sent him on this quest had known he would find the woman much to his liking. He had little doubt that they had indeed foreseen the possibility.

Her kiss had tasted like sweet wine on his lips and tongue. Her flavor haunted him still.

He couldn't wait to kiss her again. And perhaps they would do other things as well. He would do his best to make it so. But for now he would sit back and wait. Perhaps she would make the first move if he were patient enough.

Chapter Four

"Run. Don't look back, just *run."* Anna urged the group farther down the pier toward her waiting boat, waving her free hand as she turned to fire a gun with the other. A hundred or more of the zombies were less than a dozen yards behind them and closing quite fast. She was no marksman, but she was quite proud when she felled two of them with well-aimed shots to their heads.

"Ray! Here are my keys, take them and go!"

"But what about you? You'll never make it past those bastards."

"Don't worry about me. I'll be fine with Enigma—just go, please."

Ray took the keys from her and sprinted the last few yards toward the boat. He hopped in with the others while Anna untied the docking ropes. "She'll be fine using the motor until you get farther out and unfurl the sail. Just be sure you get far enough up the coast before the air strike or else she'll rock too hard and you'll run the risk of capsizing," she told them.

"Are you sure you won't come, Anna?"

"I'm sure, Ray." Anna held a silent hope that she was making the right decision, because truth to tell she wasn't sure. She simply wasn't sure about anything much anymore.

The motor caught and started with a low hum, and before another minute had passed, Anna's new friends were already adrift and heading out of the bay with as much speed as the boat possessed.

Anna turned back and gasped as she bumped into Enigma's chest.

"Now what?" she demanded, hoping that her heated blush wasn't too noticeable in the dark.

"Now we go and find the poison that is responsible for this destruction."

"How? Our way is blocked by those things, and even though you say I'm immune to them, it doesn't mean they won't still tear me limb from limb if they catch me."

"Then we must not let them catch you." He smiled devilishly as he reached out and enveloped her in his arms. Anna pushed at him to escape, but he was immovable as stone. There was a great whoosh as his crimson-furred wings unfurled themselves, and just as the first zombie reached them they were airborne.

Anna screamed and held on for dear life.

"I won't drop you," he laughed down at her.

He thought he'd never seen anyone as beautiful as she, held safe in his arms.

She thought he was having way too much fun doing this, while she was completely terrified.

"Where are we going? Where is this poison you mentioned? How can we stop it?"

"Think hard and you will know where we are going," he told her.

Anna thought as best she could despite her terror of their flight. "There's a disease control facility in the middle of the city. I thought that maybe the plague had started there—it seemed the only logical assumption at the time."

"It was most logical. We will look there for the source."

"How will you know what we're looking for?"

"I will know."

"Then let's head that way." She pointed out the direction, hoping she was right. Everything looked different from their vantage point, several stories up in the air.

Enigma picked up speed immediately. Anna hid her face against him as the wind cold-burned her exposed skin and held on for dear life.

She tried her best to ignore his erection, but with it pressed so tight against her belly it was an effort in futility.

"I want you," he said simply, as he pressed himself tighter against her.

She wanted him too, but she wasn't about to admit to it.

"Would you have me?" he asked her softly, his warm breath stirring the thick hair at her neck.

"Now's not the time," she squeaked.

"One must find time where one can."

"I can't have sex with you in the air. Are you crazy?"

"When we land, then will you be willing?"

"I thought we were pressed for time," she pointed out.

He grinned down at her. "We are. But there is always time for love."

"Love!" she exclaimed incredulously. "Who said anything about love?"

"I did. And you will soon."

"You're totally insane. I'm totally insane. This whole thing is insane and I can't take any more of it. No more talk of love. I won't listen to it."

"I know there is much in you I could love. Soon you will learn the same about me. We are destined, you and I."

"Oh my god, I can't believe I'm listening to this crap. Look, you haven't known me for more than a few hours. No way do you love me, so don't say it. I hate lies," she spat. "Especially lies to get into my pants."

"I do not lie. You will see this eventually. I am patient enough to wait." He pressed a kiss to her temple. "We have a hundred lifetimes to make you believe."

She growled and tried not to melt against him as they flew unfettered through the cold night air.

Chapter Five

The city was deserted. Debris was everywhere. Wrecked vehicles dotted the streets, and a few small fires burned, casting an eerie orange glow about the empty streets. Trash and glass covered every square inch of ground, making it difficult to walk around without tripping.

"Tell me again why we don't just leave here and forget about all this," she urged him.

"If your people bomb this place the plague will become airborne, and the entire world would be in danger of obliteration."

"Oh. Right."

Enigma took her hand and led her through the broken glass door of the disease clinic. "This place is much bigger than it looks. A few levels are below ground. The plague will be down there, where security would be tightest."

"I don't know how we're going to figure out what to take from here. I don't know the first thing about chemicals."

"I will know it when I see it," he assured her.

They walked deeper in the pitch-black building, and with every step Anna felt as if she were leaving her old life behind her for good.

"I don't like this," she said quietly.

He stopped and pulled her into his arms. "I will let nothing happen to you, do not worry."

She held tight to him for several seconds before pushing away again, reveling in the new feeling of safety where she hadn't felt safe at all in the past week.

And that was when she slid in the puddle of blood.

Enigma caught her, but not before she saw the body the blood belonged to.

"Oh shit," she cried, quickly looking away from the gruesome sight.

She had killed many in the past week, but none of them had been human. Seeing this person now, she was reminded that all the zombies she'd felled had once been living just as she was. It wrenched at her soul, frightening her as nothing else had before.

Enigma seemed to understand without her having to tell him. "Don't think about it. Just know that you put those poor creatures out of their misery. It was you or them, and I am glad you had the strength to look out for yourself."

There was a sound behind them and Anna whirled to see a zombie running toward them. Without thinking she drew her gun out of her belt and shot it in the head, felling it but a few feet away from them. Seeing the corpse of the zombie and the human so close together had her biting back a sudden sting of tears.

"I can't take this anymore," she said. "Let's find that fucking plague and get the hell out of here. I can't wait for them to raze this city to the ground."

They walked on hand in hand, in a silence both eerie and total. The only sound was the scrape of their soft footsteps in the dark.

Then Anna could stand it no longer. "Why did your people choose me?"

"Because you can kill the zombies, where I cannot."

"What?" she exclaimed. "Why can't you kill them?"

"There is a covenant between the Fae and human races. We cannot harm one another—it is an unbreakable law. I need you to keep them from harming me and me from harming them, simply because in doing so we could break the covenant, unleashing chaos in both our worlds."

"That's the stupidest thing I've ever heard," she snapped.

Suddenly he had her back up against the wall, pressing hard. "Stupid or not, it is the way things must be," he said fiercely. His pale blue eyes seemed alight with an inner flame that dazzled her in the darkness.

He lowered his head against her, subsiding in his intensity.

"Lie with me," he whispered.

Anna's eyes widened. "You mean here? Are you mad?"

"Yes, here. Now."

"I don't think that's a good idea." Why then was she melting into him?

"Surrender to me."

Anna swallowed hard and let her head fall back weakly against the wall.

Enigma seemed to take it as all the acquiescence he needed. His lips pressed hotly against the vulnerable arch of her throat. Anna shuddered uncontrollably at the delicious sensation of his lips on her skin.

His hands moved to her t-shirt, lifting it. She wasn't wearing a bra, so the burn of his hands was unfettered against her breasts as he took one in each hand. Her nipples immediately hardened against the rough scrape of his palms and fingers. She gasped and arched up more fully into his touch.

It was then that she knew their coupling was inevitable.

It seemed hardly the time or place, but she couldn't help herself and had no intention of stopping him. "Make me feel alive," she begged, gasping the words into his ear as he continued to press kiss after kiss into her throat. "Make me come so hard that I don't have to feel all of this death around us anymore."

"As my lady wishes," he vowed, laving his tongue sensually against the shell of her ear. "So shall it be done."

He pressed his erection even tighter against her belly. Then, with a low growl of masculine dominance, he lifted her against him and fit himself into the vee of her thighs. Anna shuddered and held fast, reveling in his kisses and in the touch of his fingers on her nipples.

She pushed her own hands up under his shirt and felt the ridge of silken fur along his spine. It felt softer than down and richer than velvet at the same time. His mouth moved up to her, claiming her lips with a fiery passion that had her swooning. His tongue slid along hers like a liquid flame, tasting of spicy lust and sweet desire.

He set her back down and she impatiently pushed at the waistband of his jogging pants, but he stopped her with a hand on hers and took care of it himself. His erection sprang free and hot into her hands and she gasped. Never before had she seen such a large cock—it had to be at least twelve inches in length and it was far too thick for her fingers to wrap around. His testicles were heavy and large, but hairless, which surprised her.

He reached up and pulled his shirt off, exposing the incredible muscles of his chest. Indeed, he was hairless all over, smooth and hard like living marble. Anna buried her face in his chest and rubbed his scent into her skin like a kitten. He smelled of rain and wood and sweet, rich soil. His cock felt so hot and hard in her hand, and a small droplet of pre-cum dotted her palm when she stroked him from base to tip. Shameless, she brought her hand up to her mouth and tasted him with a dart of her tongue.

The darkness shielded him from her sight, but she learned the look of him with her questing hands. She moved up from his sex, to his rippled abdomen and towering chest. His shoulders were twice as broad as hers and stronger than stone. His neck and throat were thick and as well-muscled as the rest of him. His arms were strong, with their own rigid muscles flexing as he held her tightly to him.

His mouth moved to her throat and collarbone and down farther still. He noisily slurped one nipple into his mouth and suckled her until she gasped. He used his teeth against her and she whimpered her excitement, pressing her cunt against him eagerly.

As if sensing her need, he moved his hand down to cup her. Her pussy, moist and hot, flooded anew with her growing desire so that she was dripping wet and ready for him. "Fuck me, please," she begged wantonly.

He needed no further urging. With one hand he pushed her jeans down around her ankles and shoved one long, lean finger deep into her pussy. Anna cried out and moved against him for a deeper penetration then stepped out of her pants to widen her legs further for his intrusion.

His fingers spread her pussy lips wide, playing with the hardened kernel of her clit, pinching and pressing against it until she saw stars behind her tightly clenched eyelids. He speared her again and again with his thrusting finger until her body made wet, sucking sounds with each press and pull of his digit within her.

"Please. Now," she begged. "Fuck me, *please*."

He lifted her easily up over him. And with one long, savage thrust he drove himself into her.

Anna screamed.

Enigma caught the sound with his mouth, thrusting his tongue deeply into her as his cock speared deeply into her wet and shuddering body.

He stretched her and filled her as no one had before. Her pussy burned and adjusted to his size as if made for him. She touched her clit as he began pumping his hips into hers and gasped into his ravaging mouth.

She clenched one hand in his white-blond hair as the other rubbed her clit. Within seconds she neared climax. Until he pulled her hand away and brought it up to join her other one about his neck. Anna moaned in despair, but he quickly replaced her hand with his own and sent her flying.

Her orgasm washed over her like an ocean of fire. Her body arched into his until she was almost bent backward over his steadying arm. He thrust into her as hard as a battering ram and her head butted against the wall. Her body was so wet and wound so tight—even in release—that she shook with every breath.

Enigma took her breast into his mouth again and suckled savagely, still pumping into her. Her body gave one last quiver and she fell spent against him. With one last violent thrust, he found his own release and spilled the liquid fire of his desire deep within her body.

Several long moments passed as she tried to catch her breath. Enigma shuddered against her again and one last spurt of his cum burned its way deep into her womb.

For the first time in she didn't know how long, she was at peace with herself.

He whispered something against her temple in a language she didn't understand.

"What did you say?" she asked.

"I said that you and I were destined."

She rolled her eyes. "Not that again."

"Did you not feel the rightness of our mating?"

She had, but she was loath to let him know. There was no need to romanticize it. It had only been sex.

Or had it?

Her hands were shaking so badly she couldn't put her pants back on, so Enigma helped her with a tiny, smug smile playing about his mouth. He righted his own clothing and leaned in to kiss her softly.

"You're beautiful," he said again. "Not only your body, though that is truly incredible. But you, your very soul, is beautiful beyond compare. I have never seen it's like before."

For pillow talk it was incredible.

She tried not to let herself feel as if his words forged some sort of bond between the two them. For although his body had mastered hers, she did not want her heart to belong to any man. Especially a man who was more than that—a Fae.

"Come on, let's hurry and get out of here before we're blown to smithereens," she mumbled, and turned to lead the way deeper into the bowels of the building.

Chapter Six

Anna came to a halt when she saw the man waiting for them.

"Hello, Pestilence," Enigma said at her back.

"You know him?" Anna asked in shock.

"I know *of* him. He is the cause of all of this—he is the carrier of the plague. The beginning of it. And the end."

The man looked like a skeleton, wan and thin with the same graying skin of the zombies. But his back sprouted thick black wings like those of a bat. "Hello, Fae. I suppose you have come to try and stop me?"

Anna was shocked to hear Enigma's response.

"No, Pestilence, not I."

"If this is about that silly little pact between us and them," he nodded toward Anna, "then you're a little too late. Again."

"No. This time we will right it before total war is declared between our kinds."

"And how do you plan on doing that? In case you hadn't noticed, I've already destroyed this entire city of pitiful humans."

"You haven't destroyed Anna here," Enigma pointed out.

Pestilence's eyes widened like black pools into the heart of hell. "You think to sic your human on me? What can she do to stop me? Soon the bombs will fall and this entire city will be razed to the ground. And I, Prince of the Unseelie Fae, will be free to spread my plague over the face of the world. There is nothing she can do now."

Anna looked from one Fae to the other.

"There is something," Enigma insisted.

"And what is that, pray tell me?"

Enigma placed his hands gently upon her shoulders and answered, more to her than to Pestilence. "She can forgive you."

"What?" both Pestilence and Anna asked incredulously.

Enigma took her into his arms and looked down at her face. "Pestilence has transgressed against your people. You can disarm him and release him back into his own realm if you can find it within you to forgive—truly forgive—him."

"Why the hell do you think I'd do something like that? I can't forgive him for all he's done—everyone I know is dead because of him!"

"Does not your practice teach compassion? Does not your soul long to forgive and forget in order to save this world you so love?" Enigma asked her softly. "This is why you were chosen."

Her yoga practice did indeed teach compassion, but this was too much for her to take. How could she genuinely forgive him when her heart hated him for all he'd done to her and her people?

"It's the end of the world, Fae," Pestilence spat. "Already the planes cross over this land to release their weapons of mass destruction."

"Look at him, Anna. This is why you were chosen. Look closely at him and see if there is an ounce of forgiveness within you to give."

"What if I can't?" she wailed.

"Then we have failed in our mission."

"Shut up, Fae," Pestilence growled. "Can't you see that she wishes to kill me herself? Human woman, why don't you draw your weapon and shoot me?"

"Don't do it, Anna—he won't die. He cannot die, he is immortal."

"Then how are the bombs going to spread his plague if he doesn't die in them?"

"He will use that strike on him as a strike against the peace accord between Fae and human—he will become unstoppable."

"But he started it—"

"It matters not. He is Unseelie, pure evil. He can do almost anything he wants to. But he cannot continue on his quest if you can forgive him."

"Okay, I forgive him," she lied.

Pestilence laughed, a cold, cruel sound.

"You have to mean it, Anna," Enigma told her softly.

Anna let out a long breath and closed her eyes. She blocked out all sight and sound and emotion, meditating on her breath and on the moment at hand. Her yoga had indeed taught her discipline and strength, but she wasn't sure she was ready for this. No. She pushed all doubt aside and stayed grounded in the moment.

After what seemed like hours, but must have been only a few moments, she opened her eyes and looked at Pestilence again.

He looked sickly and pale. Not at all strong enough to end the world, though she knew he would if given the chance.

She vowed not to give him such an opportunity.

Anna counted out her breaths and let her body relax. She looked into Pestilence's eyes and saw . . . fear. Fear of her.

"I forgive you," she said, and this time she meant it. Anything to stop him from succeeding in his evil intent. "I forgive you, Pestilence. Now be gone from my realm." The words came to her naturally and felt right. "And never return."

"Noooooo," Pestilence screamed. "You cannot do this. You haven't the power—" But that was all he managed before he disappeared completely before her very eyes.

Anna stood there in silence for a long while, amazed at how suddenly it had all ended.

"Come, we mustn't dally. We haven't much time before your military strikes against this place."

Anna took his outstretched hand and together they ran from the building.

They took to the air, Enigma's crimson wings unfurling like a giant cape as he held her tight in his arms. They escaped mere seconds before the building exploded behind them in a blaze of complete destruction.

Chapter Seven

They landed in a forest dozens of miles away from the blast, but still Anna could feel the ground shuddering beneath her feet.

She burst into tears the minute her feet touched earth, and collapsed onto the ground. Enigma came down beside her and held her cradled to him as she sobbed out all the long days of terror and uncertainty into his chest.

When her sobs faded into hiccups, Enigma put his finger beneath her chin and lifted her mouth to his kiss. He licked her lips, deliberately infusing her with the scent and flavor of his mouth.

She tasted of honey and tears.

"How do we know if he's really gone?" she asked him on a shaking breath.

"He won't be able to try again for another five hundred years or so. Such are the laws of our people."

"I can't believe it was so easy."

"Was it really all that easy?" he asked her.

No, it hadn't been. "All those people are dead. Everything I knew and loved is lost forever."

"Not everything," he said, and claimed her mouth once more.

She clung to him desperately, thrusting her tongue into his mouth with eager intent.

Within seconds they were both naked and lying on the soft bed of the forest floor.

Enigma traced every line of her body, first with his fingers and then with his mouth. He suckled her breasts, dipped his tongue into her navel, and licked her pussy like a cat licking cream from a bowl.

Anna screamed when he laved her asshole with his tongue. She screamed again when he placed his mouth over the whole of her cunt and suckled hard.

He flipped her over and spread her ass cheeks to better kiss and lick and suck the moue of her anus. He licked his fingers and gently pressed them into her until she keened with the wild pleasure of it. He lifted her up before him and shoved his cock into her with one mighty thrust.

His fingers filled her ass and his cock filled her pussy and the wet, slurping noises of their coupling echoed in the woods around them. He used his free hand to slap the cushion of her ass and she cried out.

"Do that again," she panted.

He spanked her again, hard enough to make her skin sting deliciously. He leaned over her and bit hard into her shoulder and she moaned, thrusting back against his questing cock and fingers.

"I don't believe it, but I think I love you," she panted, unable to call back the words.

"Such a romantic you are," he teased her.

"I mean it," she said, and did.

"I *know* I love you, my Anna," he told her. "And I know you love me, too." Enigma thrust deeper into her. "Join me. Come for me," he urged her.

He pressed yet another finger into her ass, stretching and burning her until she was sobbing with the overwhelming pleasure. Anna came with a savage scream that echoed about the forest, frightening off the birds in the treetops.

Enigma flowed into her like a molten river, spurting deep.

But he never stopped thrusting.

Once Anna was able to catch her breath, Enigma turned her back over and hooked her ankles behind his ears. He leaned forward and took one of her breasts in his mouth. He reached down and thrust a finger inside her, alongside his cock. His wings unfurled and wrapped around them like an iridescent crimson blanket.

Anna sobbed and pulled wildly at his hair, and he continued to suckle hard on her breast.

He thrust both his cock and his finger into her, over and over again, touching her womb with his great length.

Her nipple popped free from his mouth, wet and chilled in the night air. "Say you love me and mean it," he demanded.

She only gasped.

He increased the pace and force of his thrusts, using his other hand to reach around and squeeze the cheeks of her ass. He rotated his hips into hers, mashing against the swollen pebble of her clit with each movement he made.

He lifted her higher against him, delving deeper into her body until she cried out. His wings spread out impossibly longer around them, each furred inch of them caressing her body like a thousand questing fingers.

She came with a roar. "I love you, Enigma. I love you so much," she yelled, pulling at his hair and clawing at the arms that held her suspended against him.

Enigma gave a mighty shove into her. And another. And another. And then he, too, came with a roar that shook the heavens from their slumber. His wings shuddered and seemed to change color, shifting from a dark crimson to a glowing, fiery red.

It was a long time before Anna found her voice again. "Now what do we do?"

Enigma smiled down at her and kissed her mouth softly. His hips began pistoning into hers again, his cock still hard and thick and demanding. "Now you come to live with me in my realm."

"How?"

"I will show you all you need to know," he said.

"Nothing will ever be the same," she sighed, moving with him now.

"Nothing ever is. Change is inevitable. But I'll be with you every step of the way. We've a thousand lifetimes to learn everything about each other, and I know I'll enjoy every moment of it."

He thrust into her again and again, making her see stars.

"You're so beautiful," he told her.

"So are you," she said, and smiled up into his ice blue eyes.

He plumped her breasts in his hands to kiss and lick each nipple noisily. "I will love you forever," he vowed. "Your courage and your valor have saved this world, but you've also saved me, my love. You've saved me from an eternity of loneliness and duty. You are my heart now and I'll never let you go." His wings wrapped around her once more, enfolding her in his warmth and scent.

Anna nearly swooned with his words, and when he touched her clit with his fingers . . . she did swoon. It was bliss. And for the first time since the end of the world, Anna felt as if she'd come home at last.

Legacy of the Snake

Elizabeth Jewell

Chapter One

On his twenty-first birthday, Heath went to the place where his grandfather saw fairies.

Grampa Cabot had owned twenty-five acres on a mountain in Clear Creek County, Colorado, which, as of today, belonged to Heath. There was a cabin on it—nothing particularly special about it—but behind the cabin a well-worn path wound its way up the slope, made circles around the mountain, forked and separated. One fork led to the mountain's peak, at nearly ten thousand feet. There a spring sang its way out from between the rocks, bubbling and laughing, as a spring should. The spring made a pool, and in the pool, Grampa Cabot had seen fairies.

It was commonly felt among the Cabots and the Pierces—Heath's father's folks—that Grampa Cabot was one or two cheese sandwiches shy of a picnic. But Heath had always liked the old man, and had absorbed the fairy stories with rapt attention.

"Them fairies ain't little pixies, neither," Grampa had told Heath. "You go there once you're eighteen or so and you'll be doing yourself a favor." He'd winked broadly at Heath. Heath, being ten years old at the time, had had no idea what Grampa was talking about.

Grampa had died last month, not unexpectedly. What was unexpected was the will leaving the twenty-five acres and the alleged fairy pool to Heath. Ownership to be made legal as of Heath's twenty-first birthday. Today.

He'd come out to the property to check things out, but most of all to walk up the mountain to the clear, cold spring and the fairy pool. For not only had he remembered that old story, and Grampa Cabot's broad wink, but Grampa had also left him a letter.

Winded from the altitude and the long hike, Heath came finally to the end of the long, meandering path. He could hear the laughter of the spring before he could see it. The sound settled into his soul. Made him smile. He rounded the last curve and stopped just to look at the scene laid out before him.

Had the hike not been so strenuous, he would have enjoyed its beauty more. Every turn the path took, it exposed a new panorama of green and blue and brown. Born and raised in Colorado, he'd thought himself immune to the spell of the mountains. He'd been wrong.

The music of the little spring was unlike anything he'd ever heard before. Like the tinkling of glass, wind chimes, or a thousand tiny, crystalline voices. Just the sound made him believe in fairies.

He sat on a large, round stone next to the quiet pool and pulled the often-folded, many-times-read letter out of his hip pocket.

Dear Heath,

I am leaving you my land and access to the fairy pool because I don't think any other damn fool in the family ever believed a word I said. At least you used to listen. Besides, you're a good, strong, young man. Them fairies'd kill your dad.

Please take good care of this drawing I made. It's a little sketch of a friend I met in the fairy place. If you see her, tell her I said hello.

Thoughtfully, Heath unfolded the drawing. As many times as he'd looked at it, he still couldn't get his head around the idea that his grandfather had drawn it. Even though it was obviously old, and so Grampa must have been a young man. It was hard even to imagine Grampa as young, much less young and drawing a picture of a naked woman.

For naked she was, extremely so. She lay back on a low couch, her head thrown back, her thighs open, and her hand between them. It reminded him of the sketch from that girlie *Titanic* movie, but pornographic. The woman had a blissful smile on her face, vacant but not stupidly so. More orgasmically so. The pencil drawing was black and white, but the shading implied blonde hair—on her head and between her legs. Her eyes were half closed but the irises hadn't been shaded in. He assumed, then, that they were blue.

And she was beautiful. Full, round breasts, a softly curved abdomen. She was heavier than the current trend in fashion models, but Heath had never liked that anorexic look, anyway. This was a real woman. Fit and firm, lush of breast and hip. He liked them like that.

As long as he didn't have to think about Grampa Cabot drawing them naked. Naked and masturbating. It was a disturbing image.

But a beautiful woman. And, if truth be told, that was the real reason he was here now, at the pool where his grandfather had seen fairies.

He sat on the big stone for a time, listening to the laughter of the spring and staring at the still, cold water at his feet.

Was this it, then? The cold water, the green and lovely mountains, the tinkle of the spring that sounded like fairy laughter? He looked again at his grandfather's drawing. The woman looked normal enough, mortal, and she didn't have wings or anything. Was she a fairy-woman or just an ordinary girl Grampa had met there? He hadn't really said either way.

Heath folded the picture and the letter back into a neat square and slid them into his breast pocket. Maybe Grampa *had* been crazy, as most of the family believed. Maybe Heath was crazy too, trekking all the way up here to look for fairies that were nothing more than the delusions of an old man.

Oh, well. Even if there were no fairies, this was a beautiful piece of land, a lovely spring, a nice place to come to sit and think—

Heath blinked. Something had flickered in the still surface of the pool. He came to his feet, bending over the water to look more closely.

His own reflection stared back at him, his blue eyes intent, and a furrow between his blond brows as he peered down at himself. Beyond his own reflection he could see only the occasional ripple on the surface of the water, smooth-worn stones on the bottom of the pool—

There it was. A flash of gold, of white. Heath jerked around, looking over his shoulder. He was certain he'd seen another face reflected in the pool beside his own. But there was no one else here who could have cast a reflection. He was still alone, surrounded by the whispering sound of aspens, the laughter of the spring.

Slowly, he turned back to the water. The sound of the spring *did* sound like laughter, even more so than before. Was it laughter? He looked closer.

The reflection was there again—still there?—and it was laughing at him.

This time he didn't turn to look behind him. This wasn't an average, everyday reflection. Somehow, this came from below the water, not above it.

Without thinking, he plunged his hand into the water. The spring was ice-cold. He let out a gasp of shock, but pushed his hand deeper, until his fingers met the round, smooth stones at the bottom of the pool.

Amongst the ripples formed by his intrusion, the face smiled back at him. Laughed, even. It was a woman's face, lovely, with uptilted eyes and a wide, white smile. Her smile was lovely but off-putting, as if, behind the flash of teeth and the pretty face, lurked danger Heath could only begin to imagine.

He saw this, but wariness didn't even occur to him. Right now he was irked, almost angry, as the woman continued to laugh silently under the water, amused beyond reason at Heath's expense.

He withdrew his hand and bent closer, trying to see more of her. If she was beneath the water, where was the rest of her?

"Show yourself, you little bitch," he muttered, glaring down at the laughing, rippling face.

Angry now, he lifted his hand to strike the water, hoping to disperse the annoying image this way. But before his hand could strike the water, other hands grasped him firmly by the ears and dragged his face into the icy cold pool. Lips met his and kissed him, hard and hot. His face was under the water, his mouth full of a questing, probing tongue, his nostrils on the verge of sucking in the pool if they were deprived of oxygen a moment longer.

It didn't come to that, though. Suddenly the ice-cold wet was replaced with heat, warmth, and air, and he began to fall.

And fall. Into the pool, down through the water except there was no water, only warm, soft air.

It took a long time to reach the bottom. Ridiculous, because the pool hadn't been that deep. Impossible, because the pool had been a pool.

Heath struck bottom, grunting at the impact. How far had he fallen? He looked up, trying to look back where he'd come from, but there was no hole in the ceiling, no tunnel—nothing to indicate how he'd fallen through the little mountain pool into this dark, damp cave.

He sat for a moment, feeling bruises rise, then pushed himself to his feet. He had fallen what seemed to have been a long distance, but he hadn't broken anything, and he'd come through water, but he wasn't wet. The woman—if she'd been a woman and not just an apparition of some kind—was nowhere to be seen. In fact, Heath appeared to be completely alone.

Okay, so maybe Grampa hadn't been such a nutcase after all. This was certainly weird enough to have something to do with fairies. Or maybe Grampa Cabot's insanity was hereditary, and triggered at the age of twenty-one by the sound of tinkling spring water.

Whatever the case, Heath found himself in what appeared to be an underground tunnel. The roughness of the walls gave it a sense of having been naturally formed. There was water here too, perhaps seeping down from above, coating the uneven textures of the walls with a sheen of damp. The passageway seemed to go on forever in either direction, as far as he could see, before the distant reaches disappeared in the darkness.

Which way to go? The light—which had no apparent source—was uniform in either direction. Both directions looked exactly the same in every other way, as well. Maybe it didn't matter. He took a few steps forward.

Then he heard singing. Faint, distant, inarguably lovely. He froze, listening. It was coming from behind him.

That way, then. He turned and headed resolutely toward the sound.

Chapter Two

He walked for a year. Or that was what it felt like, as he trudged on and on, through the passage that smelled of wet stone and, increasingly, of a mustiness that might have been mildew. Each forty paces of corridor was identical to the preceding stretch, the same lumps and humps of wet, gray stone, the same vein of green stone in the left-hand wall. His legs were starting to ache, and he was hungry. He had no idea how long he'd been walking—his watch had stopped at twelve-fifteen, which was, by his estimation, about the time he'd been dragged down into the pool.

And the singing was the same, barely audible, just faint enough to make it impossible to tell whether there were words or only a tune. No matter how long he walked, the sound seemed to get no closer.

He trudged on. The delicate beauty of the singing was starting to grate on his nerves. Too high-pitched, too pure, with words that seemed to be there but somehow weren't, hovering just outside his ability to perceive them.

Suddenly he stopped dead and shouted, "Enough of this bullshit! Somebody tell me what the hell's going on!"

The music stopped, instantly replaced by a shower of giggling. Heath clenched his teeth. He wanted to find the gigglers and knock their heads together.

"You dragged me down here, now somebody answer me!"

Nothing. He glared fruitlessly at the emptiness around him. His anger faded, replaced by a dreary hopelessness. He trudged on.

He noticed the fog a few steps later. It seeped from the floor, rising to cover his feet, then his ankles. Drifts of it wafted up to his face. His eyelids began to sag.

"Shit," he muttered. There was no odor, no taste, but somehow he knew the fog was what dragged him down as he took a few more, staggering steps, then sagged to the ground, unconscious.

He woke to the pleasant but disturbing sensation of someone sucking his dick. The "disturbing" part didn't register right away, first the "pleasant" part had to crest high enough to awaken him completely. Then he remembered where he was—or where he'd been last—and realized he had no idea who might be going down on him, or why. He opened his eyes.

He was alone in a small room, lying on a bed that appeared to be perfectly normal. The room had a girlie feel to it, with flowery wallpaper and lacy pillowcases on the bed. He lay on top of the quilt. It was lacy, as well. He was naked. Erect too, and his dick felt wet.

He sat up. There was, indeed, sheen on the skin of his penis, as if the interrupted blowjob had been more than just a dream. But there was no one else in the room, and he wasn't capable of sucking himself.

He swung his legs off the side of the bed. He still ached, his cock demanding that someone finish what they'd started. He tried to ignore it, but he'd been so close to orgasm his balls were drawn up tight, and he couldn't seem to shake it off.

Forcing himself to ignore it, he walked—a bit stiffly—to the bedroom door. It was locked. The room had no windows.

Wherever he was, he was stuck here for a while.

What the hell? He sat back down on the bed and went to work.

From her tower bedroom, Elena watched. She smiled as the young man curled his hand around his firm, erect cock. He ran his thumb over the head, catching the beads of fluid, slicking his shaft with it, then setting to work with a quick pull-and-slide, pulsing his cock through his fist.

Watching him brought her to a state of arousal nearly as desperate as his seemed to be, but she held hers off, enjoying the sensation as her body lit up with heat. Something about him appealed to her. Maybe his straightforward efficiency—up and down, quick, even, practiced jerks—as he pleasured himself. No extra indulgences, just a quick solution to an obvious problem. Or maybe it was just his bright blue eyes and the soft curl of his blond hair against his shoulders. She wasn't sure.

Nevertheless, she found herself bending closer to the mirror on her wall, unwilling to miss anything. As he bent his head back, giving himself up to his climax, she bent forward, licking her lips, her nose almost touching the mirror's glass. She could imagine what his cock would feel like, taste like in her mouth, could almost feel the textures of his skin under her tongue. Her hand strayed to her own breast, caressing its full curves, her fingers teasing her firm nipple.

She jerked back from the mirror, suddenly aware of what she was doing. She looked at her fingers, which had strayed, then at the mirror, where the young man had fallen back on the bed, coated with a sheen of sweat.

Then, slowly, she smiled. This one just might be worth the effort.

* * *

He sat in the bedroom for another year, or so it seemed, and was about to rail fruitlessly at nothing and no one when the door finally swung open. He turned, tense, to face whoever had opened it, too tired, hungry and just plain pissed to worry about the fact he was still buck naked.

"You want to explain this shit to me?" he demanded, and then registered whom he was addressing.

She was tall and proud and painfully beautiful, with wheat-gold hair done up in a French twist not quite disciplined enough to be matronly. She wore a black leather corset, a flowing velvet skirt and small black boots.

She tilted her head haughtily at him, crystal-blue eyes examining him with some amusement. "I am under no obligation to explain anything to you," she said coolly, "but I will. Eventually. For now, is there any immediate need I may assist you with?"

A dozen answers tripped through his brain, most of them obscene. But they were also triggered by anger rather than lust, so he bypassed them. "Well, right now I mostly just need to take a piss."

She smiled a little. "Come with me."

She led him down the hallway to a door. "Here are the facilities you require. There are clothes, as well." She gave him a long, sweeping glance from his naked head to his naked feet and everything naked in between. His cock stirred from the touch of her eyes; he wondered idly what her hands might be able to accomplish.

But he gave her only a thin-lipped glare as he opened the bathroom door.

He tended first to his straining bladder, then investigated the clothes hanging on the back of the bathroom door. A white t-shirt and black leather pants. He rolled his eyes. What did she think he was? Her whore? Even so, he put them on. Anything was preferable to nakedness.

The woman was still standing outside the door when he finished. She gave him another appraising look and smiled.

"They fit," she said.

"Barely." The pants were a shade too tight, but he assumed they'd stretch.

Her eyelids lowered, her smile widening on one side. She took a step closer and closed her hand over his crotch. He flinched, but stayed put, holding her gaze, meeting her challenge. He had no idea who or what this woman was or how much depended on his tolerating her fondling.

She cupped his balls, lifting them. Her hand seemed unnaturally hot. But as her fingers manipulated him—gently, not quite sensuously—the tightness in his trousers eased. She slid her fingers up the fly, up the length of his partial erection, and here too, the leather eased its grip. Not fondling, then, in the truest sense, but rather some kind of magical clothing alteration. She stepped a little closer, her face a breath away, her lips nearly touching his, and closed her hands around his buttocks.

"Better?" she said as she withdrew.

"Yeah," he managed. Arousal lay thick in his throat, heavy between his legs. There was a thin smugness to her smile now, as she looked at him. He swallowed. "Yeah, that's better. Thanks."

"Good." She turned and walked down the corridor, away from where his room had been. "Come with me."

He looked back over his shoulder, wondering if he'd be able to find his way back. Then, deciding it probably didn't matter, he followed her.

Meekly. Obediently. Like a puppy.

This was bullshit. Unfortunately, it seemed he had little choice. At least for now.

The big house, its halls and doorways, seemed to warp or wave around him, until he no longer knew where they were going, where they'd been or even if the place was real. He thought they walked side by side down a long corridor—far too long, actually—then suddenly they came around a corner and were in a long, bright dining room.

Heath's head spun. He pressed his fingers to his forehead, blinking.

"Yes, I know," the woman said. "It's difficult if you're not used to it. I'm afraid there's a great deal of unharnessed magic in the estate. I've been working on getting it under control, but it takes time."

"I see." The room wavered in front of his eyes, then settled. It was a long room with a long table, many chairs, tall windows draped with orange and yellow curtains. Sun slanted in from outside, creating more streaks of sunset-colored orange and yellow. A big sunshine room. For a moment the light was too much, then his eyes adjusted to the vivid colors and the brightness.

"There's a guest house where you may stay," the woman went on. "I'm sure you'll be more comfortable there. There's very little magic to be mined in that part of the property."

"Mined?" he repeated, then, "Never mind. I don't want to know that right now."

"Is there anything you *do* need to know right now?"

"Your name. Do you have a name?"

"Of course I have a name. Elena. And you?"

"Heath," he said. "Heath Cabot-Pierce."

"Pleased to make your acquaintance." She tilted her head and perused him again, making him feel vulnerable. He fought the feeling, fought the flush trying to rise into his face. Her blue eyes seemed depthless.

"So," he said after her silence had gone on too long. "What now?"

She came back to herself quickly, jerking her gaze from his and approaching the table. "I must eat."

"You have to? Now?"

Settling into the chair at the head of the table, she slanted him a look. "There's something else you wish to do?"

"I thought I could go to the guest house."

"No. Not now. I must eat."

"Okay . . ." He took a chair next to her.

"Are you hungry?"

"A little." In truth, he was ravenous, though he'd only just noticed.

She snapped her fingers and a heavily laden plate appeared on the table in front of him. Rich smells instantly assaulted his senses—finely marbled beef, vegetables, rice. Everything seemed *more* than normal, the odors stronger, the colors brighter. He suspected the tastes would have a similar intensity.

In front of Elena, though, was only a small, silver, covered tray.

"Eat," she said, nodding toward his plate of food. Gracefully, she lifted the lid from her own plate. It held only a white slab of meat. It looked like fish, but Heath couldn't really tell. Whatever it was, it was unappetizing.

He turned his attention to his own food. The beef was so tender he barely had to chew it, the vegetables drenched in butter, the rice light and fluffy, flavored with herbs and bits of finely chopped onion and peppers. It tasted too good to be real.

Time seemed to warp again as he ate. He took two bites, then suddenly he was lifting the last morsel of beef from the plate. Elena watched him with an indulgent smile. She had eaten very little, as far as he could tell—perhaps a bite or two of the small, white brick of meat on her plate.

He stopped chewing in sudden realization. Was this like one of those myths where the protagonist was fine as long as he didn't eat anything in the mysterious land of Fairy? If so, he'd screwed things up pretty thoroughly for himself.

It was too late now. He'd cleaned his plate, drunk the wine. Looking into Elena's satisfied smile, he felt his stomach drop.

"I'm stuck here forever now, aren't I?" he said, his voice dull.

"You will be given a choice in that matter," she said, "when the time is right."

"Thank God," he said, before thinking to wonder who might be the one to decide the right time.

"It's time for us to go," Elena said, coming to her feet. "I'll take you to the guest house."

He stood, looking at the food still sitting on her plate. "You said you needed to eat. You hardly touched your food."

"I have taken what I require." She walked toward one of the wide, sun-drenched windows, which opened like a door as she approached. "I will show you now to your quarters."

He followed her through the door, out onto a wide stretch of grass whose intensity of green made his eyes ache. Everything here was just a little beyond normal. Normal enough not to completely disorient, but strange enough to come disconcertingly close.

A small stone cottage stood not far from the main house. Looking back over his shoulder, Heath saw a hint of the vast sprawl of the estate; it looked like a small city more than a single building. And even from out here, it wavered, the towers and wings seeming to exchange places from time to time, its vast outline never settling comfortably in Heath's vision. He turned back toward the cottage. This was more stable, more normal. He could look at it without getting dizzy.

"It's small," Elena said, "but it should be large enough for your purposes." They took a few more steps and were suddenly at the door. It had seemed farther away. It probably had been. "There will be fairy sprites to attend to your every need, if you wish them."

She opened the front door and he stepped in. "Fairy sprites?"

"Yes. They visited you last night. I trust you enjoyed their ministrations?"

"Actually, I found it a little creepy. What are they, anyway?"

He walked into the small cottage. Light poured in from an open window, but here the couch, carpet and curtains were a dusky blue so the sunset light seemed not so overwhelming.

"They are creatures of magic and little else," Elena explained. "They come when they are summoned and disperse when dismissed."

"How do you summon them?"

"You simply desire something. Express a need. They will arrive to fill it."

"I was right. They *are* creepy."

"They're quite useful."

"I'm sure they are." He remembered the sensations that had awakened him—a mouth on his cock, licking and sucking him. He didn't know whether to be aroused or disgusted.

Pushing the thought aside, he turned his attention back to the cottage. A squat, black, wood burning stove stood in the middle of the room. It was made to cook on as well as to provide heat to the little building. Across the room, a half-open door led to a bedroom. On the opposite wall of the main room, across from the wide windows, was a kitchen sink, cabinets, a small refrigerator.

"All the amenities," he commented. "Indoor plumbing too?"

"Yes." She had come only a step or two past the front door, and now took a step back. "I must go. Make yourself at home. Remember, if you need anything, the fairy sprites will see to you."

"Yeah. Let's hope not, okay?"

She smiled. "I'll see you later."

"Wait," he said as she began to move out the door. "When will I be able to leave?"

Her eyes raked down his body again, leaving him feeling naked in the wake of their gaze.

"When I grant you permission."

Carefully, silently, she closed the door behind her. Heath looked around the pretty little cottage, then sank into the blue couch.

"Damn," he muttered. "Fairies totally suck."

Chapter Three

The cottage seemed comfortable, but it was small, and it didn't take Heath long to investigate every corner, nook and cranny. There was a fridge but no freezer, a toilet but no TV. The bed was wide enough for two. Just the sight of it, obviously meant for sharing, made his loins stir. He was far too sensitive, maybe just because of the constant, supple caress and give of the leather trousers, or maybe because the image of Elena loomed freshly in his mind. There was something about her that aroused him more than could be considered normal. Sure, he could sport a boner at the sight of a pretty woman as well as any other man could, and her outfit had fairly screamed, "Fuck me," but this was still more. He kept remembering the way her hand had fit against him, cupping his genitals through the leather of his pants. Her long, slim fingers fondling him, just for those few moments. He couldn't stop himself from picturing her on her knees in front of him, taking him into her mouth.

He forced the thoughts and images back. He'd never accidentally shot his wad in a pair of leather pants, but he had a feeling it wasn't a wise idea.

Still, the house seemed to reek of sex. He had to either strip down and attend to himself, right there, or get out of the house, distract himself with some fresh air.

Outside, the orange sunset that had lit the dining room had begun to fade. Dusk lurked just behind it, casting shadows over the brilliant greens of the estate grounds. He wondered exactly how long he'd been here in this place, and how much time had passed back in the "real" world.

What had happened to him, that he could accept this so readily? Since when had he believed in magic, or fairies, or anything of that ilk? Was it in his blood somehow, that he could accept these occurrences with so little question? It wasn't a question he wanted to deal with in too much detail, for fear he might not like the answer.

The evening breeze had turned cool and questing, fingering through his hair, cooling the back of his neck. He found himself retracing the path Elena had led him on, heading back toward the dark bulk of the estate. Even from the outside it seemed abnormal, its dark outline changing, wavering, so it didn't seem like quite the same building from moment to moment. It made him vaguely queasy just to look at it.

On the soft breeze, a voice wafted to him. A woman's voice. Elena's, he realized after a moment. It seemed to be coming from a copse of trees to his right, up a small slope. Beyond the copse, the trees thickened into the edge of a large wooded area. Curious, he crept in that direction, careful to step as quietly as possible.

It was darker there, where the trees cast deep shadows in the growing evening. He saw her there, with the fading sunset gold on her hair, but at first he thought she was talking to herself. Her voice was soft and he couldn't make out her words, but her tone was sweeter than it had been before, with a different music to it.

"It will be well," he thought he heard, but wasn't sure. Still, the sound of her voice gave him that feeling more than the words, a feeling of peace and calm.

He crept closer, as close as he thought was safe. From behind the dubious shelter of a shrub, he watched.

She was not alone. She stood with a tall stag. He was still and elegant in front of her, his head lifted, his wide antlers proud and deadly. Elena's hand cupped his face, caressing his jaw. And she was talking to him.

Heath still couldn't quite hear what she said, whether because he was still too far away or because her words weren't meant for his ears. She spoke, smiling, then paused, regarding the stag's elegant face. Then she spoke again.

Heath watched, entranced both by Elena's loveliness and the elegant, feral beauty of the stag. He was missing something, he was certain. Some element of what he watched continued to elude him. But the beauty was quite within his comprehension, and it moved him.

He wasn't sure how long he stood there, taking it in, but finally Elena lifted her hand away from the stag. The animal stood still for another long moment. Then, to Heath's surprise, the stag bent one knee, lowered his head, then came to his feet and vanished with a leap into the thicker trees.

Heath carefully let out his breath, unaware until that moment that he'd been holding it. Elena looked with a soft smile at the place where the stag had disappeared into the trees. Then she too, disappeared, but not by leaping into the forest. One moment she was there, the next she was not.

Heath blinked. There was too much here to absorb—why was he having so little difficulty accepting it? Maybe because somehow he knew there was magic here, as if he could smell it, or feel it against his skin. He felt like, if he just moved his hands the right way, or said the right words, he could use it.

He flung his arms out, feeling the night breeze, touching the edges of the magic that permeated this place. He was close, but not close enough.

His attention shifted to the estate. What could he learn in there? Could he even find his way around?

It seemed worth the risk. In fact, the risk seemed low, at least given what he knew. He headed for the estate.

Its image shifted in front of him as he drew closer. The door he'd intended to enter was nowhere to be seen when he actually came within touching distance of the building. He found himself instead in front of the door to the dining hall. Not exactly where he wanted to be. But, looking around, he could see no other entrances nearby. He shrugged and opened the door to the dining hall.

It was dark and empty, the table cleared, curtains drawn on the big, darkened windows. He thought he heard a vague murmur of voices, muted, or distant, or ephemeral. *Fairy sprites*, he thought, though he had no way of knowing if this were true. Elena had made them sound like magical, animated sex toys, but maybe they did dishes too. Or maybe the estate sported a crew of human servants as well as magical ones.

Keeping his steps as silent as possible, he moved across the room. The voices seemed to be coming from the long room's far end. There must be a door there, leading perhaps to a kitchen area. If he could sneak up on the fairy sprites, catch them in action, then—

Well, then probably not much of anything significant, but maybe he would learn something about this strange world he'd fallen into.

But when he reached the end of the table, he saw no door. The wall appeared to be as solid as all the others. He could still hear the voices, though, like wind chimes tinkling in the distance.

Frustrated, he turned back toward the table. The room was very dark now, and he saw no way to light it up—certainly he didn't see anything as mundane as a light switch. Candles, maybe, but he didn't remember seeing any candles at dinner.

Then, suddenly, what little light there was snagged his attention, glinting silver off something on the table. Surely not—

But it was. He took a step closer to be certain.

The table had been cleared and reset, but one thing remained from the dinner he'd shared with Elena. The silver dish from which she'd eaten still sat in front of her place at the table.

This was odd. But what in this place wasn't? Curious, he lifted the silver lid.

The meat was still there. It was a brick of white flesh about four inches long and two wide, perhaps an inch and a half thick. He clearly remembered her taking a bite out of it, but it was intact now. Maybe it wasn't the same piece of meat. But why would it be left out on the table overnight? Wouldn't it go bad?

Maybe the little fairy kitchen workers weren't doing their jobs. Or maybe it was some special sort of flesh that needed to be prepared this way, by sitting out all night on the dining room table.

Or maybe—and gee, wasn't this a stretch in his current surroundings?—maybe it was magic.

He bent over the dish, peering more closely at the chunk of meat. It looked like fish, but not quite. He could see the imprint of bones resembling fish ribs, but were different. Like a snake. Could it be snake meat?

Unable to resist the temptation, he poked it. It was firm like fish, as well. He bent still closer, sniffing. The vague odor provided little in the way of additional clues.

Did he dare?

He grasped a corner and broke it off. He looked at it closely in the ridiculously dim light, then popped it into his mouth.

Apparently, he *did* dare.

The chunk of meat was a bit tough. He wasn't entirely sure it was cooked. But he chewed gamely, not even sure now why he'd started down this course.

Tastes like chicken, he thought wryly, and swallowed.

Suddenly the room tipped under him. He swayed, catching hold of the table for balance. His vision went blurry, everything doubling, then blackening into nothingness. That lasted only moments, but when he came back to himself, he was sitting on the floor.

Holy shit, he thought, too wavery to speak aloud, even if there had been anyone present to speak to. *It's like puffer fish or something. Holy God, I'm gonna die.*

He drew his knees up and put his head between his knees, as if this might slow the spread of a virulent neurotoxin through his body.

Great. It's some poison she eats every night to build up her immunity. And you think of this now.

He was so busy mentally berating himself that at first he failed to notice the fading of his discomfort. Suddenly he realized the strange lightheadedness was gone. He pushed himself carefully to his feet. Whatever it had been, it was gone now. He felt perfectly normal.

He gave a quick shudder, then made his way back out of the dining hall. No more exploring tonight. With his luck, he'd end up getting himself killed.

Outside, the darkness was almost complete. Heath looked for the moon but didn't see it. Either there was no moon here, or it hadn't risen yet. There were stars, though, teems of them, wide streaks and milky streams of them, unlike anything he'd ever seen before. He saw none of the familiar constellations. In a sky that looked like this, he wouldn't have been surprised to see two or three moons on the rise.

The milky streaks of stars provided a pale and eerie light, but it was sufficient to lead him back to the cottage. Something else was different, though, something besides the darkness and the stars. There were murmurs everywhere, soft voices making words he couldn't quite discern. They seemed to come from all directions, like the nocturnal singing of crickets, but verbal. This too, made him feel strange, out of place, as if he were missing some important aspect of the situation.

He hurried back to the cottage, rattled. Once the door was shut behind him, he felt safer again. Not safe, but safer.

He wondered exactly when he might expect to be able to go

home again. This place was too bizarre. He wanted to go back to someplace that made sense.

He'd left the voices outside, or so he thought. Now he heard something else, more sounds. Not words, though. Giggling. Coming from the bedroom. Hesitant, worried about what he might find in spite of the harmless nature of the sounds, he went to investigate.

There were girls in his bedroom. Three of them, delicate and beautiful and not very well dressed. Sheets of gauze material barely disguised the lines and shadows of their sleek bodies.

He stood staring for a moment—who could blame him?—then turned and went back into the living room.

"No," he said, falling onto the couch.

"Why not?"

One of the women—the one draped in purple gauze—stood in front of him. The other two, one in pink, one in white, appeared behind her. Appeared. Out of nowhere.

"Yes," they said in unison. "Why not?"

"Because you're not real." He said it firmly, but it didn't convince him. Not totally. Not when they were there in front of him, startlingly beautiful. He told himself they were fairy sprites, described to him by Elena as simple constructs of magic.

They were constructed much better than he'd expected. These three were distinctly individual, beautiful in different ways, their bodies distinguishable one from the other. He looked into the eyes of the purple-clad woman and knew he wasn't going to be able to say no. Not unless they left.

They weren't leaving. The girl in purple climbed into his lap. Her buttocks settled against his thighs, his rapidly growing erection, and she brushed her lips against his cheek. "You're lonely," she said. "We felt it."

"We came to help," said the girl in pink.

Heath could barely breathe, much less think. He wanted them, and they were more than willing to cooperate. He tried to remember why he'd wanted to resist. Nothing occurred to him. That part of his brain had been wiped clean by a flush of testosterone.

He grasped the girl by her shoulders and pressed his mouth to hers, tasting, plundering. Her mouth tasted like cinnamon. Her tongue tangled with his, pressing, toying, dancing. She shifted in his lap, back and forth, her buttocks moving against his cock.

He made himself let go. "What's your name?" It didn't seem right not to know.

She shrugged. "Does it matter?"

"Yes."

Her smile reminded him of a Christmas elf. "We don't really have names. Give us some. We'd like that."

The other two giggled agreement. "Yes, please."

He blinked. "Okay . . . Lavender. Rosa. Bianca." Not particularly original, but expedient.

Lavender wiggled on his lap, sending waves of arousal down his thighs, up his belly. His cock was so hard it hurt, straining against the leather trousers.

She grinned. "I like that. Lavender." Bending forward, she kissed his nose. "Thank you." Then she arched her back, pressing her breasts toward his face, and let her lavender gauze drape fall from her body.

She was exquisite. Heath lifted her breasts in his hands, pressing them against either side of his face, licking the valley between. Here, too, she tasted like cinnamon. He turned his head and captured a nipple between his lips, sucked it into his mouth, laving it with his tongue. It was pebbled and sweet, and she moaned as he drew on it with his mouth.

Vaguely, he heard the other two still laughing. Looking over Lavender's shoulder, he saw Rosa and Bianca tangled in each other's arms, touching the tips of their tongues together.

"Oh God," said Heath, unable to hold it back. He let himself slide off the couch, laying kisses down Lavender's soft belly, cupping her buttocks. To his surprise, she moved back.

"I'm here to please you," she said.

He settled onto his back on the floor. "This pleases me." Clasping her hips, he brought her to his mouth.

The hair between her legs was silky soft, tickling his lips and nose as he plunged his tongue between her labia. Not quite so cinnamony here, here she had the musky taste of an aroused woman. He licked the slick inner surfaces of her sex, plunged his tongue into her vagina. She wasn't as wet as he wanted her. He brought a hand around and pressed two fingers inside, working her with fingers and tongue. Did fairy sprites have a G-spot? He pressed against the right area and she gasped. So far, so good.

Then he felt hands on him. Either Rosa or Bianca had taken it upon herself to divest him of his pants. Nimble fingers unfastened the fly, then drew the trousers down his legs. The leather didn't want to let go, but the hands persisted. His erection sprang free to land in a waiting mouth.

He froze for a moment as the hot mouth closed on him, the firm, skilled tongue sliding around the head of his penis. It suddenly occurred to him that he wasn't going to be satisfied with this encounter until all three of these women had come. He hoped he was up to it.

The thought cooled his arousal enough that he was able to focus again on Lavender. She had begun a circular movement, rotating her sex against his mouth. He matched her rhythm, feeling her clit rise and tauten under his tongue. Turning his face a little, he looked up the slope of her belly toward her face. Her expression was blanked, turned inward, concentrating on her pleasure. He smiled against her musk, tasting finally the wetness he'd waited for. A moment later he felt her body clench, felt spasms shudder through the channel of her vagina. At the same time, her voice rose in a keen of ecstasy and surprise.

He held his tongue against the trembling nub of her clit until her shuddering had stopped. But it was getting harder and harder to concentrate, as the mouth on his cock drew more and more firmly, driving him far too close to climax.

Desperate to stop it—he just wasn't ready, not yet, not quite yet—he reached around and grasped himself, stopping the working mouth as he squeezed hard just below the head of his cock.

Lavender lifted away from him. His mouth quested automatically after her, his tongue seeking the musky flavor she'd taken away. But she kept moving, then repositioned herself next to him, kissing him. His mouth tasted like all the secrets of her body; her tongue reached in after them and took them back.

He could see now what was going on below his waist. Rosa had been the one going down on him; now she hovered, her lips inches from the head of his cock, waiting for his signal.

The inevitability of his orgasm had faded somewhat. He took a careful, relieved breath. Rosa grinned, revealing white teeth, with incisors just a shade too long. Her pale blue eyes gleamed with inhuman mischief. The very fairy-ness of her made him hard again.

She lifted her slim, lovely body over him and impaled herself on his aching erection.

He had a split second to admit two things to himself. First, at twenty-one, he'd only managed to have sex with two women. He'd just doubled his lifetime sexual experience. Second, he'd never been inside a woman without the protective barrier of a condom. This was hot, bare, skin-to-skin contact the likes of which he'd only imagined. Arousal, need, desire—whatever it was, it shot from his cock to his balls straight up his spine and exploded at the back of his head.

There was no holding back. He let out a howl born partially of frustration but mostly of pure shock and the glorious intensity of completion. His loins spasmed and clenched, his vision going red and black as hot come flooded out of him.

It seemed to go on for a long time, longer than past orgasms had. Just when he thought he would expire from lack of oxygen, he breathed again, one long, convulsive, shuddering breath.

He opened his eyes. Rosa still sat on his lap, her body convulsing in aftershocks on his fading erection while she giggled giggles that sounded like the tinkle of wind chimes.

"I wasn't ready," he gasped. "I wanted to wait."

"It's okay," Rosa said. "I was. Besides, we're magic."

She slid off him. As she did, the other two moved in on him. He had the distinct feeling he was no longer in control of this encounter.

He was right. They pressed him down onto the carpet. Bianca, the only one who hadn't come yet, positioned herself over his face. Lavender settled over his loins, her fingers attending to his sagging cock. Rosa sat a little to one side, playing with her own nipples. She seemed to be waiting for the right time to assume her new role.

There was little arguing with them, so he turned his head to sample Bianca's thigh. She tasted of vanilla. He could smell the musk of her desire, though, her pale, silky hair moist against his cheek.

She squealed as he touched the tip of his tongue to her clit, as if she hadn't expected it. The little knot of flesh hardened immediately, turning tight and pebbled under his ministrations. He rolled his tongue around it in a slow circle. She began to move above him, rotating her hips to match his rhythm.

Below, Lavender curled her hand around his cock.

It was his turn to jump in surprise, a little sound of shock rising in his throat. Energy had passed from her fingers into his penis, almost like a sudden static electric shock. His depleted cock leapt to immediate attention.

"There," he heard Lavender say. "That's the way we like it."

They *were* magic. He wondered how many times they could revitalize his erection, and if there was any danger he might die from too many orgasms.

Oh well. If he died, he'd die happy.

In her tower room, Elena watched through her magic mirror. Watched as Heath gamely—and literally—rose to the occasion, bringing the three fairy sprites one after the other to screams and giggles and howls of orgasm.

She hadn't been worked over like that in a long time. Maybe never, if she was honest with herself. Most of her sexual experience had come at the hands of fairy sprites. They were efficient, focused on providing pleasure, but she'd never made noises like that. Were the sprites just faking it there in the middle of Heath's living room? Probably—sprites were good at that—but she could tell by Heath's focused attention that his was more than a cursory attention to their pleasure.

It made her wonder what it would be like to be the subject of that attention. The thought made her desire run hot and liquid. Made her hand stray down her body to cup the heat of her own sex. In the mirror Heath had coaxed one of the sprites—Bianca, he'd called her—to her hands and knees, and was humping her hard from behind. Elena's viewing angle was perfect; she could see the wet length of his shaft as it slid in and out, the pull of Bianca's vagina clutching at him.

Elena swallowed. She could almost feel the thrust of Heath's cock into her own body, the pull of her own inner membranes against the friction. She moaned, clutching her mons, her clit rising under the pressure of her fingers against the fabric of her skirt.

"You need me?"

The voice ruffled the wisps of hair next to her ear. It was, of course, a fairy sprite. His fingers curled over her shoulders, feather-light.

She shook her head sharply. She didn't want a sprite. She wanted Heath. But Heath was there in his cottage, humping away at his own trio of sprites. And he hadn't yet passed the tests, the trials that would allow him access to her body and possibly more.

And the sprite was here, now. And ready, because he was a sprite, and sprites were always ready.

She tipped her head back toward him, her gaze riveted to Heath, the clenching and easing of his buttocks as he continued to pump, in and out, in and out . . . How long could he keep this up? The sprites had cast magic on him, of course—otherwise he would have been spent after coming the first time, inside Lavender.

"Take me," she said to the sprite.

Sprites always knew exactly what she wanted—that was their nature. Had she wanted foreplay, teasing, nibbling, tonguing, caressing and playing until she was wet, this one would have given it to her. But she wanted nothing of the sort, would have had no patience with it if it had been offered. So he jerked her skirt up and speared her, driving his long, rock-hard cock deep into her slick heat.

She moaned, fists clenching against the wall. Her face was millimeters from the mirror, her panting breath covering it with vapor, obscuring her view. When the fog cleared, Heath was bending back, his mouth open in a silent howl. His buttocks were clenched tight, his pelvis moving in taut spasms as he emptied himself into Bianca. Bianca screeched in delight, writhing so Heath had to tighten his grip on her to hold her still. Elena could see the indentation in Bianca's buttocks where Heath's fingers pressed hard, holding on to her.

"Oh God, oh God," Elena breathed into the mirror, a tight spiral of need wrenching its way up her chest. She reached between her legs, finding her clit awash with arousal, hard and ready. She pressed her fingers into it, so close to coming she could hardly stand the pressure. Her sex ached—with the slick, pounding penetration of the sprite's cock, and the tight-wound tension inside her let go in a long, slow spiral of pounding.

A low, harsh sound came from her throat, rising and falling with the pulsation of her orgasm. She trembled, her thighs shaking, as she held herself there against the wall, against the mirror, helpless in the intensity of her completion. She had never come this hard before. The sprite knew what he was doing—they always knew—but just watching Heath had ratcheted her up several notches.

If just looking at him could do this to her, what would it be like to actually fuck him?

But no. She wanted more than that. She hadn't brought him here just for a good lay. There were other issues at stake, and she had to remember that.

In the mirror, the sprites had laid Heath down on the floor and were caressing him, licking him. Rosa curled up against his chest while Bianca massaged his feet and Lavender tongued his nipples. He looked beatific, eyes and cock at half-mast. They were done with him, or he was done with them. But he still wanted them there—if he hadn't, they would have dissipated already.

Tears gathered suddenly in Elena's throat. Behind her, the sprite shifted, then suddenly was gone. She sensed his dispersion. She had willed it, if not quite consciously.

She wanted Heath. She'd brought him here because there was a chance he was the right man, with the right blood, the right soul. But now it was more than that—more than the semantics of finding a suitable mate who could produce a suitable heir.

She would have given up her soul, her very reality, to have been a fairy sprite right then. To be free to be there, participating in the scene in the mirror instead of just watching, to taste his skin, to comb his hair with her fingers, to take his cock into her mouth, into her body. She wanted him that much.

A sob escaped her lips and she pressed them hard together. She slapped her hand flat against the glass of the mirror and it went black.

Chapter Four

Heath woke to the sound of voices. At first he thought the sprites were still here, but he rolled over in bed to find himself alone.

Probably for the best. He didn't think he could repeat last night's performance, magic or no magic.

The voices sounded close, but there was no one else in the room. After a moment's reflection, he realized they came from outside, drifting through the open window.

The window was right over the head of his bed. Rolling onto his stomach, he levered himself up on his elbows and pushed the filmy curtains aside.

It was a pretty day. The sun was bright, the lawn green, the distant trees greener. A few ducks meandered under his window, eating grass, or seeds and suchlike lying in the grass. Heath wasn't sure. He didn't see anyone else.

He still heard the voices, though. Thin, reedy voices.

"Damn, I feel like shit this morning," said the male voice.

A higher pitched, female voice answered, "Did you eat something you shouldn't have?"

"Don't think so. *Graack!*"

Heath blinked. Beneath him on the grass, one of the male ducks, a mallard with a teal-green head, gave a full-body shudder and said, "*Graack!*" again.

Holy shit. The ducks. He could hear the freaking ducks, and they were talking to each other.

"I know how you are," the female said, wiggling her wings into place. "You'll eat anything. What did you do to yourself?"

The male duck "*graack*"-ed again, then shook his blue-green head. "There was a pile of mash by the back door of the dining room. There might've been a lump in it."

"Might've?" The female duck sounded quite put out. "Well, whatever you ate, I hope it comes out without killing you."

They waddled away from the cottage, toward a little pond not far from the forest. Heath leaned back away from the window and shook his head to clear it. Talking ducks. It was too much.

Then he remembered. The stag. Elena in the clearing, conversing with the animal as if it could understand her. As if she could understand it.

And the mysterious slab of meat. Had it been magic? Was that why he'd felt so strangely compelled to taste it?

He rubbed his hands over his face and shook his head, trying to restore some sense of reality to the situation. It seemed a hopeless task.

Finally he rolled out of bed and headed into the kitchen. He was hungry. Ravenous, actually. Not surprising, after last night's exercise. He was surprised he wasn't comatose.

There wasn't much in the refrigerator, but he found a carton of milk, butter and a bag of grapes. In the cupboard, among a collection of canned goods and dry pasta, he dug out a can of fruit cocktail and, from another cabinet, a loaf of bread. It was enough for breakfast.

He was working his way through the pile of grapes when he heard more voices from outside, coming in this time through the kitchen window.

"Please, God, let it be people this time," he muttered, and went to see if it was.

Maybe they were people. They might have been sprites—it

was hard to tell. But they weren't ducks. They trudged across the lawn, one of them carrying a shotgun casually over one shoulder.

"I'll hack up the lot of 'em if I have to," one said to the other. "Friggin' ducks."

"Shit," said Heath. He slammed through the front door of the cottage. The men turned, looking taken aback, as he accosted them. "Hey! What's going on?"

They looked at each other, then the one with the gun said, "Lady Elena's lost a ring. We're thinking one of the ducks maybe ate it. They'll eat damn near anything, 'specially that fat drake."

Drake. Drake was a boy duck, right? Heath scrambled through his brain fruitlessly for a plan. "So what are you doing?"

"Gonna look for the ring."

"With a shotgun?"

"Well, it might be in the shit out there by the pond, but if it ain't, we ain't got much choice but to shoot 'em and cut 'em open 'til we find it."

"No, no, no." An hour ago, it wouldn't have bothered him a bit. Ducks were ducks, for God's sake—good for eating and not much else. But the drake had talked and "*graacked.*" "I don't think killing is really necessary."

The man with the gun regarded him in surprise. They really didn't seem like sprites to Heath. They were too blunt, too unattractive. But perhaps sprites manifested based on what jobs they were required to perform. Certainly the three girls of last night had been made for sex. These two seemed made for—well, for shooting ducks.

"No killin', huh? Then how do you propose we find that ring?"

Heath had absolutely no idea. "Just let me handle it. If I don't find the ring, then we'll figure out later what we should do next."

The two men shrugged. "Yeah, all right. You come look for us at the house when you get tired playin' in duck shit."

Howling with laughter, they headed back to the estate. Heath watched, his sense of triumph quickly fading to perplexity.

He had no idea what he was going to do.

Looking in her mirror, Elena smoothed a brush through her long, unbound hair. In the mirror's surface, Elena now regarded not Heath's cottage, or anyone else's sexual activity, but a man, somewhat older than herself, with dark hair and a neatly trimmed beard. Her father.

"I merely speak out of concern for you. You know that, Elena."

She sighed, very carefully, so it didn't show. Her father had a matching mirror on the other side of their connection, and though he exasperated her, she had no desire to annoy him. "I know that, Father. But I can handle this situation."

"You have been known in the past to act rashly."

"That was a long time ago." She gritted her teeth—carefully.

"Only concern, Elena. Only concern." Her father's face was gentle, and she had to admit she could actually see in his eyes the concern he claimed to feel.

"He has passed the first test." *Best to move on,* she thought, *address the issues, as he would expect to hear them addressed.* "I am prepared to move on to the next trial."

Her father nodded soberly. "I'm still not sure I like this. I would much prefer to choose a man for you myself."

"I know. But you agreed to let me do it this time. I'm old enough and strong enough to handle this. I know what I want."

"All right. But if it appears things have gotten out of hand—"

"I know. I'll expect to see you. But I don't think anything will get out of hand."

Her father's frown was grimmer than she would have liked, but she wasn't going to tell him anything else. She worked her mother's magic here, magic he had no right to.

He clenched his teeth. "I wish to make final approval."

"I don't think that will be necessary."

His eyes flashed, but his voice was even. "We shall see." He inclined his head. His image blinked out, and Elena's reflection rose to replace it. Frowning at her own face, she continued to brush her hair.

She had no intention of telling her father what was going on here. Her mother had left her a legacy of magic from her own clan, and a way of judging men that stemmed directly from her mother's bad experience with her father. The test of the White Snake—the magical flesh that allowed her to communicate with animals—had proven Heath's magical blood. Had he not been of the correct lineage, he would not have been compelled to eat, or if he had, it would have killed him.

The other "test"—Heath's reaction to the fairy sprites—was of her own devising, and the results had been as significant to her as his ability to assimilate the meat of the White Snake. She'd seen too many otherwise qualified candidates take their pleasure from the sprites—sometimes brutally—and give no consideration to the beings with whom they coupled. Heath had been different. She could still see his face buried between Lavender's thighs, his mouth and tongue working diligently—

She closed her eyes and drew a long, steadying breath. Yes, he was different. A man of proper blood, as proven by the White Snake. And quite possibly a man of proper temperament, as implied by his actions with the sprites.

She just hoped he passed the duck test.

"*Hey, you!* You out there on the pond!"

Heath felt like an idiot, jumping up and down at the edge of the pond, waving his arms like a crazy person at the group of ducks swimming near the pond's opposite edge. The drake and his—wife? Girlfriend? Duck paramour?—had already taken to the water by the time he got to the pond. He could tell which one was the drake he wanted, though. He was fatter than the others, and kept shaking his head and opening his bill. Heath could almost hear the "*graaack*" sound.

The ducks looked toward him. Some of them put their bills close together, but Heath was too far away to hear what they were saying.

"Yeah, you, yah duck-freak morons!" He started to jog around the perimeter of the pond. "I need to talk to Grack!"

"There is no one here named Grack!" one of them hollered back in his reedy, annoying voice.

"*Graaack!*" said the drake.

Heath pointed. "Him! I need to talk to him."

"You address me, sir?" Grack called. He swam tentatively toward Heath. "You wish my fat self for dinner, perhaps?"

"No, not at all," said Heath. He spread his hands. "I don't have a gun. I just want to talk." The duck came closer. "And don't be so pretentious."

Grack ruffled his wings as he approached the shore. He stepped out of the pond and stood near Heath.

"*Graaack!*" he said, then, "What the hell do you want?"

"That's more like it," Heath muttered. "Look, I heard you talking this morning under my window. You ate some mash you found by the dining hall. I think you swallowed one of Elena's rings."

"Oh, dear God. She'll have me shot and slice me open before she loses a ring."

"Yeah, she sent some guys out to do just that, but I told them to let me take care of it."

The drake bobbed his head. "Then I am in your debt, most gracious human-creature."

"I take it you haven't crapped it out yet?"

The drake looked affronted. "Not that I am aware."

"Can you barf it up or something? Can ducks vomit?"

"That may not be necessary. I believe—*graaack*—I believe it may be lodged in my throat."

"Let me look." Heath dropped to his knees and held out a hand.

Grack tipped his head, eyeing Heath from one bird-black eye. "You touch my neck, you damn well better not twist my head off."

"Not much you could do about it if I did, is there?" He wiggled his fingers. "Just come on. I'm not gonna hurt you."

Tentative, the duck approached him. Heath gently slid his fingers down the curve of Grack's neck. Sure enough, there was a lump about halfway down. "If this was solid, you would have choked to death."

"It is quite uncomfortable, nonetheless."

Carefully, Heath felt the round lump of the ring, wedged in the duck's esophagus. "Let me squeeze it and you cough and let's see what happens."

"Ow," Grack protested, as Heath pressed below the ring, trying to move it upward. "*Graack!*" said Grack.

"It moved." Only a little, but it had moved. "Here, do it again."

"*Blerk!*" said the duck, his voice reedier and a little choked. "That is quite painful."

"Just hack again."

"*Graaaack!*"

The hard lump under Heath's fingers gave abruptly. Something bright and gold flew through the air. The drake shook his head sharply and took a step back. "My goodness!"

Heath had tried to follow the arc of the flying ring, but it had moved too fast. He fixed his attention on a spot in the grass where he thought it might have fallen and headed that way.

"You wanna help me find this?" he called back to the duck, afraid to look over his shoulder for fear of losing his focus on the spot in the grass.

"*Blerk!*" said the drake.

"Useless pile of poultry," Heath muttered. He went to his hands and knees, combing through the grass with his fingers. A moment later he touched something round and slick and scooped it up. Sure enough, a circle of gold lay in his hand. "Got it!"

He got up and turned around to show the ring to the duck. But Grack had already slipped back into the pond.

"Thank you!" Grack quacked in his reedy voice, then paddled hard toward his wife and the other ducks. The female duck met him halfway, tapping his neck affectionately with her bill.

Oh, well. What had he expected? Grack was just a duck, after all. Heath put the ring in his pocket and headed back to the cottage.

Intending to finish his breakfast, he went into the kitchen. And heard voices again. Tiny voices, so faint he could barely make them out at all. What the hell was this, then? He didn't see anything untoward . . .

Then he approached the counter, reached for the remains of his breakfast. It was covered with ants.

He recoiled in disgust and looked around for a magazine, a newspaper, anything to squash the insects. But there was nothing at hand. And then he realized where the voices were coming from.

Shit. He couldn't even squash ants now? Hesitantly, he bent closer.

"C'mon, good sandwich, good sandwich." The voices were barely audible, even though several were speaking in unison. Heath peered intently at the insects, trying to make out which ones were talking.

If he could understand them, they must be able to understand him. "Could you get the hell off my food, please?" he said.

"We're hungry! We're hungry!"

They spoke in little chorus groups of ten or twelve, each at a slightly different pitch. The result was, once Heath could hear it, alternately harmonious or dissonant, depending on the pitches. Still, he could barely hear them. He bent so close he could see the tiny antennas waving.

"Look, if you're hungry, you can have that food. But first get off it, go outside, and wait by the door. I'll bring it out. If you promise to stay out of my house, I'll leave you something outside every morning."

The ants congregated in a group. A vague buzzing rose from them as they apparently discussed the proposal among themselves. Then a group detached from the others and came toward him.

"Your offer is generous, but we would be greatly appreciative if you could supply a meal at morning and evening."

Heath leaned even closer, until he could make out each individual ant's set of fine pincers, opening and closing.

"You're pretty bold, considering I could wipe out the lot of you with one hand." He waited for a reaction, but got none. Ants, he realized belatedly, didn't have facial expressions. Or faces, really. Just bug-eyes and tiny pincer mouths. "All right," he said finally. "Morning and evening it is. Now get the hell out of my house."

Obediently, they marched down the counter, across the floor and out the door. Heath picked up the dish and set it outside, watching the last few ants leave the room.

He shook his head. "Un-freaking-believable."

Well, so much for breakfast. He might as well get the ring back to Elena before her sprite-or-not-sprite-goons came back with that shotgun. Careful to avoid the ants, he stepped over the doorstep and headed for the estate.

"He sent you back?"

Elena forced herself to work up a miffed expression as she regarded the two groundskeepers. It helped to cross her arms firmly over her chest, so she did. "And you obeyed him?"

The larger of the two workers screwed up his face. "We figured we didn't wanna kill no ducks if we didn't have to."

"Fine." Elena spoke sharply, though inside she was pleased. "Go on about your business, then. Check the roses."

"Yes, milady." They trudged off.

As soon as they were gone, Elena grinned and clapped her hands like a little girl. Heath had rescued the ducks. This was perfect.

Heath had entered the mansion through the dining hall door, but somehow he wasn't in the dining hall. He was, instead, in a regular hallway-type hall, that went on and on and seemed to lead absolutely nowhere.

This was nuts. All he'd wanted to do was see Elena, give her the ring, and go back to the cottage, or possibly find something else he might be allowed to do in this place. Instead he wandered an empty hallway with her ring in his pocket. He slid his fingers over the round, smooth surface. It was oddly warm, as if it carried something of her in it, enough of her essence to keep the metal perpetually warm.

"Okay, what's the deal," he muttered. "Is there some way to get through this nutty place?"

"This way."

He stopped, staring. The voice seemed to have come from the walls, but it was Elena's voice.

"Pardon?" he said.

"Just follow the twinkles."

Oh, of course. Twinkles. He shook his head in disgust as a sparkling shimmer formed in the air in front of him. A little ball of fairy dust, he thought. Just like what a fairy might sneeze out during fairy allergy season.

The shimmery thing zigzagged down the hallway. He followed.

The trip proved surprisingly short. In a matter of minutes, he found himself standing in front of a door, which opened to show Elena behind it, smiling. Her long, white shirt was unbuttoned halfway down, her rich, blue, velvet skirt clung to the contours of her thighs.

"What may I do for you?"

Heath fingered the ring in his pocket. Its warmth rested comfortably against his fingers and for a moment he didn't want to give it up. Then he withdrew it and held it out to her. "I just wanted to return this."

"Oh! My ring!" She took it from his hand and looked at it, smiling, then slipped it on her finger. "Where did you find it?"

"One of the ducks—it was caught in his throat. I got him to cough it up."

"Eww, lovely." She gave an adorably disgusted crinkle of her nose.

"Um . . ." Heath put fingers to his forehead, gathering himself. "The ducks . . . they were talking to me."

"I know." At his befuddled look, she gestured with an elegant hand. "Come in. Please."

He did, brushing past her. She closed her eyes at the contact, at the heat that passed through her at his touch.

"So what's the deal?" he said. "I mean with the talking ducks and all that."

She didn't want him asking questions. Not right now. The stakes were too high and it would be better for everyone if she closed the deal before her father found out what she'd discovered a long time ago.

At least she hoped it would close the deal. If not—well, she could handle that later.

She pushed the door shut behind her and ripped open her shirt. He stared at her. Elena was not a woman who believed in subtlety. Or bras. His eyes flicked over her bare breasts.

"Do you *really* want to talk about ducks?"

He closed his gaping mouth with a snap. "No. No, I don't think I do."

"Good. Because neither do I." She closed the distance between them and pressed her breasts against his chest. "Touch me."

He stared down at the pale mounds of her breasts pressed against him, but somehow couldn't bring himself to actually touch her. If he were honest with himself, he would have to admit that he was more than a little afraid of her. And being afraid of her didn't exactly make him want to rush to get her hands into his pants.

"What's wrong? I know you're functional." She closed her hand on his crotch. It was, of course, impossible for him to hide the erection he was sprouting. "See? You want it inside me, don't you?"

"If you're going for romance, it's not working."

"No romance. Just sex." She pulled his t-shirt up to his armpits and the warm mounding of her breasts against his bare chest made him close his eyes and draw a breath. There was just no sense fighting this.

"Okay. As long as we're clear." He bent his head and took her mouth.

She was hot and soft and it occurred to him that she smelled like a woman, not like cinnamon or vanilla, like the fairy sprites. Just like skin and desire. It was enough.

He pressed her mouth open with his, plundering, tasting, her tongue hot and eager against his. She pulled his shirt the rest of the way off, tossing it to the floor, and he gathered her in to him, his arms around her.

It never occurred to him to wonder why she was so eager. After all, he'd pleased three women quite thoroughly last night, so why shouldn't one woman succumb to his charms? Even though this woman seemed quite in control of herself and nothing at all like a fairy sprite summoned specifically for his pleasure. This was not a time for the asking of questions. This was pretty much just the time for the grabbing of opportunities.

For a few seconds, Elena felt guilty, knowing she was using him for her own ends. But he was willing and able, so what difference did it make? There wasn't much leeway here for niceties. She knew what she wanted, and why, and it was time to claim it.

His mouth was eager enough, finding her breast, drawing hard on it. His hands slid down her back, pulling her closer, trying to make this softer, more poetic than there was any call for it to be. She wanted pure sex—wanted him to mark her with it. She tore at his trousers, pulling the annoying things out of her way. What had she been thinking, giving him leather pants? They were too damn hard to get off.

She managed, though, and was rewarded with the hard, jutting length of his erection, springing forward into her hand as she reached for it. He was hot and hard under her fingers and she grasped him firmly as he moaned into her ear.

"Not so fast," he said.

"I like it fast. Fast and hard and up against the wall. Don't you?"

He was breathing hard, his blue eyes gone gray with need. "I like whatever you like."

"Then go for it."

He shifted her, getting her skirt out of the way, and she clung to him so she wouldn't fall as he adjusted her thighs against his hips and pushed himself hard inside her.

The sensation caught her off guard, and she stared into his eyes for a moment, her own eyes wide and blinking. There was no logical reason he should feel so different, but he did, and every millimeter of his hard flesh, embedded in her soft body, made her desperately aware he was not a fairy sprite.

He didn't seem to notice her slight hesitation. He held still for a breath, his eyes closed, as deep inside her as he could get.

Poised, she thought. Waiting for something. She had no idea what.

Finally he looked at her again and smiled. "Sorry. That just felt so good I had to savor it."

She melted. His smile, his blue eyes, the genuineness of his voice—it tore her up inside in a way plain sex could never do. The need inside her had become so intense she wasn't sure she could stand it.

Back to the sex, then, she thought. *Hang on to something you can understand.* She clenched herself down hard on his cock, until he let out a gaspy grunt.

"Don't just stand there," she said, though the melted place just under her heart kind of wished he would.

But he smiled, and kissed her, and then proceeded to ride her, supporting her against the wall and giving it to her fast and hard, just as she'd asked. She closed her eyes, fighting back the mewling kitten noises building in the back of her throat.

His cock inside her was hard but his mouth went soft against hers as he continued to kiss her, his tongue tracing her lips, then opening them. He pressed his tongue against hers, curled the tips together. One of his hands cupped her breast, rolling her nipple, mounding her soft flesh against her body.

No fairy sprite had ever touched her quite like this. Because the fairy sprites could only give her what she wanted, and she'd never known she wanted this. Fast and hard between her legs, soft and gentle on her face, her throat, her breasts. His mouth climbed over her as if he had never tasted female skin before, his tongue soft on her flesh, his hands roving but still securing her.

She felt safe. Profound. And as he suddenly bucked up hard between her legs, his release pulsing inside her, she thought she might even feel loved. The thought made the curling fire inside her come together and fly, filling her blood as she shattered and shouted with a climax that made her heart pound and her thighs shiver and the mewling of kittens come unfettered from her throat.

He kissed her softly until her shivering faded, still holding her carefully against the wall.

"Was it good?" he said, smiling.

"Good," she answered, and her voice trembled. "Yes, good."

He lowered her to the floor. "What now?"

She could only stare at him for a moment, still overwhelmed by the pounding and the melting of her body, of her heart.

"Stay with me," she said. "Stay until morning."

He nodded. His smile looked less satisfied than content. "I can do that."

He did, and they made love again as the sunlight began to spill in through the windows. This time she let him lead, and his gentleness made her want to weep. Wrung and weak, satiated beyond imagining, she drifted back to sleep in the circle of his arms.

Chapter Five

Elena was awakened by the sound of a familiar voice coming from the other room. A very loud familiar voice. Loud and angry.

Her father.

"Elena! Turn this mirror on this instant!"

She took a long breath. This didn't sound good. Not good at all.

Next to her, Heath stirred and blinked. "Geez. Who's mad?"

"My beloved father," Elena drawled. She swung her legs out of the bed and grabbed a robe. On the way into the other room, she made a mostly futile attempt to straighten her hair.

Heath rolled over so he could watch her. She covered her sleek curves too quickly, before he could get the full view.

She looked worried, though. Why was she worried? Was her father a scary person? Curious, he followed her out of the bed, stopping in the doorframe. Even in Fairyland, it couldn't be a good thing to get caught naked with an angry guy's daughter.

"It's a little early," Elena admonished the face in the mirror. It was a long, angular face, the chin darkened with beard, the eyes flashing with anger.

"Explain yourself," the man snapped.

Elena crossed her arms over her chest. "Explain what?"

"You told me you had a candidate. You told me you would test him appropriately. You never told me who he was."

"If he passes my tests, does it matter?"

"Yes, it does, and I think you know why."

"Your quest for vengeance has nothing to do with me."

"It does now. You made sure of that." The mirror went black.

Elena threw up her arms. "Shit. I should have known this would happen."

Heath took a step toward her, wondering if he should try to comfort her, or just stay out of the way. He opted for the latter. "I don't understand. What is this all about?"

She turned toward him. "It's about your grandfather. Your grandfather Cabot was of the Blood. He found his way here through the pool—the same pool you came through."

Heath watched her pour juice into a glass, focused on the curve of her wrist where it emerged from her sleeve. "The Blood?"

"Human-fairy mix. Certain branches of mixed blood resonate with certain deposits of magic. Your family's heritage is rooted here. This magic is your magic."

"So I'm . . . part fairy?" It was a strange concept.

"That's right. Genetically speaking, it goes back pretty far, so it's quite diluted. Magically speaking that doesn't matter. All it takes is one gene cluster."

"Really?"

"Really."

She put the juice away and settled across the table from him. He had barely touched his eggs and toast, more concerned at the moment with her story. "So you're looking for what? A suitable stud?"

"Don't be so cold about it. I need someone of the right bloodline to father heirs, yes, but that's not all I'm looking for."

He sipped his juice, trying to resist the urge to put the worst possible spin on everything she said. "So what's the deal with Grampa Cabot?"

"He found his way here, like I said. And there was a woman."

He nodded. "I've seen pictures."

"Yes. Well, that woman was, at the time, my father's wife."

"Oh."

"'Oh' is right. Your grandfather stole her away and my father never forgave him for that. He remarried, they had me, and I'm all magically worthy, but he's never let go of that wound."

"So this is bad for me."

"It's very bad for you."

"And the fact I knew nothing about this doesn't work at all in my favor?"

"Not as far as my father's concerned."

"So . . . what happens now?"

"I don't know. He's coming here, I know that much. After that—I guess we'll find out."

Elena's father, Lord Conal, was a large and intimidating man. He stood at the head of the dining room table—which had reappeared somehow, along with the long dining room—and glared down at both of them.

"Elena, you knew this would be unacceptable. Why did you go through with the testing?"

Heath dared a surreptitious glance at Conal, then looked quickly back down at the table. He'd had some bad experiences with girlfriends' fathers before, but as far as he knew, none of those men had been capable of turning him into a frog. Or worse.

Elena, however, met his ire with a steady glare. "I saw all your candidates, father. They were weak, spineless men, or they were brutal bullies. There was no in between."

"They were men I felt capable of leading you, or of being led by you."

Elena's lips thinned. "This man, father, is capable of leading *with* me. That's what I want."

Conal glared at Heath. Feeling the scrutiny on the top of his head, Heath looked up, then fought the urge to look away. He was pretty sure it would help Elena's cause if he could manage to show some backbone. "I am not my grandfather," he said firmly.

Conal scowled. "You look like him."

This startled Heath. Grampa Cabot had been old and wrinkled and frankly not that attractive. But he'd been young once. He must have been young when he'd been here.

Which begged the question—how old was this Lord Conal? For that matter, how old was Elena?

He gave her a sharp, questioning look, but she was focused on her father. "He's right. He's a completely different person and he deserves a chance."

Conal's eyes narrowed. "Okay. Fine. I'll give him a chance."

Elena stiffened a little, becoming more wary in spite of her father's apparent acquiescence. "What kind of chance?"

"I will set him a series of tasks. If he can accomplish these tasks, then I will grant him your hand."

"No, father. I grant him my own hand."

"Along with various other parts of your body, I wager, and you probably did that ahead of time."

Elena came to her feet. "Yes, in fact, I have. Therefore we are already bonded. Therefore your dissent means nothing."

"Bullshit." Conal's voice was steady but his hands trembled against the table. "My dissent means everything. You will marry no one without my approval."

Elena ground her teeth together, but said nothing.

Heath didn't know how the rules worked here, but he knew enough to realize Elena was up against a wall. And not in the fun way, like she'd been yesterday. Apparently she had no real choice but to follow her father's wishes.

Finally, in a dead voice, she said, "You're going to kill him."

Conal's smile made Heath cold. "That's entirely up to him. If he's truly such a wonderful candidate, he'll come through this with flying colors." He turned to Heath. "You'll find your instructions."

"Where?"

"Where they are. That's your first challenge. Find them. And you—" he pointed an accusing finger at Elena, "you may not assist him in any way. If you do, I'll know about it and the tests will be invalidated."

With a cold half-smile, he lifted his hand and disappeared.

"You son of a bitch!" Elena shouted after him.

"I heard that!" said Conal's disembodied voice.

Heath shoved his hands through his hair. "This really can't be good."

"You're right. It isn't."

She slid her hand comfortingly over his shoulder. "This is too much. Let me send you home."

"First I want you to answer a question." His voice came out harder than he had intended, and she drew back from him, her eyes widening a little.

"What?"

"The tests. You told your father you tested me. What did you do?"

Her eyes remained wide and startled for a moment, then she gathered herself. "The snake."

"Snake? What snake?"

"The meat. I ate it at dinner, I left it out for you, you ate it later."

Heath stared, trying to process what she'd said, while she met his gaze firmly. "That was dead snake?"

"It's magical." She squared her shoulders, defiant, as if he might challenge or reject her. "Consuming the meat allows you to talk to the animals. It was the final proof of your fairy blood. If you hadn't had the Blood, if you hadn't been of the right family, the magic in the meat wouldn't have worked on you."

"What *would* it have done?"

Her jaw clenched, then released. "Theoretically, it would have killed you."

"Wonderful." This was the worst fairy tale ever. "So you just left it out for me to eat, knowing it could kill me?"

Shifting her shoulders again, Elena lifted her head and glared him in the eye. "Theoretically. But in actuality, if you hadn't had the appropriate blood, you would have had no desire to eat it."

Heath considered that, then nodded slowly. "I see." He remembered the compulsion. It had certainly had the intensity of magic. "How long will it last?"

"I don't know. I have to eat again about every six to eight months. It could last less time with you, or longer."

"My fairy blood is less pure, so it shouldn't last as long."

"It doesn't work that way. It's not predictable."

Although her voice was relatively normal, her body remained taut, as if expecting a blow. Heath eyed her for a few more seconds, then let out a long breath. "Fair enough."

She relaxed abruptly. "Now, please, let me send you home before my father kills you."

She was trying to hold back her emotions, but tears had sprung into her eyes in spite of her careful control, and her voice had shivered. Thinking about last night, about what they'd shared, he clenched his teeth in resolve. "No."

"I don't think you understand what you're getting into."

"I think it's probably better that way." He bent forward and kissed her, hard and firm. "But I'm not leaving, so don't try to make me."

She smiled sadly. "All right. It's your choice. But I can't help you." She stood. "I'm going now, but I'll see you later. I can't help you but I can see you. I just have to make some preparations."

Wondering what she meant, he nodded. "All right."

"Be careful," she said, and she too, disappeared, leaving Heath to make his way out the sissy human way, through the door.

The sun was about halfway between its zenith and sunset, and Heath still had no idea what he was looking for. He'd spent the hours since this morning meandering over the property, poking through the woods, scanning the fields, even trying to search parts of the mansion, though that hadn't gone well and he'd had to summon a sprite to lead him back out. But all his efforts so far had proven fruitless.

Now he stood next to the lake, watching the twinkle of sunlight on the rippling water. Under the shush of the wind he heard vaguely the voices of insects, exchanging their impressions of the weather. There were so many voices they blended together, becoming an indistinct hum of sound. Only an occasional word reached him, enough to convince him bugs rarely talked about anything remotely interesting.

The lake was about the only place he wouldn't be able to search with any kind of thoroughness. Sure, he could swim, but he didn't have any scuba gear, so it would be hard for him to check the bottom, or any of the deeper water levels. It followed, by his own logic, that this was the most likely place for Conal to have hidden the first set of instructions. But after two hours of standing there staring at the shining water, he was no closer to a plan.

One of the groups of bugs started talking about a new batch of flowers, somewhere to the east. Heath listened for a moment, not sure why he cared. Then he realized it wasn't the flower conversation that had caught his attention. It was something else, another voice.

"Help! Help!"

That wasn't a bug voice. He didn't think it was human, and it didn't sound like a duck, either. So what was it? He bent his head, taking a step forward at the same time.

"Help us!"

The voice wasn't much clearer, but he was definitely heading in the right direction. He took a few running steps, shifted his direction just a bit, then stopped again.

"Help! Here! Help!"

The voice was right under his feet now. He dropped to his knees, trying to find its source.

Fish. Three medium-sized koi-type fish lay just to his left, struggling feebly in the long grasses. Heath grabbed them, one by one, by the tail and tossed them back into the water. They shimmied off, glinting. He watched with a smile. What good was it to be able to talk to animals if you couldn't do some good with it?

"Dammit!" What good was it to be able to talk to animals if you didn't take the opportunity to get them to do useful things for you? Like, for example, search the damn lake. Smacking himself in the forehead, Heath straightened.

"Hello? Hello, human person?"

Heath squatted again. "Yes?"

The fish had swum right up to the edge of the lake, almost into the grass. It poked its orange mouth just out of the water to speak. "Thank you for saving me. I am most grateful. If I can ever do anything for you, please call me. My name is Fish."

Well, that was original. He wondered what the other fishes' names were. "Yes, Fish, you can help me."

"I can help you now? How extraordinary!"

It seemed like a big word for a fish. He explained the situation as briefly as possible. "So if there's anything in the lake you don't recognize, could you maybe bring it up here for me to take a look at?"

"Of course, human person. I will bring things here. Wait for me."

"You bet."

Heath found a comfortable, relatively dry spot to relax in while he waited. This talking to animals thing was freakish, but maybe it would come in handy after all. He certainly couldn't search the lake by himself, and this fish was the most logical choice for an assistant. He wondered where the other ones were. Ungrateful scaly things, anyway.

A few minutes later, the fish came back and stuck his nose above the water. "Nothing yet," he said, and disappeared again.

More time passed. Heath shaded his eyes against the sun. He was starting to see spots in his vision, afterimages from the reflection of the sun off the water. He wondered how long the attention span of a fish was. At this point, koi-boy might have forgotten what he was looking for.

But, finally, just as he was about to drift off in the heat, Heath heard a sudden splashing. He straightened. The fish was struggling with something, just below the surface of the water. Heath leaned forward and reached under the fish, catching hold of what it was carrying. His finger snagged in a loop of cloth, attached to something that wasn't particularly heavy, but was definitely a bit much for a medium-sized koi fish.

"Oh, goodness," said the fish, as Heath relieved it of its load. "That was quite cumbersome."

Again with the big words. Did they have fish dictionaries down there at the bottom of the lake? "Do you think it might be what I'm looking for?" It was a long tube with a cloth loop at one end. He pulled at the loop, trying to get the lid off the tube. It was fastened on quite tightly, undoubtedly to ensure it would be waterproof.

The fish had dunked its head back under the water, producing waves of bubbles. Catching its breath, Heath thought. When it came back up, it said, "I asked some of the crustaceans in the area and they said it fell into the water only a few hours ago. It was embedded in a bit of a mud bank, so I apologize for the delay in bringing it up."

"Not a problem."

"I'll be back," said the fish, "to see if this is the right thing. But right now I must swim a bit."

"Sure. See you in a few."

The fish flipped its tail up as it disappeared under the water. Heath yanked again at the cloth cord. Still, the lid didn't give. He grasped it firmly and twisted it, and finally it moved a little. A few more, forceful twists, and it came off. Inside was a piece of parchment, neatly rolled. Heath pulled it out and read it.

> Congratulations. You have completed the first phase of my series of tests. Rejoice in your victory, as it is probably the last one you will have.
>
> For your next instructions, meet me in the field.

"Asshole," Heath muttered. He stood, looking back across the field behind him. He thought he could see Conal in the distance, but with a soft curve of hill mostly blocking his view, he couldn't be sure.

"Is it what you need?" the fish's voice said from behind him.

"Yes, it is. Thank you very much."

"Good. Then my debt is repaid." It shimmied back into the water, disappearing into the blue depths.

Heath shoved the parchment back into the tube, then trudged back across the field, toward the dark speck that might or might not be Conal. As he drew closer, cresting the small hill, he discovered it was, indeed, Mr. Bigshot Lord of Fairy.

Conal looked none too pleased as Heath closed the distance between them. Stopping a few feet away, Heath lifted the tube. "Got it," he said.

"I see." Conal's voice and expression were sour. "How did you manage that? You're not even wet."

"Trade secret," Heath replied. "So, what's the next bit of nonsense you have prepared?"

"You might wish to address me with more respect."

"I might. What's your deal, anyway?"

Conal twitched a broody eyebrow. "My deal? I don't like you."

"You don't know me. You don't like my grandfather. And, news flash, he's dead."

"Good."

"So deal with me. Talk to me. What is your problem with me?"

Conal glared at him, eyes sparking. They were blue, like his daughter's. "You fucked my daughter."

"No, I didn't."

"You deny—"

"I made love with your daughter." Heath broke through Conal's anger. "If you don't know the difference, then it's no wonder Grampa stole your girl."

Conal's eyes went cold and hard. For a moment Heath was afraid. Any minute now, there would be the hopping legs and the slimy skin and he would say nothing but "Ribbit," for the rest of his life. Conal was shaking with rage. Maybe Heath would get lucky and he'd just get the shit beaten out of him.

But, suddenly, Conal turned, whipping his arm into the air. From his hand flew sparkles of gold, hundreds, thousands, more than his fist could have possibly contained. A smattering of them struck Heath's face. He looked down to see the gold sifting into the grass. Grain, tiny kernels of wheat.

With his back still half turned toward Heath, Conal growled, "Find them. Find them all. By sunrise, or I'll see you banished from this realm." Then he stalked away.

Wonderful. He wondered if the task would have been a little easier if he'd kept his mouth shut. Probably not. Conal seemed to have it in for him.

He sank to his knees and scooped up a handful of grain. There was no way this was going to get done by morning, if ever. He was well and thoroughly screwed.

He tried, though. He tried for hours. He found maybe a bushel, piled it up in one spot, and started work on another. By sunset he had two piles, but wasn't even a good start. Judging by what he'd seen of the field, Conal had scattered the grain over a good three-acre area. Between the sheer volume of the area and the long grass that hid the kernels, it was hopeless.

But he refused to give up. Maybe he was just an idiot, but somehow he couldn't throw his hands up and say, "Screw this." He kept thinking about Elena, her blue eyes and golden hair and her soft, sweet body. Maybe, he thought, he was actually in love with her. Why else would he be out here on his hands and knees, slicing his fingers on the damn grass, making piles of wheat kernels?

When the sun set, of course, it became even harder. He couldn't see what he was looking for, and he didn't have any sort of artificial light. Conal hadn't said anything about using a flashlight or a lantern, but then again he hadn't said it wasn't allowed, either. Maybe he should go back to the cottage and find something . . .

"Hello? Hello? Hello? Sandwich person?"

The little voices sounded familiar. Peering down at a bare spot on the ground near his left knee, Heath saw a small collection of ants. "Yeah? What's up?"

"You promised us food at sunset? Why is there not food at sunset?"

"Sorry. I'm a little busy, here."

"Doing what? What is this strange task that you do?"

"I have to pick up these wheat kernels. There's like a jillion of them."

"Go away," said the ants. "We will do this. You go and make us sandwiches."

Heath stared. Again, a perfectly obvious solution. Why hadn't he thought of it? Except . . . "There's only about twenty-five of you there. Can you do it yourselves? I need to have it done by sunrise or they're throwing me out of the country."

"We cannot have you leaving the country. We must have

sandwiches. There are many jillion of us in this field. We will do this for you. Now, please go make sandwiches."

Many jillion. Of course. Where there were ants, there were always more ants. And where there were sandwiches, there were many, many more ants. "You got it," he said. "What kind of sandwiches do you want?"

The ants buzzed among themselves for a moment. "Peanut butter and jelly," they finally said. "Except, please, no peanut butter."

"Honey?"

"Honey is most excellent."

The ants began to scatter into the grass. Heath pushed himself to his feet, and walked back to the cottage to make sandwiches.

When he came back, there was already another pile sitting next to the two he'd collected. These ants were efficient workers, that was certain. He settled down on the grass to watch.

The ants swarmed over in groups to devour the sandwiches. When they were done, there was one left, so Heath ate that, then stretched out and stared up at the moon. He might as well go to sleep, he thought. There was nothing else he could do here, really. If the ants weren't able to complete the job, he was shit out of luck, because there was no way he could do it himself. And he had a feeling any help he offered the ants—aside from making sandwiches, of course—would be no help at all.

The moon was bright and pretty. After a time, Heath's eyelids drooped, and he fell asleep.

Chapter Six

A harsh voice woke him. "What is this?"

Heath jumped, jarred out of a dream he could no longer remember. There'd been sprites in it, though. Naked ones. He peered up into a pale, near-morning sky to see Conal looming over him.

"Good morning," Heath said. "How goes it?"

Conal scowled. "Far too well for you, it appears, but your actual accomplishment remains to be measured."

Heath sat up. All around him were piles of wheat kernels. Ten, twelve—he couldn't see them all from this angle. But they were neatly arranged, and the sweep of grass over which Conal had scattered them last night looked clean and well picked-over.

Heath smiled, then pushed himself to his feet. "Let's measure it, then."

Conal glared at him. Then, stiffly, as if he had no desire to do this, he trudged past the piles of wheat, into the open field. He lifted his hand sharply. Nothing happened. Heath held his breath, wondering what that meant. If nothing happened, was that good or bad?

Apparently it was good, because Conal leveled a glare at him. The older man walked farther into the field and repeated the gesture. Still nothing. He walked farther away. Again nothing.

Heath rocked back on his heels. Apparently this was going to take a while.

He was right. Forty-five minutes later, Conal came stomping back from the farthest edge of the field, his expression dark and glowering. "Congratulations," he growled. "I don't know how you did it, but you did."

Heath smiled, trying not to feel smug. "Thank you."

Conal stopped next to him, crossing his arms over his chest. "Do you care to share what magic you used to accomplish this?"

Heath shook his head. "Sorry. Cabot family secret."

Conal gritted his teeth so hard Heath could hear it. "Fine. You're not finished yet. Meet me in the dining hall at noon for your next assignment." He stalked away.

"M'Lord," Heath called after him. Conal stopped, but didn't turn around. "If I may be so bold, how many more tasks do you have planned? Because if this is just going to go on forever, I might look into going over your head."

He had no idea if there really was a way to go over Conal's head, but Conal turned around then and the fire in his eyes told Heath he'd struck a nerve. "There will be one more task," Conal grated. "If you accomplish that, then you will have my daughter and my kingdom."

He spun and headed back toward the estate, making a quick gesture behind him. At first Heath thought he might have just been flipped off, but the piles of grain abruptly disappeared with a sharp hissing sound. No insult then, just an afterthought of magic.

Heath frowned. One more task. Somehow he knew it was going to be a doozy. After all, he had to prove he was worthy of Elena's hand. And to rule the kingdom. He hadn't thought much about that part of it. He knew what to do with Elena—what the hell was he supposed to do with a Fairy Kingdom?

He headed back toward the cottage. Just outside, the ants waited.

"More sandwiches, please. We have worked hard all night."

Carefully, Heath stepped over them. "You betcha. Wait right there."

In her room, Elena anxiously awaited her father's appearance in the mirror. He'd promised to talk to her this morning, to let her know how Heath had done with the latest test. She sat in front of the mirror, chewing her fingernails and waiting.

The whole thing infuriated her. It would have been easy enough for her to spirit her way out of this room and go help Heath herself, but she knew if she did, her father would likely just hack Heath's head off and send it back to the real world in a box. And if he found out she'd helped him, he was likely to banish her at the very least. He was already mightily pissed. Vendettas were ridiculous, she thought. Just a huge waste of time and energy.

Finally the mirror began to glow blue, and after a few seconds of buzzing, clarified into an image of her father's face. He didn't look happy. Elena held back a smile.

"He has passed the test," Conal said. "I will set a new one at noon. I want you to be there. In the dining hall."

"You can't just test him forever," she said. "If you try to drag this out, I'll go straight to Milisande."

Conal gritted his teeth at the name. Milisande was the High Queen of this section of Fairy, and while the majority of the inhabitants of the realm cared little for the law, when they did go to Milisande for help, she stepped in quickly and firmly. One got the impression she enjoyed throwing her power around and didn't get enough opportunity to do so. One also got the impression she favored women over men in her decisions of justice.

"There will only be one more test," Conal said. "I assure you, only one more will be necessary." His tone was anything but reassuring. He was trying to hide it, but Elena could sense an underlying smugness.

"Father—" she began, but broke off. If she challenged him now, she would have no hope of sneaking around him later. She forced herself to bob her head in obeisance. "As you wish."

Conal nodded, and the mirror went black.

At noon, as bidden, Heath stepped into the dining hall. Funny how it had become stable again—this was the second time in two days he'd been able to walk right in, rather than wandering the halls looking for it as he'd done before. Elena was already there. She looked worried. Heath settled into a chair next to her.

"No," she said. "Sit over there." She pointed across the table.

He shrugged and did as she'd said. "So what do you think he's going to do next?"

"He's going to give you an impossible task. Then you just have to do the best you can."

"He already did that. Twice. Or at least once—the first one wasn't quite as impossible as the second one."

"This will be worse." She looked across the table at him, straight into his eyes, one hand sliding over the tabletop toward him. "Don't say anything when he tells you what he wants you to do. Just nod and get started right away. We'll figure things out afterward. Whatever happens, I'll do whatever I can to help you."

"What if he finds out?"

"He won't. I know what I'm doing. He has no idea what he's dealing with here. He doesn't know about the Snake."

"You mean he doesn't know I ate it?"

"He doesn't even know it exists. It's a secret from my mother's family—it has nothing to do with him."

Heath nodded sagely. This was good. Maybe there was some vague hope, after all.

"Just—" Elena began, but then Conal appeared, popping in out of nowhere to stand next to the head of the table. He leveled a dark look on his daughter.

"Just what?" he said.

Elena straightened, meeting Conal's severe gaze. "Just sit back and see what happens." She looked at Heath. He had the feeling that was exactly what she'd intended to say in the first place.

Looking suspiciously from Heath to Elena, Conal took a seat in the chair at the head of the table and folded his hands in front of him. "I have given this considerable thought. The man who marries my daughter must be of extraordinary skill and talent, particularly if he comes from a family of obvious disrepute and villainy." He paused, as if expecting Heath to protest the statement. Heath said nothing. "Therefore I have posed a great task, worthy of the skill and talent I would expect to see. You will—" Here he turned his attention to Elena, though his words were meant for Heath. "You will retrieve an apple from the Tree of Life."

Elena shot to her feet. "I knew it! That's not fair, Father. I'm going to Milisande and I'm doing it before day's end."

"Wait," Heath said. "I don't understand. What's the deal? Just tell me where the tree is and I'll go get the stupid apple."

"That's just it," Elena snapped. "No one knows where the damned tree is. No one's ever found it. Nobody even knows for sure if it exists."

"Oh. Well, that could be a problem."

Conal smiled thinly. "I have it on great authority that it does, indeed exist. I will even furnish a clue for your paramour, here." He glared at Heath. "Go west."

"West is good." Heath sank back in his chair. This was more complicated than clearing a three-acre field. He didn't think the ants would be much help to him here. Or the fish, for that matter.

"This vendetta has gone on long enough." Elena's voice shook. "I will not have you refuse a perfectly acceptable candidate because of your own stubborn prejudices. I'm going to Milisande."

"Wait," said Heath. He wasn't sure who Milisande was, but he was sure that aggravating Conal further wasn't likely to be the best idea at this point. "Give it a chance," he suggested. "I'll get started, and if I make some headway, then I'll continue. If not, then I'll leave it up to you."

"Do you see?" Conal said to Elena. "He knows how to behave like a man."

"And will you give him any kind of credit for that?" she snapped back.

Conal turned his dark glare back to Heath. "Go west," he repeated, standing. "Take a horse from my stable and begin. I expect you to be out of my kingdom by sunrise tomorrow."

He disappeared with a flash of light and a disdainful curl of smoke.

"Oh, nice," Elena said. "Visual effects always help." She stepped away from the table, shoving her chair back into place with more than necessary force. "Come with me. We're going to go have a chat with someone."

"Elena, I appreciate your wanting to help, especially since this is so arbitrary, but I really don't want to bring this to this Milisande, not yet. I'd like to at least have a go at this."

She shook her head. "Not Milisande. Someone else."

"Okay." He shrugged and followed her out of the dining hall.

She took him into the forest. He followed, not inclined to ask where they were going. It seemed unimportant, and he trusted her. Wherever they went would be relevant to the situation.

She moved tautly, anger at her father apparent in every step. He didn't blame her. Conal was being unreasonable. He was acting like this was Romeo and Juliet, something crucially dramatic, some kind of . . .

Some kind of fairy tale.

That irony struck him across the face. What else could it be, with the magic and the talking ants and the Snake and everything else? And when Elena stopped in a small clearing, some distance into the forest, he held his breath and remembered once again that he was in another world.

Not far away among the trees, he could see the dark brown arcs of a stag's horns. Elena made a soft, whispering noise and the animal turned his head sedately. He blinked, studying her for a moment with deep, inscrutable brown eyes, then slowly stepped toward them.

A few steps away, he stopped and said, "Yes?"

"I wish to ask a question," said Elena. She had let her body relax, Heath noticed, and kept her head slightly inclined, not quite meeting the stag's eyes.

The stag lowered his head, lifted it again. "Continue."

"The Tree of Life. Does it exist?"

"Yes."

"And are there apples?"

"This time of year they will be green, but yes."

"Can it be reached by humans?"

This time the animal paused. "I cannot answer."

"Why?"

"I do not know the answer."

Elena nodded. "Which direction does it lie?"

"West." He lifted his head suddenly, testing the breeze with wide nostrils, then abruptly bounded away. Heath jumped, startled.

"Dogs," Elena said. "The stable boys exercise them around this time of day." She sighed, turning toward Heath, and took his hands in hers. "So it's true. It's there, and it lies to the west. What do you want to do?"

"I'll get a horse and head west. I don't see that I can really do anything else."

She nodded. Her brows were drawn together in concern. "I wish I could help more."

Squeezing her hands, he bent forward and kissed her gently. "I'll be all right."

But her eyes looked sad. "I wish I could believe that."

If she cried, he was going to lose it completely. Let her send him home, live the rest of his life without her—whatever it took to make the tears stop. But she didn't. Instead she looked up into his face and said, "We have until daybreak."

He nodded. "My cottage is closer."

"Not really," she said, "not if you know the right magic. But yes, let's go there."

"There may be ants."

Her smile wrenched at his heart. "I like ants. They're good conversationalists."

They turned, walking toward the cottage, and he squeezed her hand. "Are they really? I thought mostly they were just after sandwiches."

There were no ants. The plateful of sandwiches Heath had left for them on the doorstep was empty, not even a crumb left behind. He pushed it out of the way with his foot and bent to sweep Elena up into his arms. She buried her face against his neck, her mouth warm on him as she kissed his collarbone. Desire rose hot in his chest and he nearly stumbled, carrying her into the cottage, across the main room, into the bedroom.

He fell with her onto the bed, pushing her skirts up as they went, and landed half on top of her, his mouth latching to her body, her belly, up until he found her breasts through her light silk tunic. The material went quickly wet and slick beneath his tongue, her nipple hardening against his tongue while he teased the other with his fingers.

She writhed under him, straining, her legs clutching his hips. She was naked under her skirts, and her sex slid hot and damp against his stomach. Grinding into her with his body, he drew hard on her breast with his mouth, her desperation feeding his, until she gasped under him, the sound walking the edge of pain.

This might be the last time. He knew this all too clearly—that after tonight he might never see her again. The thought was more than he could bear, and hot tears flooded his eyes. He blinked hard to get rid of them, but they gathered thick in his throat, instead, and refused to be swallowed no matter how hard he tried.

He drew his head back from her breast, scraping his teeth over her nipple as he did so, making her cry out softly and clutch his shoulders with her hands. The musk of her arousal rose to his nostrils and he breathed it hungrily, then bent his head to lick her thighs, the soft jut of her hip bones, her navel. Finally, he pressed his mouth between her legs and tasted her.

Her hips lifted under his mouth, pressing toward him, her thighs falling farther open as she offered herself completely to him. He thrust his tongue inside her, tasting the thick, hot wetness of her arousal, licking it out of her, her sex tightening, shivering at the invasion. Fingers wove into his hair, pulling too hard, making him dive deeper into her. He caught her clit against his upper lip, drew it into his mouth, sucked and laved it until she wrenched at his hair, her back arching under him, her body shivering, her voice rising in a long, high cry of desperate ecstasy.

She yanked his head up, pulled him up her body to bring his salt-wet mouth to his. He settled onto her and she lifted her legs, opened her thighs a little more and shifted. He moved with her, impaled her, sank deep inside her, her heat clutching hard on his cock, drawing him in farther than he thought he could go. Magic, he thought, but it wasn't. It was only her, her body, her sex, her plain, human, woman's magic. A tear fell hot down his face; he couldn't help it.

"Take me," she whispered, her voice hitching in her throat. "God, do it hard. I want to feel you."

Her thighs rose higher against his sides, her knees tucking in under his arms, and he shoved into her as far as he could go, let his body take over. His hands found hers, his fingers weaving between hers, tender, as he pounded her, rough and hard, spearing her. She was tight and hot, clenched on him, and the heat coiled up into his abdomen, insistent, animal lust that rose and rose and suddenly wrenched loose and he exploded into her, his voice grinding out in a bestial howl of completion.

He let it carry him, his orgasm so intense it almost hurt, Elena taut as a bowstring beneath him, her body shuddering, also, in another wave of completion. Finally, when he was wrung and empty, he opened his eyes and looked down into her face. Her eyes were wet.

"Come back to me," she said. "It's all I ask."

Bending down to her, he kissed her gently. "I'll try," he said. He could promise nothing more than that.

Chapter Seven

Just before daybreak, she went to the stables with him and helped him pick out a horse, though he could have done it himself. The one he finally saddled was gray, with a white star, a laid-back attitude and a bit of a Southern drawl.

"Dunno where this tree might be, but we'll go take a look," he said. "Haven't been out on a good ride in I don't know how long."

They'd called him Shadow but he said his name was really Bob. He encouraged Elena to pack the saddlebags as heavily as they could be packed. "Put a magic on 'em if you can. Make 'em refill themselves when they're empty."

"I can, but the spell will fade the farther you get from my realm," said Elena, pulling the saddlebag buckles tight. She turned to Heath, smiling but still sad-eyed. "I'll contact you when I can. I mean, when I'm pretty sure Father won't find out about it."

He grinned. "You just be careful. Stay in touch as best you can."

He kissed her one last time, hard and deep, then rode out.

It wasn't long before he began to wonder why, exactly, he was doing this. Did he really love Elena so much that he would risk himself in this way? For all he knew, this was a fool's errand meant to be the end of him. In fact, based on Conal's gloating and Elena's reaction that was exactly what it was. So why not turn around, head back, and demand to be sent back home?

Something about the blood in his veins, he thought. The same blood that had compelled him to eat of the White Snake now compelled him to take on this task, impossible as it might seem to be. He could barely remember what the real world even looked like anymore, much less why he would want to go back there. This place seemed more real to him than anything else. Here he had what he wanted—a woman, a place to be earned, some power to wield. More than he'd ever dreamed of back there in what he could laughably refer to now as reality. What was reality? If this place was more real, then wasn't this the true reality?

He rode until dusk, then stopped for a rest and a meal. Relieved of the weight of the saddle, Bob shook himself thoroughly, then settled down to eat.

"Mighty good grass here," he told Heath. "We could stay the night. We're right outside Elena's domain."

"Good to know. Thanks." He settled down on the ground to try to light a fire. The horse was silent, absorbed in his grazing. One thing about Bob—he wasn't very talkative. Heath had decided he liked that in a horse.

With the fire underway, Heath set about to figure out how to set up the tent Elena had tied behind his saddle. He'd expected metal rods and ropes, stakes to hammer into the ground, but when he unrolled it, it suddenly leapt out of his hands and busily set to work putting itself up. Handy, Heath thought, then yanked a corner of it to drag it away from the fire before it set itself ablaze.

Inside, the tent seemed bigger than it had on the outside. Perfectly possible, he thought, for a tent that erected itself. There were blankets inside, and a bedroll. Heath wasn't sure how they'd gotten there, and so assumed this, also, was one of the tent's magical properties.

He arranged the bedroll, then went back to check on Bob. The horse was standing near a tree, dozing, so Heath left him alone. He didn't think it was necessary to hobble or tie him for the night. He seriously doubted Bob would run off.

He ducked back into the tent, then froze, startled.

Elena lay on his bedroll, draped in a long, transparent blue garment that could barely be called a nightgown.

"Elena?" he said.

"Sort of," she replied. "Actually just a magical projection. But come here." She lifted a hand and beckoned him. He came to her and knelt, and she kissed him. Her mouth felt real and warm, plundering his with soft fire.

"Heck of a magical projection," he said, drawing back.

"Would you like another?"

"No." He kissed her again. She tasted real too, but now that he knew she wasn't, he noticed the absence of smell. The odor of her skin was vague, not as pure and rich as it was in real life. "You're fine."

"I mean a second one. Two women." A second figure appeared in the tent with them, a small woman with dark hair. She stepped closer with a sultry lowering of her eyelids. "Like that. Would you like that?"

He looked at her, then at the other woman, the other projection. "Can she be you too?"

Elena smiled. "You're sweet." Instantly, the second woman became Elena, as well, with her wheat-gold hair and luscious body. "Much better." She came toward him, and he looked at both smiling Elenas, identical but not the same. The second one stopped in front of him and kissed him, pulling at his mouth with hers, teasing his lips with her teeth. The other shifted behind him, wrapping her arms around his waist.

"Lie down," they whispered. "Lie down and let us tend to you."

So he closed his eyes and let the women ease him down to the pallet. One belly-to-belly with him, the other belly-to-back, they set to work.

Back in her room at the castle, Elena lay on her bed, partly in magical trance, partly aware of her manipulation of the spell she performed. She felt everything—every contact with Heath's body from both of the magical projections she had sent him. It made for a strange, doubled layer of sensation. His chest against her breasts at the same time as her breasts pressed against his back, legs tangled from too many angles, long stretches of skin sliding over each other. It was almost more than she could handle.

It was almost more than he could handle—Elena's lips on his, stroking and probing, her hands caressing his chest, pressing against his nipples. At the same time, Elena behind him, kissing his neck, scraping her teeth over his shoulders, her hands reaching around him from behind, slipping down his stomach, curling around the hot length of his cock.

He didn't know where to start. But Elena—both of her—seemed to have things under control. Maybe it would be best if he would just relax and go with the flow.

"The flow" soon involved hands on his buttocks, a knee pressed between his thighs. Then, from the other side, a mouth on his cock, drawing him in, hot and wet. He arched back to find himself closed in Elena's arms from behind, her hand caressing his face, his hair. She kissed his neck, his shoulders, the backs of his ears. Her other self drew hard on his sex, her tongue circling the head of his penis, curling around the glans, drawing a wave of heat from the base of his spine, through him, into her mouth. He clenched down on the building orgasm, feeling it rise, refusing to let it crest.

Elena—the real Elena—threw her head back on her pillow. She'd never tried this kind of magic before and it was more intense than she had imagined it could be. It was almost more than she could take, filling her chest, her loins, with liquid fire, tingling down to the tips of her fingers, filling her whole body. It was like soft explosions scattered through her. An orgasm here, another one there, lots of little orgasms everywhere . . . and one big one, building in the bowl of her pelvis, spreading hot and melty down her thighs but not quite ready yet. The magic had disabled her own voice but she could hear the laughter, the soft moaning coming from the projections of herself. She would have screamed if she could, just for the delight of it.

Heath let out a growl, deep and shivering on the edge of satisfaction. She almost had him, the Elena who had just pulled his balls into her mouth, easing her tongue between them through the skin of his scrotum. God, it was good, like the fairy sprites but like Elena as well. Best of both worlds.

As if sensing he was hovering, holding himself back from the final plunge, she let him go. She slid her body up his, his penis tracing down between her breasts, down her belly to her sex. She straddled him, gave him a few more seconds to regain control, then she drew him up inside herself and he bucked under her, pressing high and hard into her. She cried out joyously, arching back on top of him.

"Don't forget me," said the other Elena. She positioned herself on his chest, her crotch near his chin. Her hair tickled his skin and he could smell her arousal. She was wet and ready. He looked up, past the curves of her belly and breasts to meet her eyes. She smiled.

"Go for it," she said.

She shifted just enough, bringing her sex into contact with his mouth. He stroked his tongue inside her slick folds, rolled the tip around her clit. It was hard to concentrate on both women at the same time; on the Elena riding his erection and the other riding his tongue, but somehow he managed it. He felt her clenching on his cock, felt her begin to shiver under his tongue.

For Elena, back in the castle, it rapidly became overwhelming. She could feel both orgasms building at the same time, feel all the layered sensations of his hard length inside her, his mouth and tongue on her. All the layers came back together in her own body, there where she lay entangled in the spell. They came together and peeled away and floated off her in streams of filmy heat. It seemed to go on forever, and for a moment she thought she might die with it.

Her voice was disabled on this side of the spell, but her counterparts, the constructs with Heath, both threw their heads back and keened in ecstasy. Heath grasped Elena's hips, the ones by his face, then the ones over his own hips, as he too, shattered into climax.

She couldn't hold the constructs anymore. The Elena on Heath's mouth disappeared, leaving him with only one. He clung to her, feeling her body clutch on him convulsively, until suddenly, abruptly, she was gone.

He sat up straight, groping fruitlessly for her as her image disappeared. "Elena!"

"I'm sorry." Her voice was wan, but audible. "Too much for me to hold it. Too intense." He could almost see her, a vague shadow of her face. She smiled. "Thank you."

"Elena—" But she was gone.

He hurt in the morning. His thighs and buttocks ached from riding, his heart hurt from having watched Elena leave him the night before. He packed and saddled Bob, but led him, walking.

"What's the matter?" Bob asked. When Heath explained, the horse gave a whinnying laugh. "Gotta get back on that horse, bub. It ain't gonna get any better."

Eventually he did get back on, but not until after lunch. He forced himself to stay in the saddle until nightfall, then collapsed into sleep almost before the tent had finished setting itself up. If Elena came to visit, he didn't know.

After a few days the pain was less, but he still had no idea if he was on the right track. He stopped a few animals here and there, those who didn't run away from him. They all said, "Go west," from the squirrel to the bluebird to the garter snake that hissed across their path.

"West's a long way, I guess," said Bob.

"Yeah, it looks that way."

And on he rode. On and on. West and farther west. Perhaps he could ride all the way around the world in this place.

One day he opened his saddlebags to find them exactly the same as they had been the night before. No refills. Elena's magic was waning. When he crawled into his bedroll that night he saw her above him, a waft of an image.

"Too far," her voice whispered. "You go on without me now. Best of luck."

He almost told her to contact Milisande, to report this as an affront to any kind of justice, but instead he only said, "I miss you."

He loved her. He was certain of that now. He woke with her in his thoughts, went to sleep with her in his thoughts, dreamed of her through the rest of the day and through the night. Had he thought it would get him anything but dead, he would have ridden back and challenged her father hand-to-hand. But there was no point. If he was dead, he couldn't have her at all. Best to keep riding.

West and more west.

Finally there was very little in the bottom of the saddlebag. He began to wonder how he would eat. He'd started looking along the path for edible plants, but his knowledge of herbology was limited. He certainly couldn't kill anything, not when everything that moved and breathed in the forest could beg him for its life.

The birds and squirrels helped, though. Braver than other small creatures, they brought him seeds and nuts from time to time, though the squirrels especially had very short attention spans and often forgot their promises. But they kept him alive.

He had no idea how long he'd been traveling when he heard

the raven. It was crying out with what seemed to be its last breath, weeping a dark cawing into the sunset.

Heath searched through the trees until he found it. It lay on the ground, its wing wrenched and broken. Gently, he reached toward it. "I can help you," he said.

It looked up at him with a round, black eye. "How do you speak to me?"

"Don't worry about that. How long have you been here?"

"Suns. As many suns as there are eggs in a nest." It threw its head back. "I have waited for a wolf or a fox to end my suffering but none has come. Kill me, please. I wish only for death."

But Heath was in no hurry to kill, even if he'd been asked. Instead he bent closer, examining the twisted wing. "I think I can help you. Would you let me?"

"Awwk," it said.

He wasn't sure if that was agreement, but he carefully eased the bird up from the ground. He mounted his horse and settled the raven in front of him, then took his waterskin and carefully dribbled water into the bird's beak.

"Ah, water," it said when it had swallowed a fair share. "That is a help, I must say."

"I have food, as well. Here."

As they rode, he fed the bird with water and bits of bread, and when they reached a suitable place, they stopped for the night though it was only a few hours past noon. Heath set the bird's wing, tying sticks along the broken bone. It slept quietly next to him through the night.

In the morning, the bird was much more alert. "This is better," it told Heath. "You have been most kind."

It rode the next day perched on the saddlebags, and they chatted. Heath told the raven about his quest. It occurred to him that he had no idea how long he'd been traveling now—a month? Two? A year?—nor did he know if he was still on the right trail.

"It's to the west, yes," said the raven. "West and more west. I've never seen it myself, but I know those who say they have. The apples will be pink by now. Not quite ready to eat. Not quite."

So they rode on. After a time, the raven began to test its mended wing, and finally it flew away.

Chapter Eight

The departure of the bird for some reason made Heath feel lonelier than ever. That night when he set up his tent and stretched out on his blankets he felt drained, empty. He felt like turning back in the morning, or better yet, packing everything back up and turning around right now.

Fatigue was the only thing keeping him from the latter course of action. He was in the middle of an imaginary conversation with Bob, too tired to actually get up and talk, when he drifted off to sleep.

And found Elena. She was there in front of him, in a drift of mist, or fog, or wishfulness, draped in a length of sheer, white gauze.

"Heath." Her voice was as ephemeral as the mist, as the gauze that barely covered her.

He didn't bother to say her name but simply closed the distance between them, his hand reaching out to her suddenly enclosed in his. He drew her to him and kissed her, tasting the familiar warmth of her mouth.

"I miss you," he whispered. He wondered if this encounter existed anywhere outside the dream, if Elena experienced anything of this where she was. Could she feel the heat of his body as he folded her against him? The flutter of his tongue against her lips?

Or was there no magic at all here—only the construction in his mind of his deepest desire of the moment?

It didn't matter. For these moments, however long he could hold to the dream, he was with her.

She was soft and sweet in his arms, her mouth filling his with the hot taste of passion. He clung to her, pulling her as close as imagination would allow. The gauzy thing she wore was like nothing between them; and then it *was* nothing, it was gone, and the heat of her skin found the heat of his.

It had been so long. His mind, confused by the endlessness of his travels, couldn't puzzle out how long it had been. He only knew he wanted her, and with more than just the ache in his body—with an ache in his heart. In his soul.

He brought her close to him, sliding his hands down her back, cupping her buttocks. He lifted her in his arms until she was wrapped around him, her legs around his waist.

"How long has it been?" he asked her, his lips against her ear now.

"Too long," she murmured back. "No questions. Love me."

"I love you," he said, and the words surprised him. They felt so true coming out of his mouth—truer than anything he'd ever said before.

It wasn't what she'd meant, though, and he knew that. He kissed her again, then carried her to his pallet on the floor. Gently, he laid her down. She reached up to him and brought him to her, until he covered her with his body. She held him with hers, her legs around his waist.

He wanted her so badly he could almost weep with it, the pain in his heart trying hard to spill out of his eyes. Bending his head to her again, he pressed his mouth against her breasts, caught a nipple in the curl of his tongue. She arched backward, gasping, and he slid his hand behind her, drawing her closer, drawing her breast deep into his mouth, tasting the warmth and softness of her flesh.

Even this dream version of Elena knew what she wanted. As his mouth pulled greedily at her breast, she caught his hand and drew it down between her legs, guided his fingers into the slick, hot wetness nestled between her thighs. The realness of the dream startled him for a moment; he could feel the soft tickle of her hair against his palm, the slickness of the channel of her body. Her muscles clenched on his fingers, drawing him deeper.

This had to be real. On some level, it had to be real. Was she back in her rooms, dreaming even as he was, writhing under his ministrations? The thought of it made him steely hard, made him groan in the depths of intense need.

He would treat it all as if it were real, then. He would give her everything he had to give. With his fingers buried in her heat, he found her clitoris with his thumb, pressing and rolling until she twisted and cried out beneath him. He wanted inside her, wanted his cock deep inside her body instead of just his fingers. But he held on, working her, listening to her gasping, moaning, keening as her body clenched on his fingers. He found her mouth again, kissing her hard, feeling her journey to orgasm as humming against his lips.

Finally, she shuddered beneath him and he felt her pulsate around his hand, felt her completion as she moaned it into his mouth. Only then did he shift his own body, find her center, and press himself deeply into it. So hot, still shaking with the aftershocks of her climax. So real. More real, even, in its way, than their actual encounter. Because then, when he had had her in reality, he hadn't known what would come. Hadn't known he could love her.

He held himself still for a long breath, afraid of his own release, afraid it might come too soon. Opening his eyes, he looked down into her face. She smiled up at him, dreamy pleasure in her eyes. "Hard," she whispered. "You can't hurt me."

He blinked, swallowed, and then drove into her. Hard. She whimpered and at first he thought he might have hurt her, but she was still smiling, her eyes still locked to his. Her mouth slanted up in a wicked, daring smile. "You can't hurt me," she said again.

"I wouldn't."

"I know."

"I love you."

She smiled again, then her hands grasped at his buttocks, pulling him deeply into the cradle of her body. She clutched him and he rode her, the rhythm he set fast and hard, until he could hold back no longer, and spilled his ecstasy into her.

And she was gone. He bolted awake with his body alight and aching, not quite satiated because of the ending of the dream, and his eyes damp with tears.

"This is a lonely trail, Bob," Heath commented one morning. It had been chilly when he'd awakened, and he wondered if they'd ridden as far as fall by now.

"Yes, it is." Even the horse seemed to have lost his enthusiasm. They just went on and on, mile after mile, west and more west. Still the birds and the squirrels said they were on the right track, that the tree was real, that the tree was to the west.

Suddenly, Heath pulled back on Bob's reins. "This is insane."

"Sorry?" said Bob.

"We have no idea where we're going. I have no idea how long we've been gone. I could spend the rest of my life going west."

Bob stood silent, waiting.

"I don't know if it's worth it."

"Should we go back?"

Heath shook his head. "I don't know. If I go back, I lose her. But if I stay on the trail . . ."

"Maybe you find this apple and maybe you die riding."

"Yeah." He slid down from the saddle, patting Bob's shoulder. "Let's just stop here for a bit. I want to think."

He took Bob's bridle and saddle off, then sat on the grass, looking up at the clear, blue sky. What had it been like, watching the sky from a Colorado mountaintop? If he went back now, would he be happy with that life? Because that would be what he would have left. No Fairyland. No Elena.

No Elena.

He could live without magic, without fairies, without the brilliant night sky with its unbelievably beautiful stars, without the talking animals. He wasn't sure he could live without Elena.

Hell, she was just a woman. There were plenty of other women in the normal, mortal world. He should go back, let Conal send him home, and look for love somewhere else.

But something deep inside, something he hadn't even been aware of until this moment, told him that would be impossible. Something in his blood sang out to the soil he'd left behind in Elena's kingdom. Something else in his blood sang out to Elena herself. He was bound to both, irrevocably, because of ancestry he'd never been aware of until she'd brought him through the pool.

He took a long, slow breath and closed his eyes, letting the sun beat against his face, his closed lids. It seemed he had no choice. He would go on. He would ride, west and more west, until he found the apple or died trying.

"Hey, Heath," said Bob suddenly. Heath looked up. The horse was watching the sky now. "Do you see that?"

Heath squinted into the bright sky. A dark form approached them, small but growing larger. "What is that?"

"A bird, I'm thinking."

Heath sat up. He shaded his eyes with his hand. Strangely, his heart had sped up, pounding so hard he could feel it in the back of his throat. The horse seemed similarly enthralled, tipping his head back and forth to bring the approaching bird into focus.

Suddenly, Heath pushed to his feet. "It's the raven."

"You sure about that? That bird we carried a while back?"

"Yes." There was no way he could be sure, but he was. Somehow he knew this was the same bird. It came closer, and finally veered over the tops of the nearby trees, swooping over Heath's head. Heath ducked. As the bird swished by, barely missing his hair, it dropped two round objects on the ground in front of him.

"For you!" the raven called. "I'll be right back."

Heath straightened, staring at the ground. At his feet lay two apples.

He looked up again. The raven made a long circle, then came back, landing on the ground next to the apples. "Sorry. Had to drop my load first." It shook its wings into place. "Sorry I took so long. That damn tree is *west,* I'm telling you."

"So I'd gathered." Heath picked up the apples. They looked like normal apples, but the moment he touched them, he could feel the magic, cool and almost moving under his hands. Slowly, he smiled. "I don't know what to say."

"No need to say anything," said the bird. "You saved my life. Now we're even. One of the apples is to give your lady's father. With the other, you can wish yourself back to the castle."

It shook itself again, then launched into the air. Heath watched it go. Only when it had disappeared into the sunlight did he feel the tears on his face.

As she had every night for the past four months, Elena watched her mirror. In it she saw nothing. She'd seen nothing since Heath and Bob had passed out of its range. It was keyed to Heath's energy, and as soon as he got close enough again, the mirror would again show her his progress.

But it was blank. Again.

Was he dead? Had he given up and found some way back to his home? Or was he still riding, riding and riding, west and more west, to a tree apparently only the animals knew how to find?

She'd done some asking around, among the birds and squirrels. She wished she could talk to the insects, as Heath could, because she had a feeling the bees knew a great deal about the world. But a bird she knew had spoken to a bee who'd said its family was part of the honored group in charge of pollinating the elusive tree. Oh, yes, it existed, in that place west of west that no one could quite say how to reach.

She leaned back in her seat, caressing the curve of her belly. She'd spent the last several weeks deflecting questions from her father, who had noticed the slight change in his daughter's silhouette. She was eating too much, she'd told him, because she was worried about Heath. That ruse would last only so long before it became obvious what truly widened her waistline. Her child. Heath's child. She had an heir of the Blood growing within her, but it would be so much easier to give this child its due if Heath were here, and married to her, and approved by her stubborn father.

Sighing, she rubbed her tired eyes and looked at the mirror again.

And rubbed her eyes again. Had the surface of the mirror changed? Lightened?

It had. She leaned forward. The black mirror was slowly turning blue. Please, not just a message from her father, she prayed. Please, be Heath.

Suddenly the blue turned to green and there he was, perched on Bob's saddle, smiling. With a jolt, she recognized the terrain behind him.

He was right outside the estate.

With a shout of pure joy, she leapt from her cushions and ran, out the door, down the hallway, across the field. Heath met her halfway, caught her in his arms and spun her around.

"You're home," she said, sobbing with elation.

"Yes," he said, and kissed her. "I'm home." Lowering her to the ground, he cupped a hand over her belly. "What's this?"

She smiled. "Your son."

"Really?"

"Really." She laid her hand on top of his.

"Would it hurt him if we . . . ?"

"No."

"Then let's."

She took him to her room, shortening the corridors on the way so it only took half the usual time. He laid her down on the bed, unbuttoning the front of her long, gauzy gown. Spreading the sides of the dress open, he exposed the round bulge of her belly. His hands shaped it, caressed it, then he laid his ear against it and closed his eyes.

"This is the most beautiful thing I have ever seen."

She smiled as he turned his head to kiss her, there on the mound of her stomach. "Are you sure he'll be okay?"

"He'll be fine. He'll know his father loves his mother. It's a good thing."

Heath seemed hesitant, but then he smiled and kissed her belly again, then lower, then he unbuttoned the rest of her buttons, all the way down to her calves, and tossed the gauzy folds of her dress out of the way.

"I love you," he said. "I think I knew it before I left, but it took the time away to make it really clear. I love you more than anything I might have left at home. If there's any way at all for it to be possible, I want to be with you."

"I think we can arrange that."

"But your father—"

"It'll be all right."

"How?"

"I don't know, but I know it'll work out somehow."

"How do you know?"

"Because it has to."

It wasn't much of an answer, she knew, but it was the truth. And he seemed finally to accept it, as he lowered his head between her thighs. She shivered as he licked deep into her folds.

"You taste different," he said. He tickled her clit with the tip of his tongue and she cried out, half laughing with the sensation.

"You remember what I taste like?"

"How could I forget?"

"It's been so long . . ."

"Longer for me. At least it seemed that way." He kissed the inside of her thigh. "I missed you."

"I missed you."

He turned his attention back to her sex, setting his lips against her labia and humming. She didn't recognize the tune, but its vibrations sent her gasping. She was more sensitive now, since the pregnancy, and when he added his fingers to his efforts, sliding one, then two, inside her, she shimmered suddenly into climax, spinning and floating, lost in a timeless moment before she came back to hear his soft laughter.

"Come inside," she murmured, barely able to summon her voice.

He lifted his head and cupped his hand again around her belly. The swell of her womb had clenched hard around her orgasm and he took a moment to explore the new, tighter contours as it gradually relaxed. She loved the way his hands felt on her, claiming her body, claiming his child.

Then he claimed the deepest parts of her, sheathing himself in her with a move like hot velvet. The hypersensitivity of her body made him feel bigger, harder, than he'd ever been before. Moving in a long, slow glide, he brought her back to the heights, until she broke and wept and shuddered again. He kissed her as she climaxed, his lips soft on hers. Then she felt him pulse inside her, pouring the essence of his body into the essence of hers.

"I take it back," he whispered. "Love just isn't a strong enough word."

There was still Conal to deal with. Elena cast magic and watched the mirror intently until she saw him in the field, near the pond. Then she waved to Heath to come with her.

Still half naked on the bed, Heath rolled off, dug up a pair of pants, and followed Elena out the door. Casting magic in front of her as they half-ran down the corridor, she shortened the distance between her room and outside by two hallways and an antechamber. Heath was just buttoning his pants when they hit the grass.

Elena collected herself, slowing her pace to a lope, heading across the lawn to her father. He stood stiff and erect by the pond, and even when they came within earshot, he made no attempt to turn or to greet them.

She stopped a few feet behind him, facing his straight, stiff back. Heath curled his hand around her elbow and she nestled backward into him a little, strengthened by his presence and his support.

"Father," she said.

He turned around slowly. There was no surprise in his eyes as they found Heath, only the hard, flinty light of anger. He had known, then, that Heath was back.

"Unless you have conjured lies and aided this man against my orders, this is not possible."

Elena lifted her hand. A light sprang from her curved palm, then the apple appeared, rotating shiny and golden just above her skin. "It is possible."

"He could not have done it by himself." He looked older, Elena thought. Five, maybe ten years. Had his anger done this to him?

"I didn't do it by myself," said Heath, his voice soft but solid, with power in it. "But Elena did not help me. I did not ask for her help, nor did I wish it. My own powers took me as far as I needed to go."

"You have no powers."

"Apparently I do."

Conal took a step toward Heath, his body taut, his mouth pressed hard against his teeth. The fire in his eyes was feral. Instinctively, Elena covered her abdomen with one hand and took a step back.

"You do not belong here," Conal growled. "I will not have you in this land, much less ruling here with my daughter."

"You have no choice," said Elena. "He did as you asked. He retrieved the apple."

"He wasn't meant to. He was meant to disappear."

"Do you think I don't know that?" Elena swallowed tears. She was far too emotional of late—no doubt because of the baby. "You sent him off to die. But he didn't. Now you have no choice. You must step aside and allow us to rule."

"I will do no such thing."

"You will."

For a long moment they stood, Heath and Conal locked eye to eye, Elena waiting, almost holding her breath. Then, suddenly, she let it out with a gasp.

A stag had emerged from the trees. The same stag, she was certain, with whom she'd held so many conversations. The one who had told Heath to go west. Head held high, he crossed the field toward them. He looked at Elena and dipped his head slightly, then turned. Directly in front of Heath, so there was no mistaking to whom he made the gesture, the stag bent one knee and bowed.

Conal gaped. "What is this?"

"There are forces at work here over which you have no control," said Elena. Her voice shivered, with fear and anticipation. Her father knew nothing of the Snake—that was her heritage. His lack of knowledge would be his undoing.

The stag straightened, then looked back toward the woods. Out of the trees came more animals—squirrels, rabbits, foxes, a lone wolf with golden eyes. Prey and predator walking side by side, neither seemingly aware of the other. All came over the grass to bow at Heath's feet. Some stayed to stand by the stag in homage while others retreated to their homes. Either way, their meaning was clear. The animals, and thus the land, pledged loyalty now to Heath, not to Conal.

After a time, the stag looked toward Heath. "You are a good man. This one was good in his time but his hatred has destroyed his heart. We will follow you." Then he bounded back toward the trees, followed by the others in a meandering line.

Conal was shivering with anger. "What have you done to me?"

"I have done nothing," said Elena. "What you have done, you have done to yourself. You are old, Father, and more, you refuse to let go of your hatred. The land has made its loyalties known."

He was defeated. Elena knew it and now Conal knew it. Heath seemed perplexed, but he stood silent while father and daughter faced each other. Some of the rage faded from Conal's eyes, replaced by weariness. "I don't understand."

"Heath received power from the land, from the legacy of my mother's people. Had you spent any of your life loving her, instead of hating the man who took your first wife, you might also have been granted this legacy." Elena paused, gathering herself. The confrontation had tired her with the rawness of its emotion. "Heath took the power he was granted and used it with love and compassion. Thus the land has chosen him."

"Then I can do nothing." His voice grated with helpless anger.

"You can do nothing."

Conal looked at Heath, his teeth clenched. At first Elena thought her father might make some move, some effort to mend what he had broken. But he only stood for a moment, staring at his rival—his conqueror—then lifted his hand and disappeared.

Elena blinked back tears. “I wish him healing,” she whispered.

Heath slipped his arm over her shoulders. “Perhaps it will come,” he said. “Grandbabies can do wonders.”

She smiled up at him, appreciating the effort. This land was hers now, she realized. Hers and Heath’s, their children’s and their children’s children. It was as it should be. She caressed the vague curve of her belly and leaned into Heath’s half-embrace. Together, they walked back toward the estate.

Toys 4 Us

S. L. Carpenter

As usual I dedicate everything I write to my wife.
The love of my life.

This book was inspired by a dear friend of mine,
whose honesty and friendship I admire. Dot, this book is for you.

Chapter One

Kathy's Party

Nervous and scared she would forget how to *do* it, Dana looked into the bathroom mirror, staring at her reflection. *Just like riding a bike,* she thought to herself. Everyone does it; she just hoped she would remember everything about *it.*

She set her purse on the nightstand, adjusted her breasts, tugged her underwear down to keep it from riding up her rear end and walked out to face her fear.

There were fourteen women in the living room, all giggling and laughing. A nervous tension filled the air. Dana walked out to her little table, smiled at the ladies and began.

She reached into her bag and took out a six-inch dildo with a stand and stood it on the tabletop. "This is a dildo. This is life-size and has a smooth latex skin covering it. There are bumps and veins around it to give it the feel of a real penis and is what most women are accustomed to with a man."

The women sat looking somewhat bored, first at each other then back up to Dana. She started every party with a matter-of-fact approach to the toys. Dana looked over to Kathy, who was throwing the party, and winked.

"*This* is what a woman really needs!" she yelled as she pulled out a flesh-toned, twelve-inch vibrator with a clit-tingler on the side that rotated as it hummed. The women burst into laughter and whistled.

"Now *that's* what I'm talkin' about," a woman blurted out.

"This isn't reality; this is what men *wished* they could have for their woman."

Dana had broken the ice. Kathy winked back and Dana continued showing her toys to the group of women.

For almost an hour Dana explained the different toys, beads, games, oils and accessories to add pleasure to a couple's sex life. Every party made her more comfortable and more open about sexuality. Often, she would touch on her own rather tame past.

Even though she was rather new to the whole experience of selling pleasure toys, she loved how she could finally feel as if she were helping women as well as men. She hadn't had the couple parties yet with the guys staring at her showing them toys. But she knew that what she did at the all-girl parties the guys benefited from, in a lot of ways.

Dana had been sheltered and held back by her former boyfriend and he had left her feeling inadequate as a lover. It wasn't her fault the men in her life were insecure and blamed her for their own lack of knowledge and technique. Being told how to please a man was her basic education. *The man was supposed to know what to do,* or so she was made to think. Her experience was more "Thanks, babe, you were great!" then a smack on the ass and sleeping in a sticky wet spot.

A while after her breakup with Ronald, Dana was asked to go to a pleasure party put on by a girlfriend. Janice was a consultant for the Pleasure Parties Company. Dana saw how everyone reacted and opened up to Janice during her demonstration, and she was hooked.

After the party, Dana met with Janice in the back room and they started talking about how Janice started and their friendship grew from there. Janice was always so free and alive. Dana envied her.

After attending three parties with Janice, then assisting at three more, she finally agreed to become a consultant. Of course, she did massive hours of research—in-depth research—and she wanted to be sure she had a real knowledge of the products she would sell.

It was a demanding task. For hours and hours, night after night, she experimented. The different sizes, colors and shapes of the toys and intensity of her multiple orgasms were the price she paid. It was a dirty job but one that needed done.

Dana was finally awakening to the sexual being she never knew existed inside her. She realized that the pleasure derived from understanding her sexuality was the key to the treasure that lay within her.

She had maxed out her Visa and felt ready to try selling the toys. Of course, some free samples and the tax write-off were added benefits. It was her time to shine.

Ronald had moved on and left her for another woman. Now she could move on and spread her wings—and legs—and find herself.

Dana finished her presentation and had given out a few door prizes and massage oil samples. The girls still giggled and chatted in the living room and Dana went to the back bedroom to take orders and answer more personal questions.

One by one, the ladies came into the back bedroom and asked Dana about the toys and purchased things in privacy. Dana was so happy and it also aroused her to explain and see the way her subtlety and nonjudgmental words helped ease the ladies' preconceived notions that wanting to buy something like a fourteen-inch, double-ended, pulsating, rubber dildo was dirty and nasty. Her own thoughts followed theirs and she kept mental notes of things to try.

Most of the women knew exactly what they wanted, either from a friend's recommendation or because the simple sight of it got them hot. She had sold seven vibrators, two pairs of handcuffs, a fluorescent yellow whip, three sets of pleasure balls and a partridge in a pear tree.

The last woman, Lisa, sat browsing through the catalog and pointed to a slender pink vibrator. "This looks nice."

"So what size would you like?" Dana asked the petite woman.

"Well, I'm not sure. I have never had one. My husband is a computer salesman and leaves for weeks at a time. Patty asked me to come to the party. I figure this might curb the tension a little. What do you recommend?"

"What size of man are you used to?" Dana asked, trying to make her less nervous. "Here, look at this." Dana held up her hand, extending her middle three fingers. "Is he this wide?" she asked holding up the three fingers.

"No, smaller than that." The woman blushed.

"What about this?" she asked again, holding up one finger.

"Noooo, he is wider than that."

Dana held her index and middle fingers up. She placed the fingers between her lips and sucked them into her mouth. "I'd say he's an average-sized man then. Hmmmm, let me think," Dana mumbled as she looked Lisa over and saw how she still acted a little nervous. "You ever hear of a 'Pocket Rocket'?"

Blushing, Lisa answered, "Well, the girls were whispering about those. They said I should get one."

"I highly recommend it."

Dana noticed that Lisa seemed to be squirming a little. She looked her in the eye and still sensed a little apprehension.

"I have one," Dana said, winking and raising her eyebrows at her. "I love it."

"*Sold!*"

Lisa paid her with cash and Dana dug one out of the case she brought that held some supplies. She didn't keep too much with her, but some of the best sellers sold quicker if the ladies could take them home after the party.

After the party ended, Dana was picking up wrappers and things in the living room. She knelt down to pick up a receipt and when she stood up she saw someone in the doorway.

"*Ahhh!*" she screamed, shocked by the shadow. "Oh God, it's you, Will. You scared the crap out of me."

Will was Kathy's husband and he had gone bowling with his buddies while Kathy had the party. He was a big, good-looking man with a moustache and a hint of gray in his whiskers.

"How'd the party go? Kathy was really looking forward to it. She and her girlfriends were giggling all week."

"It was a blast. We had a lot of fun and Kathy spent about two hundred bucks on toys. Uh-oh, I'm not supposed to tell you that," she giggled.

"You look great, Dana! You know where the *boss* is?" Will asked.

"I saw her go down the hall. Tell her I'm almost done and will let myself out. Take care. Bye."

Dana picked up her little folding table and started walking toward the entryway.

Damn, forgot my purse in the bedroom. Dana walked down the hall and saw her purse on the nightstand. She leaned over and picked it up.

She dug her keys out and glanced over toward the bathroom. The door was half open and she saw Kathy's reflection in the mirror. She was kneeling down and had a bathrobe on. As Dana continued walking she saw more of her.

Warmth swept through Dana as she stared, seeing Kathy sucking down Will's cock. His pants were opened and he leaned against the sink, letting Kathy devour him.

Should she go? Should she watch? She was transfixed on seeing

Kathy tease Will's thickened cock as she licked and sucked it between her lips.

Dana's mouth salivated. Will was a very nice-looking man and she could see why Kathy never complained or joked about her love life. She seemed so joyous as she pleasured him. Dana stepped quietly toward the door to get a closer look. She looked down toward Kathy's feet. Kathy's hand was moving between her legs.

Biting her lower lip, Dana tried to see her friend's privates. Kathy wiggled and spread her thighs farther apart. Dana saw a light purple color between her legs.

Kathy had bought a small purple vibrator at the party. Will must have walked in on her trying it out in the bathroom.

Kathy stopped sucking Will's cock and held the rigid shaft in her hand. She gasped as she plunged the vibrator in and out.

Dana was becoming increasingly wet and felt her panties becoming damp from the heat. She couldn't stop watching. Her own desires made her uncomfortable. She gazed down and saw her nipples straining within her silk bra. Dana set her purse down and grasped her breast. It filled her hand, and the nipple was sensitive and ached.

"I can't take this. I want to fuck you right *now,*" she heard Will command.

Kathy freed Will's cock from her stroking hand. She shuddered when she pulled the vibrator from her hot pussy. As soon as she stood up Will smothered her with a deep, wet kiss.

Will's hands groped at her bare ass and full breasts with a begging need to feel her. He seemed desperate. Dana's hand crept between her legs as she stared at her friends in a passionate embrace.

Kathy turned around and leaned across the vanity, sticking her ass out in front of Will. He wobbled, pants falling around his ankles, and stood behind her. Kathy looked across the vanity and saw Dana looking in. Dana stood with a shocked look on her face, hand on crotch and her heart sank from embarrassment. Kathy winked and smiled wide, knowing her friend enjoyed her blissful state.

This eased Dana. She felt less worried because her friend seemed pleased she was watching.

Dana watched Kathy's expression more intently when she saw Will bend his hard cock down between the cheeks of Kathy's ass. Kathy let out a deep, open-mouthed sigh as Will sank into her pussy with a long hard thrust.

"Mmmmmm, damn, you feel good," Will mumbled. "You must have had a lot of fun at that party."

"Shut up, Will. Just do it, just do it, mmmmmm."

Kathy's eyes closed and she had a devilish grin on her face as Will plunged harder and deeper into her wet cavern.

Dana couldn't take her eyes off her friends. Will was grunting and she saw the thick shaft pull free then disappear back into Kathy. She closed her legs against her hand and squirmed.

Kathy moaned and Dana saw she was in extreme pleasure by the straining muscles of her face and her short gasps of air. "Oh fuck, Will, harder, harder . . . I'm . . ."

Will grunted and slammed hard into Kathy. The muscles in his legs were flexing and his face was tight. His jaw was shaking and he winced as he pulled on her hips. It looked like he was about to explode. Kathy's body shook on the vanity and Dana felt lightheaded. She saw her friend climax and almost felt as if she were part of it. She needed her own release.

Will arched his back and picked up Kathy. As her ass elevated, Will bent his knees and groaned.

Dana couldn't stand it. Her knees buckled and she banged into the dresser behind her. Scared from the racket she made, she scurried out the door. Perspiration wetted her forehead and she was flustered. Most of all she was incredibly horny.

She climbed in her car and tried to locate her keys in her purse. She was aroused to a desperate point and also embarrassed by getting caught watching Kathy and Will. As she found her keys, she felt a small plastic container.

Ben-Wa Balls. Dear Lord, the temptation.

The feeling they gave her had always brought her such pleasure. They were the first "toy" she had ever bought. She used to slip them inside her pussy at lunch and spend the day at work squeezing them for hours.

Her pussy was slippery and she wanted to get home as fast as she could.

Sitting in her car at the stoplight, Dana's hands were still shaking. Her nerves and the experience she had watched, had her all flustered and on fire. A loud *honk* blared from behind her when the light turned green and she was lost in a daze. She stepped on the gas and continued her ride home.

Dana couldn't shake the images of Kathy and Will from her mind—his strong, muscular legs flexing as he pushed his large cock into her; the way Kathy's face glowed and the wicked smile of passion across her lips. It was beautiful and nasty at the same time. For Dana, it was like looking into Kathy's fantasy.

While her mind flashed the scenes of sex, the fire between her legs became hotter. She was almost soaked through her underwear. The burning need of sexual tension began to overwhelm her.

Chapter Two

Home Sweet Home

Pulling up to her apartment driveway, Dana stopped suddenly. She stared down at her legs, watching them quiver. Dana knew she needed to finish off this built-up tension. She reached over and grabbed her case on the passenger seat. It fell and spilled its contents onto the floorboard.

Brought back to reality, she leaned over and started picking up samples from the case she had taken to the party.

Her underwear pressed against the puffy, engorged lips of her pussy and she laughed, looking at what she was picking up. Her hand was drawn to a firm, glass dildo that shimmered in the dim light inside the car. The long, smooth shaft fit snugly in her hand as she grasped it. The glass was cold from the night chill, but it felt so soothing. Dana bit her lip and her underwear seemed to squeeze the juices from her. A warm feeling slid along her inner thigh as she tightened her legs.

Fuck the stuff in the trunk. I have to get inside!

Dana hit the automatic door locks and scurried up the stairs to her apartment with her bag thrown over her shoulder. When she reached to open her apartment door she didn't even notice she had walked along the hallway and up her stairs with an eight-inch glass dildo in her hand.

Fumbling with her keys she heard a voice in the hall. She

stood still by her door and saw Mrs. Canerly peeking out her door to see what the noise was.

"Hello, Dana. You okay?" she asked.

Becoming anxious and wanting to get inside, she held back from telling the old bat to *fuck off*. "I'm fine. There, I got the door open. Goodnight."

As she started closing the door she heard Mrs. Canerly say something, but she really didn't care.

Dana set the dildo on her table by the door and tossed the party bag onto the floor. It fell with a loud "thud". She ripped off her coat, walked into her kitchen and hit the message machine.

"Hello, dear, this is your mother. Please . . ." She pressed the delete button quickly, knowing her mother's routine of asking fifty million questions about everything.

"Dana, this is Kevin. I'm sorry, but I have to go out of town so I have to cancel our date for tomorrow night. I was looking forward to it and . . ."

"Asshole." She deleted his message and slipped her heels off.

Dana wasn't too upset about Kevin's cancellation. She didn't really like him that much. Their last date was at the movies seeing Tom Cruise's new flick. She had been feeling frisky and slipped her hand under the popcorn bucket Kevin was munching on. After a few seconds of squeezing Kevin's cock she had unzipped his pants and slid her hand inside. Much to her disgust, he blew his load onto her hand and she couldn't eat popcorn through the rest of the movie. He had joked about it being buttered but the mood, as well as her hand, was a mess.

She grabbed a bottle of brandy from the cabinet. She unscrewed the top and poured a small portion into a short crystal glass. Downing it, she breathed out a sigh.

Setting the glass down, she looked up and saw the glass toy on her table. It was almost calling to her with a translucent glare from the lights, and again she felt the temperature rise between her legs.

Grabbing the bottle of brandy, she walked to the table and took the dildo with her down the hall. She set it on the sink in the bathroom and started a bath.

Looking into the mirror she remembered Kathy and Will in the bathroom. They were so sexual. Will looked so hot to her. She knew Kathy was a sexy woman, but damn.

Dana hadn't been with a man in a while. She liked Kevin but wasn't thinking about sleeping with him. He just didn't stir her like some other men did.

Unbuttoning her blouse, she drifted into her thoughts, letting the top fall to the floor. She unfastened the clasp on the front of her bra and freed her breasts from the tight garment. Her nipples were tight from arousal. They looked like two nickels on her breasts. She smiled and gave a playful tug on each one.

She shimmied out of her skirt and had to pull her underwear from between her legs. The wetness made them stick to her pussy and when she pinched the fabric to pull them down, a jolt of excitement shot through her spine as she touched her pussy.

Dana grabbed the bottle and poured a mouthful of brandy. She closed her eyes and swallowed the drink. It burned a little but brandy always relaxed her. She also needed to be a little looser; she was so uptight and yet excited.

She stepped into the very warm water. It was perfect to relax in and let her aching muscles soak in the heat. She glided back into the bath. It soothed her so much. For what seemed an eternity she lay in the water, melting to its caress. She looked down and saw her nipples peeking up. She caressed her smooth, wet skin and cupped her breasts. Her eyes closed and she thought back to what she had seen earlier.

She saw Will's backside and the tightening of his ass while a pair of hands grasped it. Dana's vision was different, as the woman in the image transformed to her. She saw herself sucking the long, firm shaft of Will's cock into her mouth and tickling the back of her throat. The fantasy was taking on more feeling as

Dana pinched the tips of her nipples, sending a message to her already aching pussy.

She envisioned Will's hands on the back of her head, enjoying the pleasure she gave him. She loved oral sex and seeing what Will had with Kathy made her crave the taste and control she could have over a man.

Dana's mouth became dry from her panting. This dream made her so hot. She reached over and poured another mouthful of brandy. As she swallowed it, the burn she felt became the hot seed from his loins spilling down her throat in her fantasy.

Her mind wandered to the ache between her legs. She spread her thighs apart and toyed with her pussy in the water. She was in a painful state of need. She reached over to the sink and fumbled, trying to grab her new toy. She grasped it firmly and sat back into the tub. She set it on her chest between her breasts. The glass was translucent and had oil or something inside. It was a swirl pattern that made Dana contemplate screwing it into her scorching-hot pussy. She stroked the length of the shaft in her hand. It was extremely stiff and firm with a slope to the right like a man's penis. The head had a deep ridge around it. Just like where the tip of a cock joins the shaft.

Dana couldn't help but want to feel this inside her. She held the shaft in her hand, brought it to her lips and kissed the tip. Dana closed her eyes, slid the glass shaft in her mouth and envisioned looking up at Will and pulling his cock from her mouth.

She felt a little awkward fantasizing about Will. He was a hunk, but a married one. Her mind swam through an ocean of men she had fantasized about as she slowly turned the glass cock within the wet confines of her red lips.

Antonio Banderas, Hugh Jackman, Carrot Top . . . different men of her dreams. Her fantasy needed reality. It needed an actual face she desired. Someone that made her wet.

Her fantasy took another step as she moved it to a large bed of pillows. She saw herself lying naked with Derrick above her.

Derrick was someone she'd always dreamt of fucking, but it had never happened. Derrick would fuck her tonight.

The toy became alive and she could feel the throbbing of his heart through it, his large hard cock toying with the opening of her pussy. She was so hot she almost begged him to fuck her. His long hard shaft slid into her with a forceful, steady thrust.

Dana put her wet hands to her face. The water refreshed her skin. She lay in the tub, letting the glass toy fill her pussy. Her muscles clenched tightly around it. She wasn't accustomed to something this hard and long inside her. The extreme physical pleasure put her on the brink of passion's door as she felt the pressure of the dildo touching the entrance of her womb.

She reached down and slowly pulled it back out, then thrust it in deeper. Her mind saw Derrick flexing and sinking his cock into her. Dana pulled her leg out of the water and hung it along the edge of the tub. The shaft seemed to ease in and out better, and she envisioned Derrick driving into her like a man possessed and overwhelmed with hot, dark lust.

Dana was absolutely blissful at how the toy filled her so deeply. The friction rubbed against her G-spot like no man had ever done. Derrick's body and image was her fuel for the intense amount of sexual tension she felt, and this toy became the lightning rod to let her storm of frustration loose. Dana whimpered and tightened her pussy around the hard glass shaft in spasms. She was so close that anything more would cause her to erupt.

Her eyes strained shut and she cried out as she pushed the toy deeper and twisted it. Her inner walls gripped the shaft and her orgasm ignited a deep fire buried within her. She shook and smiled widely as it pressed against her G-spot. Over and over she clenched the toy with her pussy. She pulled it out beneath the water and had to close her legs together.

A chill swept over Dana while she stared over the edge of the tub. She giggled when she pulled the plug to the tub out with her toes, not wanting to move. As the water lowered, she became cold. Dana struggled to get up with her arms wobbling and holding firmly on to the toy. She grabbed a towel and wrapped herself with it.

Relaxed and soothed, she walked down the hall to her bedroom. Dana flopped onto her queen-size bed and rolled onto her tummy. She opened her nightstand, dropped the toy into the drawer and covered it with her underwear. *That one is definitely a keeper. Gonna have to recommend that one at my next party.*

Chapter Three

I Don't Like Mondays

At work the next day, Dana answered calls from customers and tried not to let the constant bitching faze her otherwise good mood. Being a senior customer service representative for a high-profile advertising company had its good and bad points.

She had great benefits, and she had actually worked there long enough to have some freedom with her schedule of hours.

The bad part was that it was a large corporation . . . very big on their image. Image was their selling point and they were sacred to the idea that if they were clean as a whistle the clients would like them, because image was their business. There was no way they would condone one of their senior account representatives selling what was considered "porn toys." They constantly posted memos and flyers on company perspectives and issues. Most employees didn't bother to care about it because they just put in their forty hours a week and went home.

Dana didn't really worry too much, but she kept her little side job a secret. A few of the girls knew about it but she kept it pretty quiet. What she did after hours was her business, not theirs. Maybe if some of the people running the place would loosen up they wouldn't be so fucking anal about other people's affairs.

The week went by without much change going on except for William, the CEO, complaining about cost and net worth. Maybe if he didn't buy so much personal shit it wouldn't be a problem. Who needs all those silly "power ties" anyway?

Pam's Party

The party had been a huge success, probably one of Dana's best. She sat in the back bedroom filing away all of her paperwork.

There was a knock on the door and Pam poked her head in. "How're things going, Dana?"

Pam was a friend from college who ended up getting a high-profile job with too much responsibility, and she was overworked. She was successful in life but lacking in love.

Smiling, Dana answered, "I'm doing great. Thanks for having the party. It was one of the best ones I have ever had. You have a couple of pretty wild friends."

After closing the door, Pam went and sat next to Dana on the bed.

"Ummm, Dana? I wanted to wait until you were done to come talk to you." Adjusting her seat she looked back at Dana and said, "I haven't been with a man before. I mean, I'm not a virgin—there was this boy in high school—but you know what I mean. I'm rambling now, sorry."

"It's okay. What do you want to say, Pam? You can tell me." Dana was trying to be helpful but in the back of her mind she was thinking, *I hope she doesn't ask me to hop in bed with her.*

"This is so embarrassing. I have never had a vibrator and wanted to know how to use it."

"Is that it? What are you so worried about? A lot of the women at the parties I throw don't have a lot of toys. Some don't have any. Now, that Kris woman knew what she wanted and seemed to be very knowledgeable."

"Can you, ummm, show me what to do with it?"

"*Excuse me?*"

Embarrassed, Pam blushed a bright red. "Nooooo, not like that, I just mean, well . . . you know, what is a nice way to get off? I can't see getting intimate with something that has 'Made in Taiwan' written on it."

Dana shook her head, giggling. "Well, the most important thing is to be relaxed and comfortable with yourself, Pam. Just take a nice bath, relax, drink a tall glass of wine and mainly . . . picture the hottest guy you know wanting nothing more than to fuck you like an animal."

Pam grinned widely. She was flushed red and biting her bottom lip. "That would be Tony. Mmmmmmm, he's a definite beefcake. He's tall, dark and handsome. Mmmmm, saw him at the company picnic in his swimsuit."

She leaned over saying, "I could see the outline of his cock in the suit and the head almost hung out the leg of his shorts. Damn, I'm all warm thinking about him!"

"Well, this is the perfect kind of mood for a little teasing." Dana reached over to her bag and pulled out a small, pink egg-bullet. She unwrapped it and set it in Pam's palm.

Dana smiled and turned the egg on.

Pam's hand jerked back as she felt the fast vibration electrify the nerves of her hand. The humming made it move in her palm, causing Pam to giggle.

"Now what am I supposed to do with this?" Pam asked. In a way she knew, but wanted Dana to tell her.

"Well, press it against your, ummm, well, you know." Dana closed Pam's hand around it. With a jerk Pam pulled her hand back. It startled her at first.

"That kinda tickles. I mean, it feels like it is moving, not just vibrating."

"You have no idea what these little babies feel like inside your pussy. We're talking, climbing the walls." Dana smiled back and lowered Pam's hand toward her lap.

"Now rest your hand right here."

Pam had her hand resting between her legs over her dress. The slow melodic hum vibrated and swirled in her hand. It was soothing and she could feel it through her body.

"Close your eyes," Dana whispered. "Now turn your palm over and press it against your pussy."

Closing her eyes, Pam could feel the pressure of the egg against her pubis. The vibrations crawled through her body. She felt the delicious wetness of arousal growing inside her. Her smile showed her delight.

The sight of Pam's pleasure started getting to Dana. She began to get very turned on. The glow of arousal from Pam ignited the fires inside her.

Whispering again, like a guide, Dana said, "Now let the egg massage your pussy."

Pam turned her head slightly and the rhythmic swirl of vibrations now echoed through her wet cavern. "Mmmmmmmmmmmmm, this feels nice."

Dana pulled back as Pam tugged her dress up and rested the egg against her now-wet panties. The glimmer from her arousal was shimmering on the red silk.

Dana found herself staring. Not like a lover, but as an admirer. She hadn't ever seen another woman pleasuring herself this close. There were times she had seen movies or watched herself with a mirror. This was different, and very stimulating.

"Ohhhhh, this feels so goood. Mmmmm, talk to me." Pam was captivating and sexy.

"You seem to be doing just fine. God, you are so beautiful, Pam. You should see yourself." Dana found herself lost in the beauty of another woman. For a brief moment she saw what a man sees in a woman. Dana's underwear became moist while she watched Pam.

A deep moan radiated from Pam. "I think I found my clit. Ohhhhhhh, I, mmmmmm."

Knock, knock, knock.

Pam dropped her egg and Dana shook herself back to reality.

"Hello? Anyone here?" The door opened slowly. "Sorry, hon, I was just letting you know I was home." Pam's boyfriend, Eugene, waved to Dana and then closed the door.

Dana looked at Pam. "That's Eugene, huh? You sure you don't need extra batteries?"

They both smiled and Pam helped her pack up her things and then gave her a big hug. "Thanks, this was nice. I had fun with the girls."

They walked out to Dana's car and put the bags and other supplies into the trunk and backseat. Standing in the cool night air, Pam and Dana chatted a little. The coldness had an effect on both of them.

"It's getting a little nipply out here," Dana joked, noticing Pam's and her nipples awakening to the chill in the air.

"You know, if you get Eugene to use that egg on you . . . well, think about it." Dana winked at her and hopped into her car.

Sitting in her car at the longest stoplight in history, Dana looked across the street and spotted a nightclub. *I could use a nice, relaxing drink,* she thought. *And a nice relaxing fuck, too.*

After watching Pam warm up with that egg vibrator, Dana felt a little edgy and a lot frisky.

A thick cloud of smoke billowed out the door of the club as the bouncer let her inside. The music blared loudly and the steady *thump, thump, thump* of the bass vibrated through her spine. It was so cramped, so chaotic and so alive. Dana loved it.

There was wall-to-wall beefcake scattered throughout the bevy of young blonde bombshells. They were all a little younger than her but she figured she would see how different the chase was now. Dana had been out of the hunt for a while.

She sat down at the only open stool at the bar. She was basically unnoticed as she sipped a Chardonnay the young, stunningly handsome bartender gave her. Too bad he wasn't shirtless.

With his chest all wet and the heat in the club, he basically was. For a brief second Dana envied his tight, clinging shirt.

The problem was, so did about four other young women panting over him as they flirted and showed their 44DD plastic chests to him.

Dana turned back to the bar to get a refill. Looking into the mirror behind it, she caught her reflection. She also caught the reflection of a familiar face.

It was Ronald. He was dancing like the total white-boy he was on the floor with a tall skanky-looking brunette. Even though she was over him, the urges of jealousy crept back.

Dear God, don't let him see me, she thought as the music stopped. She looked down at the bar and fumbled with her drink.

A gentle tap on her shoulder made her cringe. She knew who it was. Her slow turn confirmed her assumption—it was Ronald and the skank.

"Hey Dana, what are you doing on this side of town?" he asked snidely.

"Ummm, I'm meeting some friends," Dana lied, not wanting to let him know she was alone.

"This is Celia. She's a friend of mine. We met a while ago."

Dana's eyes burned through the plastic-looking woman. She had brown hair with a perm that looked like an electric accident and wore a short black dress that showed off her petite frame. *I could kick her ass,* Dana thought.

"Looks like your friends are late like usual, huh?" Ronald always made her feel bad. Even when it was unintended.

In her mind she said all the insults she wished she could say. Comments on his penile dysfunction, the way he drooled in his sleep, the way his mother used to call him Ronny. She wouldn't stoop to his level. Instead, she forced a smile and nodded her head.

* * *

After seeing Ronald at the bar with that other woman Dana began to sulk. She also began drinking some more wine. Sitting by the end of the bar she felt pathetic. She had to drive and didn't want to get drunk, she just wanted to relax and feel bad.

"Dana? Is that you?"

Dana turned to see one of the couples from her party. Kris and Adam were a nice couple and spent *a lot* of money at the party.

Kris was a very slim woman with light brown hair and blonde streaks through it that accentuated the length. It cascaded to the middle of her back. She was dressed to kill with black boots and a plaid miniskirt with a white cotton tank top-style blouse. She obviously wasn't wearing a bra because her nipples poked out, full tilt. In most circles she was a definite hotty; in this crowd she really stood out.

Adam was as his name stated—the perfect male. He stood six feet three inches tall. As he pulled his hand through his shoulder-length, thick black hair, the muscles in his arm bulged . . . as did the package in his pants. He was broad-shouldered and had a polo shirt on that seemed to fit like the Incredible Hulk. He wore tight, navy blue khaki pants and he was what most women would call an instant wet panty male.

"What you doing here, Dana? Mind if we join you?" Kris motioned for the bartender to come over.

Adam leaned in. "What are you drinking, dear?" He breathed in the fragrance of the glass. "Hmmm, white wine, huh? You need something a little more . . . potent. Hey, Bill, get this woman a fresh drink. Make it a strawberry daiquiri." He looked down and whispered to Dana, "He's a buddy of mine. We live down the street, so we're in here a lot."

Turning to Kris, he said, "Come on, babe, I want to dance a little."

"My feet hurt. Hey, take Dana for a dance. She needs to have some fun."

"Uhhhh, I'm not a good dancer." Dana tried to think of a good excuse. She felt dumpy and wanted to just sit at the bar.

"Ohhh no, you don't. Let's go." Adam took her hand and led her to the small, cramped dance floor. A mid-tempo song was playing and they started to move together with the beat of the music.

Adam looked at Dana as she hung her head and every now and then would look in Ronald's direction. "Hey, what's wrong?"

A slow song started to play and Dana turned to leave the floor. Adam's large hand gripped her small shoulder and he tugged her back to him. "Come on. We can talk a little as we dance."

"Well, see that guy there with the brunette? He's my *ex*-boyfriend. He dumped me a while back and said some awful things. So now when I see him, I get a little down."

Adam held Dana tightly in his large, muscular arms and Dana laid her head against his chest. He felt so strong, so safe, and God, he felt so good against her.

"Really? Hey, fuck that guy. You really were happy and seemed so fun at the toy party. I can't believe you let some *asshole* make you feel bad. You're a really fine-looking woman. He's the fool to let you go."

"Ohh, you're embarrassing me. It's just that he said some things that really hurt so I am a little self-conscious when I see him. Just not as assured as I could be." Her hands dropped and went around his waist. Dana felt the firmness of his body.

The song ended and Adam led her back to the bar. Dana held his waist and watched his ass while walking behind him. Kris had her drink and a few of her friends had joined her.

Adam put his arm around Dana and she felt comfortable with these strangers. Of course, having her arm around a hunk wasn't all that bad, either. Maybe Ronald would see her with him.

"Hey, Kris, see that dorky-looking asshole over there? He dumped our friend Dana." Adam motioned toward Ronald.

Kris and her friend giggled and looked at Dana with an evil smile.

"Uh-oh," Adam said, smiling.

"Uh-oh, what?" Dana looked scared and was suddenly becoming a little looser and more adventurous.

"Come on, Dana, let's dance." Kris grabbed her hand and her other girlfriend followed.

"Yeah, I wanna dance, and shake my ass, oh yeah, oh yeah." Kris' friend, Nina, swayed her arms over her head and jiggled.

Kris joined Nina, waving her hands above her head as the uptempo sounds of Nelly started thumping in the bar. Kris stopped and looked into Dana's eyes. She took Dana's hands in hers and started swaying to the grooves of the music.

"Close your eyes, Dana. Climb into the groove with us."

Behind her, Nina grasped Dana's hips and pulled her ass against her body. The drinks were relaxing her and Dana was getting looser and having more fun as she became more in tune with the music.

Kris leaned into Dana and their lips would touch as they danced. Dana looked up into Kris' deep brown eyes and saw something that she wished *she* had. The reckless nature to just be free. Dana closed her eyes and leaned into Kris while they danced together. Their breasts would brush against each other's and the pulsing rhythms of the music were the orchestra for their erotic dance.

Dana opened her eyes and stared back into Kris'. The crowded floor seemed to disappear as Kris moved closer and kissed her. Her lips were soft and wet. Dana had never kissed a woman before and the disturbing show of affection in front of all these people didn't seem to bother her.

Kris and Nina yelled and shook their heads as they danced with Dana. The freedom was exhilarating and the sensuality was arousing. Dana was sucked into it.

Dana had no cares, no worries; she was just having fun. Kris and Nina made Dana a sandwich between them and all together they swung their hips and shook their asses to the guys whooping and whistling on the floor. Adam stood by the table, pumping his fist in the air and hand-slapping the guys watching with him. Dana felt fantastic. She was happy, she was relaxed and she was horny as hell.

The girls danced close together. They would part as they moved but when they faced one another they would touch and feel each other. Kris rubbed her nose against Dana's. Dana slid her tongue along Kris' lips.

Dana began to feel a little freer and spun around. She danced with Nina, who was a tall brunette. The men drooled looking at her. She was stunning and she had a beautiful way of moving. The three of them danced a little longer and then glided off the floor.

Downing her daiquiri, Dana was rejuvenated. She was laughing and having fun with her new friends.

She felt a tap on her shoulder and turned to see Ronald.

"Hey, you never danced like that for me before." He smiled and winked at her. "Maybe if we danced like that things would have ended up differently."

Suddenly hurt again, and mad, Dana glared up into his eyes. She was sick of his shit and wasn't going to let him ruin her night.

"*Adam?* Can you come here please, babe?"

Adam stepped up and Ronald looked slowly up to his steel eyes.

"There a problem here, sweetheart?"

"Ronald, I'd like you to meet my new boyfriend, Adam. He's shown me the way a woman should be treated. In life and especially in the bedroom."

Adam pulled his hair back again. Ronald saw the diameter of his biceps flex to the size of his leg. Adam poked Ronald's chest with a thump from his finger. "Hey, are you fucking with my woman?"

Ronald gulped, seeing how the veins in Adam's neck pulsed and his shirt stretched with the flexing of his powerful arms. "Uhhh, nope, I was just leaving."

After Ronald scurried out the door pulling his girlfriend along, the group of them burst into laughter. Dana gave Adam a big hug and thanked him for letting her *use* him. She held him for a second, almost drawn to kiss him. She hesitated then blushed a bright red.

"Well, we had a *blast* at the party and are gonna go home and try some of the stuff we bought. You should join us."

"I can't drive yet," Dana said, a little tipsy and feeling the drinks relaxing and warming her body. "Maybe I can stop by and we can talk some more, if you'd like?"

"That will be great!" Adam piped in.

"Nina? Where's Nina?" Looking into the corner she saw Nina kissing her boyfriend, Carl, in a little booth. "Looks like she has other plans."

Chapter Four

They left the bar and Kris waved to Nina, who was now tonsil-deep into kissing her boyfriend. It was a cool night and the breeze chilled Dana. She shivered and Adam put his jacket over her. It was warm and extremely big on her. But she loved his chivalry.

He had his arm around Kris and they talked as they walked the short distance to their apartment.

Kris began talking, "You know, you should have yourself a boyfriend. That Ronald guy seemed like a wimp. It sucks when someone makes you doubt yourself. That's why I love this big brute here. He does whatever I ask him to and I let him goof off with his friends."

"That's right. We respect each other and our needs. Except last Sunday."

Kris rolled her eyes. "Not that again. I told you I was sorry. I had that bridal shower to go to and needed the ride. Jeez, *end of the world, you missed the first quarter of the Steelers game*. I mean, I thought I made it up later."

"Well, yeah, that was nice." Adam had a goofy smile on his face.

"You two are so comfortable around each other. It must be a great feeling." Dana leaned against Adam and they continued walking.

"Haven't you ever felt totally happy just talking with a man? I mean, we were friends for a few years before I stole Adam away from that bitch—I mean, his ex-girlfriend." Kris smirked and looked at Adam.

Dana thought for a moment. "There was a friend of mine, Derrick, that Ronald and I knew. He was so funny, we could just talk and talk for hours. We'd flirt and joke around. He was a real gentleman, too. He was hot, though. Mmmm, I mean, yummy-looking, but I was with someone and wouldn't you know. I just liked Derrick as a friend but we really hit it off together. Another time, another place . . . who knows?"

"My advice to you, Dana," Kris continued, "is that the next time you see this guy, grab him and show him who you are now. Fuck the past, it's over. Just *go for it*!"

"Well, here we are." Adam walked up the steps and held the door open to the complex.

The apartment was dimly lit with an array of candles and a fire burning as they sat in the living room.

Kris and Adam kissed a few times as they said the normal touchy-feely lovers' comments and told Dana about themselves. Kris worked at Tony's Italian Cuisine as a hostess. Adam was a fireman. Like she needed to fantasize even more about his fire hose.

"The whole Pleasure Party stuff is just a part-time thing I fell into," Dana said. "I'm not sure where it will lead me. I have fun helping people. I've been pretty lucky so far."

"Well, I was impressed. You really seemed to have a good time and had a lot of those women laughing. It was nice." Kris winked at Dana.

"Hey, babe, I'm gonna take Dana into the bedroom. I have some stuff to ask her about." Kris reached her hand out to Dana.

"No problem. I have some stuff to do on the computer." Adam smacked Kris on the ass and walked away.

"Damn, that man spoils the shit out of me. He is so sweet, and look at that body." Kris took Dana's hand and led her to the hallway.

Dana followed Kris into their bedroom. The room was huge. They had a large bed with a deep red bedspread and a loveseat with a matching chair. A TV sat in one corner. The master bathroom was on the other side.

Kris motioned for Dana to sit on the bed then reached into the nightstand and pulled out her bag from the party. She tossed it on the bed and sat next to Dana. She unzipped her long boots and pulled them off one by one.

Dana sat watching Kris. On any other occasion she would feel uncomfortable but she was very content just sitting and watching.

Kris caressed her legs and calves after slipping off the boots. "I just wanted to ask you about some of the stuff I bought tonight."

"Sure, what would you like to know? I can . . ." Dana stopped talking as Kris slid off her underwear and unfastened her miniskirt.

Dana stared, unsure of what to do or say. She had seen her share of women at the gym and in general. But this was something different. This wasn't just a woman changing her clothes. Kris was a beautiful woman who was stripping for her. She knew Dana was watching.

As Kris tossed her shirt aside, Dana found herself appreciating the sensuous woman before her.

Kris plopped on the bed and lay next to Dana. She untied the small ribbons holding the bag of party toys closed. "I just wanted to make sure I knew how to use this stuff right."

Dana turned away. What was she doing? How was she going to get out of this? Why did she have this sudden arousal creeping through her body? Her eyes looked back to Kris' smooth flesh. The shape of her legs, her flat stomach, the small tight nipples on her pert breasts. She was beautiful.

"Can you show me how to use this new vibrator?" Kris asked as she opened the box.

"Kris? Ummm, I'm not a lesbian or anything."

"Lesbian? Who? *Me?* Fuck no. I like nothing more than a thick cock. Look at my boyfriend." Kris giggled, knowing Dana probably felt a little weird. "Hey, just because you look, touch or feel aroused by another woman doesn't make you gay. I just wanted your help."

Dana felt better hearing Kris' honesty. She was right. She lay back and rolled over next to Kris on the bed. They both looked at the new vibrator. "The Pussy-Pleaser. Perfect name." Dana laughed. "I don't have this one but I hear it's great!"

Kris rolled onto her back and lifted her knees up. Dana lay on her back next to her.

"Should I lube this thing up or . . . mmmmmmmmmm." Kris found that she was already wet enough to press the tip inside her shaved pussy.

Dana longed to feel her own vibrator. She was jealous of Kris, who had a fucking hot guy and was confident and open about her sexuality. Dana admired that. She also admired how much pleasure she was getting from the toy Kris had purchased from her.

"Oh God, my nipples are so hard." Kris closed her eyes and moaned. The hum of her vibrator dulled as she sank it in deeper.

Dana sat up and looked at Kris. She was in her splendor. Totally vulnerable. Dana reached over and touched the smooth skin of Kris' stomach.

"Ohhhhhhhhh, mmmmm," Kris moaned, feeling Dana's touch.

Dana set her hand on Kris'. She held the toy and felt the pulsing vibrations. Moving her hand away, Kris let Dana hold it within her. Kris cupped her breasts trusting Dana with the vibe that churned her juices.

Dana stared at Kris' pussy, opened by the vibe. She had seen her own in a mirror and earlier saw the joy Pam was in, but the sight of a wet pussy in want entranced Dana. She pushed the vibe in, seeing the skin grasp the shaft and stretch inward. She pulled it outward and could see the flesh gripping the vibe, not wanting to release it.

Kris moaned deeply. She had the tips of her nipples pulled away from her breasts and her back arched upward. "Mmm-mmm, I love this new vibe. It feels almost like Adam's cock."

As Dana slid the vibrator in and out she gently twisted it. "If I had a man like Adam I'd be in bed every night. He is so fucking good-looking." Dana caught herself going a little overboard with her desire for Adam.

"Mmmmmmmm, yeah, he's really hot. Mmmm, that feels good, Dana. Keep doing that."

Dana pressed on Kris' tummy as she plunged the vibe in and out. "I wish I had someone like him to just fuck when I needed it."

"Dana? Do you want him?" Kris asked as she moaned.

Dana stopped for a moment. What was she thinking? These strangers had her opening up to them. She was helping Kris masturbate and fantasizing about her boyfriend as she did it. She had to stop this.

"Yes." She spoke from her heart.

Kris grasped Dana's hand and pulled the vibe from her. "Adam? Can you come here?"

"No, no, no, no. I can't!"

"Dana, it's okay. Trust me, you won't regret it and I'm okay with it."

"No, I can't. I have to get up early, I just . . ."

Adam walked into the room and saw Kris standing naked with a twelve-inch vibrator in her hand. "Ummm, did you call me? It looks like you have your hands full."

Kris walked up to Adam, grasped his crotch in her palm and turned to Dana. "She is okay with it, babe. She wants you."

Kris sat on the chair by the loveseat and spread herself open, facing the bed.

"You do whatever Dana asks but . . . you can't fuck her. She has to beg me to let you fuck her."

Dana turned and looked at the wicked smile on Kris' face. Kris looked and winked at her, laid her head back on the arm of the chair and continued to slide the large vibrator across her breasts. Dana looked up at Adam and shrugged her shoulders, not sure what to do.

Adam knelt down and put his finger under her chin. Lifting her head, her lips were softly brushing his. Their mouths merged with a kiss. Pulling back, Adam opened his eyes to see Dana's face. She seemed so lost in the mood.

"You are so beautiful, Dana. Just tell me what to do to make you feel good," Adam said, caressing the hot skin of her neck.

"This is so weird. I mean, you are so fucking good-looking. I could never attract—"

"Shhhhhh, I am here with you now. For you, tonight, I am your man. My sole purpose is to give you pleasure. Kris is fine with this. We love each other but she knows I love women, and sometimes I can let her know there is a woman I desire. I desire you, Dana. I asked her for this. Trust me and be with me tonight."

Melting, Dana felt herself giving in. "Can I kiss you?"

She leaned forward and kissed Adam's firm lips. She shivered with nervousness. "I haven't been with a man in a long time. I'm not sure what . . ."

Adam captured her lips with a deep passionate kiss. Dana felt his large shoulders as she wrapped her arms around his neck. Her tongue seemed drawn to seek out his, so she opened her mouth slightly and tasted his hot breath. She instantly became wet, and her pussy began to burn from the heat.

"Mmmmmm, ahhhhh, oh yes," Kris moaned as she masturbated on the chair with the vibrator. "Damn, Dana, you weren't kidding when you said this was a pussy pleaser."

Adam grinned and looked at Dana while wiggling his eyebrows. "I'll show you a pussy pleaser."

Dana smiled and hugged him tight. His body made her warm and she wanted to touch all of him. She kissed him again and then let go. "Where's that massage oil?" she asked, looking around the room.

Reaching into her bag by the bed she scooted back on the bed and patted the spot next to her. "Come here, *big boy,*" she said, wiggling her eyebrows back at him.

Adam climbed onto the bed and Kris piped in, "It's about fucking time."

He rolled onto his back and Dana tugged at his shirt, trying to pull it up. Adam pulled it up over his head and Dana caught herself gasping at his body. His midsection was firm and muscular. He had a true six-pack abdomen and she licked her lips, seeing his huge chest.

"Sorry, got distracted. Okay, you take the oil in your hand like this." She poured a healthy amount into her palm. "Then you smear it where you wish to massage." Dana smeared the oil onto Adam's chest and abdomen. The crevasses were bumpy and she felt each one, as her hands became an erogenous zone. Her panties were useless at this time because they were completely soaked.

Adam reached over and unbuttoned her blouse very slowly.

Dana sat up and let him pull the blouse free from her skirt.

"Mmmm, I like black underwear." His deep voice cut through her. He unhooked the clasp on the front of her bra and her breasts burst free from the chamber that held them. Her nipples were so tight she swore they would send her over the edge if touched. "Oh, wow, you have beautiful breasts."

Oblivious to anything but her ache, she leaned down toward Adam and pressed her bare chest against his. The warmth soothed her burning need. She closed her eyes and felt his heart pound beneath her. Her hands fumbled with his pants button and zipper. She wasn't looking, just feeling her way.

Adam reached around her body and up her skirt. He rubbed the back of her legs and cupped her ass in his hands. His large hands squeezed her cheeks and she sighed. Reaching between her ass cheeks, his thumb pressed on the puffy, hot lips of her pussy. The thin fabric was the only barrier keeping his finger from becoming engulfed with her juices held inside.

"Shit, your pussy is on fire," Adam groaned as his thumb pierced the opening to her ecstasy.

"Ohhhh God," she moaned while Adam's thumb toyed with her pussy. Dana's hand slid inside his underwear and found the prize. She moaned loudly when she felt the immense girth of his cock in her hand. "Dear Lord, you are fucking wondrous."

"Go down on her, Adam. I want to watch you eat her pussy." Adam obliged by tugging Dana's underwear over her ass and down her legs.

As Dana lay on her side she held firmly on to her prize. Then she knelt over and straddled Adam's face.

He grabbed on to her ass and pulled her down. Lower, lower, until his hot breath blew through the wet flesh. Dana looked over at Kris and saw her eyes flutter as she slid the long vibrator inside her shaven pussy. She let it rest inside and pulled at her nipples. She looked so beautiful and so enriched by her freedom of passion.

Adam's tongue found Dana's clit and he flicked her hardened bud, causing her to shudder. His cock flexed in her hand and she felt his heart pounding through the veins along the base. Releasing it from his underwear, she stared at it with admiration and lust. He was extremely thick and above average in length. Without hesitation she forced the length into her mouth, touching the back of her throat.

Adam growled and the vibrations rumbled through her pussy as he pulled her lower.

As if competing, Dana vigorously stroked his cock in her hand as she licked the head of it. Her breasts slipped against the sweat and oil across Adam's stomach. Their heat was becoming almost too much for her to stand and Dana started to feel desperate to feel Adam inside her. Fucking her hard, like an animal.

With a dreamy stare Kris watched her lover and Dana explore each other and she came with the toy buried deep inside her.

Adam relentlessly assaulted Dana's clit with his viper-like tongue. Her juice flowed freely and Adam sucked up the sweet nectar from her. Adam's large hands dug into the flesh of her ass and he shook his head violently, stretching and licking her.

Dana couldn't control herself as she moaned and gasped for air while she deep-throated Adam. The salty seepage from his cock fueled the oncoming storm.

With a deep moan Dana sat upright and grabbed her breasts, putting full force against Adam's probing mouth. She pinched her nipples, tugging the tight, red ends away from her body, and became lost in her ultimate fantasy.

With a blinding flash she felt herself falling. She rode the waves of her orgasm to the restful beach of her mind. She felt blissful, but not totally fulfilled.

Adam lay with his face shiny and wet. Collapsing across Adam's body, Dana rolled off him, admiring his large cock. *Damn, I want to be fucked with that.* "Can we fuck now, Kris?"

"Kris?"

Kris had left. Adam rolled onto his side, facing Dana. "Mmmmm, you *know* what I want, don't you?"

With a nasty thought, Dana smiled and rolled onto her back.

"Just a sec." She reached over to her purse and grabbed a condom.

"Wanna see a trick I learned?" Dana wiggled her eyebrows and grinned at Adam. As she tore at the wrapper she kissed the engorged head of Adam's cock.

Sitting up, she showed Adam the condom. "Watch, no hands." Then she made an "O" with her lips and set the condom on her mouth. Leaning over the glistening tip of his hard cock, she rested the condom on the top then lowered her mouth down around the swollen tip. The condom unrolled as she slid him into her mouth.

Adam moaned as he felt both the tightness of the condom and the contours of her lips around his cock.

Sitting up, a small drip of saliva fell to his tightened balls and Dana licked them. She liked the coarse feel of the skin on her tongue. His balls flexed with the throbbing of his stiff cock. She loved the effect she had on him.

"That tickles." He laughed and Dana lay back on the bed, awaiting her treat.

Adam rolled over on top of her. His massive body dwarfed her. He pushed himself up so not to crush her petite frame.

Dana wrapped her legs around Adam's hips and looked down her body. Her breasts were heaving and she could see Adam's huge cock throbbing above her pussy. Pulling with her legs she felt her opening stretch to accept his gift.

Dana was wet and really hot to feel the fullness from a man. Her body was flushed and her blood boiled. She stared up at Adam and pulled a few strands of his hair behind his ear and lifted up to kiss him.

Adam lowered down and sank into her. "Ohhhhh, mannnn, you are soooo tight. Mmmmmmmm."

Dana tried not to whimper from the lovely strain his cock had on her as she was being stretched apart. She opened her mouth and arched her body up as he sank back into her again. The tightness was incredible and her pussy convulsed with every minute of this abuse.

"I don't want to hurt you, dear. Are you okay?"

Dana grabbed his ass and pulled on it, motioning him to go faster. Her legs twisted together along his hips.

"Hard . . . hard and fast. I want to feel you, Adam. I want to feel like I am being fucked by a real man."

Like a piston he slammed in and out of her pussy with a heated fury.

Sweat built up on Dana's chest and Adam's forehead was wet from perspiration. "Ohhh, Ohhhh, I . . . I . . .mmmmmm. I'm gonna come again, ohhhhh."

Kris walked in with only a robe on, hearing Dana's cries of joy. She knelt by the bed and looked at Dana's face as it contorted in pleasure. She stroked her face gently and smiled. Adam pounded harder into her. The bed creaked and Dana felt lightheaded. The hard bang of the headboard against the wall accentuated the power of Adam thrusting into Dana.

Kris took off her robe and lay next to them and stroked Dana's breasts with the back of her hand. The softness contrasted with Adam's roughness as he fucked her.

"Oh don't do that, I can't . . . can't handle that . . . right there, Adam, right there, ohh, mmmmm." Dana's voice wavered as she became more excited. Kris licked her fingertips and then pulled gently on Dana's small, tight nipples.

Kris leaned up and kissed Adam as he pleasured Dana. Then she turned and kissed Dana ever so gently. "Let go, dear. Just let go."

Kris' words echoed in Dana's mind and she closed her eyes and let herself go. She wrapped her arms around Adam's powerful body. Her nails dug into the flesh of his muscular back and he cried out as she raked his flesh and she came again.

Adam grunted loudly and she could feel him swell inside her. His eyes bulged and he puffed air in quickly. Adam grunted again, moaning loudly, and Dana felt him explode within her. Over and over she felt the throbbing inside her walls. It spewed hard into her from the pressure of holding it in so long. Dana looked up and pulled Adam down and kissed him. She held him tightly and the air between their slick bodies made a funny farting sound that made the three of them laugh.

Adam had a goofy smile on his face and rolled his eyes. His body was shiny from the massage oil and passion they had shared.

Dana felt him slide out of her and she just lay there, totally spent.

Adam climbed out of the bed and went into the bathroom.

Snuggling next to Dana, Kris rolled next to her and whispered, "I swear to God. That man is the best fuck I have ever met."

"I'll second that," Dana added.

Kris leaned over and kissed Dana's cheek. "You get dressed, I'll give you a ride home."

Dana's legs hurt, her ass was sore, her body ached from Adam's weight on her, but she didn't care. She felt great. And her pussy felt even better.

Chapter Five

THE NEXT WEEKEND

"Thank God it's Friday," Dana shouted as she sat in the front seat of her car.

She flicked on the radio, turned up some new Matchbox Twenty song and sped out of the parking lot. As she pulled up toward the electronic gate to leave, she stopped suddenly. Her head jerked forward and she glared out the window at the car that almost hit her.

"Hey, *bitch,* watch where . . ." Dana yelled out her window. "Whoops, sorry."

The boss's wife had cut her off and seemed to be in a terrible rush. She recognized the boss's car by the license plate saying TOP DOG. All Dana saw was her blonde hair and her hands flailing. She looked very flustered. She screeched her tires and took off down the road. Dana just shrugged. Whatever.

Deciding to just veg out for the night, Dana picked up some nice Italian food and a bottle of light, white wine. It was so relaxing to just read her latest *Romantic Times* magazine and listen to some mellow R&B music in her apartment.

After polishing off her tortellini and three glasses of the Chardonnay, Dana was relaxed. Her magazine had other effects on her. There were reviews of new romantic books coming out and excerpts. The excerpts always got to her. This month an excerpt from Elizabeth Lapthorne's new book was in it.

A sudden warmth took over Dana's body and she decided to cool off a little and change her clothes.

Dana slipped out of her dress then grabbed her silk robe. It didn't cover all that much, but it was comfortable. Ronald had always poked her when she wore it because her nipples showed through. She just loved how it gently brushed her skin. Like floating on air.

Standing in front of the fridge she stared at what she could nibble on before bed. The cold air caused her nipples to tighten. They protruded into the fabric, and she giggled at how the cold affected her body. Damn, it's cold. She grabbed the Ben and Jerry's and walked to the living room.

The fabric floated over her flesh like a breeze. She plopped down on the couch to watch some TV and relax. Surfing through a hundred fifty-two channels of nothing good to watch, she came upon a sexy movie of a couple making out. It was one of those cheap R-rated sex flicks. Terrible acting, but she liked the good-looking men in the movie.

The couple kissing intimately and the fake sex scenes were arousing Dana.

Knock, knock, knock.

Who the hell would come over at eleven p.m.? She wrapped herself in a blanket and peeked out the peephole. It was Derrick. After her breakup with Ronald she didn't see Derrick much.

Dana unlocked the door and let him in. She gave him a big hug and looked up at his eyes. "What's wrong?"

"Oh, my roommate has a girl over and he wanted to be alone with her. I saw your light on and was wondering if I could crash here a while." His big puppy dog eyes looked desperately at Dana. "*Pleeeeeeeease???*"

"Oh quit it. Of course you can stay a while. I'm winding down anyway. Want a beer?"

Derrick was an average-sized man with a broad chest and very muscular arms. He was in construction and worked with heavy things all day, and it paid off for him. He had light brown hair and steel blue eyes. A girl could get lost within their depth. He was wearing his traditional rock band t-shirt, jeans and a flannel shirt that was unbuttoned.

Dana and Derrick had felt a distinct draw to each other. They just couldn't do anything about it because of their commitments to others. Every time Derrick had broken up with a woman, Dana had Ronald. Now that she was free from Ronald, Derrick had a girlfriend. *That lucky bitch,* she thought.

"Sure, thanks. It's been a while since we talked anyway. This will be . . . ummmmm. What are you watching, Dana?"

"Oh just a silly cable movie." She laughed, wondering what Derrick thought of her now.

She strolled back into the living room, beer in hand, and with the most erect nipples imaginable.

Derrick glanced up from watching the movie and did a double take of Dana's breasts. *Whoa, must be cold.* "Nice robe." He gulped as she handed him the beer.

Dana looked down and burst into laughter. Blushing four shades of red, she tried to cover herself. She flopped onto the couch and grabbed a small blanket hanging over the edge.

"So, how have you been doing, Derrick? Since Ronald and I broke up I haven't seen you much."

The night seemed to just fly by. Dana was telling Derrick about her job and her boss and all the small talk. There had always been chemistry and a spark between them.

A few times, when Ronald had been away, Dana had thought about the typical "what-if" scenarios. What if she kissed Derrick? What if they weren't attached to others? What did Derrick look like naked? How big was his cock? Would he mind if she tore his clothes off and fucked him silly?

Derrick told her about how he broke up with his girlfriend a while ago and how he lived with an old friend and that they shared a two-bedroom apartment. Derrick left whenever his roommate had women over. Especially his new "friend" of the month. She always flirted with Derrick and he wasn't attracted to her at all and her constant gawking and accidental rubbing on his crotch made him uncomfortable.

"Well, I moved to those new duplexes down the road and . . . well . . . When you were with Ron it was cool to hang out because you were a couple and I was a friend with both of you. Now to me he was an idiot for letting you go. I know I wouldn't have." Derrick caught himself from going too far. "You are a great woman."

Dana felt herself flush, and warmth crept through her body. The wash of moisture between her legs reminded her of the stirring of desire that was filling her.

"Well, Ronald always made me feel like I wasn't good enough. Everything was about *him*. I was so hurt I didn't know what to do. It was, and still is, hard to open myself up to anyone. Ronald would always get drunk and fall asleep but you and I always had fun. I always liked that. You were the best male friend I had for a long time. I loved when you came over and we just sat around bullshitting about things. Your girlfriends, that silly car you had—we just talked about everything. Now that I am single I don't know how to act around a man anymore."

Dana leaned forward and Derrick looked down her neck and could see the slope of her breast under the cover-up.

His obvious admiration didn't go unnoticed. "Do you think I'm pretty, Derrick?"

"Silly question."

Dana smiled, knowing he did. She reached down and untied the loose belt holding her robe closed, revealing her full breasts. "A friend of mine gave me some advice if I were to see you again. I think I am going to follow what she said."

"Ummmm, Dana, this isn't fair. You know I have always had a thing for you."

"Hey, ever since I have known you there has been a line I didn't cross because we were both with someone. Now we're not. I just want to know. I always wanted to know," she said, staring into his eyes.

"Know what?" he asked stupidly.

"To know what it would be like to fuck you." Dana lunged forward and kissed Derrick's lips. Overcome with need and desire, Dana was more aggressive than ever. She had wanted Derrick for a long time and this was her chance to reopen the fantasy she had longed for.

Rolling into his lap, Dana slipped her tongue into Derrick's mouth.

As Derrick twisted his tongue around hers, he could feel his own desires opening up. He could also feel an oncoming throb in his pants. She was so hot he was growing stiffer by the moment.

"Come with me. I have something I want to show you." Dana took Derrick's hand and led him down the hallway to her bedroom.

Derrick jerked her to a stop and she turned to him. He grabbed and kissed her deeply. His hands slid down her back and held firmly on her ass.

She began to melt but maintained her control. "No, not yet, wait, I want to do this with you."

She led him to a nice, blue reclining chair in the corner of the room and had him sit down.

"Can I . . . ?"

"No, you sit here."

Dana unfastened his pants and kissed him again. Her breasts hung slightly before his face and Derrick could breathe in her perfumed skin. It intoxicated him.

Dana turned around and bent over. "You like my ass, Derrick?"

"Ohhh, yeah."

"Can you help me with my underwear, dear? They are so tight on my pussy. I need help taking them off."

Derrick laughed and tugged them down to her knees.

Dana turned around and stepped out of them. Handing them to Derrick, she again reached for his pants and slid her hand under the waistband of his underwear. She opened her eyes wide as she felt how big and hard he was.

Kneeling before him she pulled out the head of Derrick's large cock and flicked her tongue at the tip, making it flex. "Mmmmm, I shouldn't have waited for this."

Derrick scooted lower in the chair and Dana tugged his jeans down to his thighs. His underwear was tight with the raging hard-on confined within them. Dana again kissed Derrick then dragged her nails down his chest and peeked under the waistband of his Hanes and pulled them over his stiff cock. In all its glory, it was more than she had expected.

With one long motion Dana filled her mouth with the hard shaft.

"Ohhhh, damn," Derrick groaned.

Closing her eyes she pictured it in her pussy. The thought made her wet again and she slowly released his cock from her mouth. She looked at the shimmering tip and kissed it. The residue from anticipation trickled from it as it throbbed. With a wicked smile she licked the tip clean.

Putting the underwear back over his cock, Dana stood up and walked over to the bed.

"What the—??? This isn't fair. I can't . . ."

Derrick stared at Dana as she pulled a vibrator out of her bag by the closet door. Puzzled, he wasn't sure if it was for her or him.

Dana hopped onto the bed. She went to her knees and spread her legs apart, sitting on her feet. "I want you to watch me, Derrick."

"But, what about . . ."

"Oh don't worry. If you do this for me I am going to make you come so hard you'll see the back of your head."

"Uhhhh, deal."

Dana sat up and rubbed the gleaming flesh-toned vibrator against her neck. "Talk to me, Derrick, I need your voice."

"Damn, you look so good. I want you so bad it hurts."

"Mmmmmmm, you like me touching myself?"

"I just wish it was me."

Dana closed her eyes and let the vibrator explore her flesh and Derrick's voice explore her mind. The steady hum vibrated against her pubis, making her wet. She pressed the toy against her clit and felt shocks of pleasure shoot through her body.

"Ohhhh, Derrick, my clit is throbbing. I wish you could feel how wet this makes me. Mmmmmm, damn, I want to fuck you, mmmm, damn." And with a single thrust, she slid it into her dripping pussy.

"Oh fuck, this is too hot." Derrick did all he could not to grab his cock to relieve the pressure building inside him.

Dana rubbed her breasts and tugged at her nipples as the toy vibrated and churned the inner walls of her pussy. A tear trickled out from her eye as she felt freer than ever. Her body was burning like a fire out of control. She grabbed the base of the vibrator and began the motions of sex in and out, in and out. Her other finger found her clit as it pulsed and hardened.

She opened her eyes and looked at Derrick. He had his cock in his hand, trying not to burst.

Dana fell back onto the bed. She plunged the toy in and out of her pussy imagining it was Derrick's stiff cock filling the aching void of her desires.

Dana grabbed her breasts and twisted the nipples, sending a jolt to her pussy. She had a breast in each hand and the vibrator was being drawn in and out of her. She looked over and didn't see Derrick sitting in his chair anymore.

He had taken the vibrator in his hand and controlled how Dana was to be fucked by her toy. Strong, deep thrusts filled her inside. Even with this much pleasure, she longed for the real thing. A man pounding hard and deep into her pussy.

A hot wetness covered her clit. She looked down and saw Derrick's head between her legs and his tongue was engulfing her pussy with hot saliva. The peak of her orgasm was upon her and she tightened her pussy around the toy and Derrick sucked hard on her clit, sending her over the edge.

Lost in the bliss of her orgasm she breathed short gasps and tried to relax.

Standing up, Derrick tugged his shirt off and slowly pulled up his t-shirt. His muscles rippled on his abdomen and Dana squirmed.

Dana wiggled her body and scooted to the end of the bed. Her head hung off the edge and she grabbed Derrick's cock and pulled it to her mouth. With a slow stroke Derrick slid his cock into her mouth. He reached down and grasped her breast, squeezing it gently.

"Oh damn, damn, damn, this is so sexy."

Dana's legs widened. He could see her labia lips purse and couldn't stand any more. He leaned forward, sliding his cock down her throat and brushed her pussy with his fingers. They were wet from his mouth and hot from her orgasm. His finger slipped between the lips and along her still swollen clit.

Dana's hands held firmly on to the back of Derrick's legs and while his fingertips toyed with her pussy, her mouth drooled as his cock filled it. She would no longer want for a man; she would take the man she wanted.

Stepping back he slid his cock free of her mouth and grabbed her.

"I can't handle any more. I'm gonna explode. Fuck, I want you so bad."

"You really want me, Derrick? Really?"

"Oh yes, yes, yes."

Dana smiled and rolled onto her stomach. She propped her ass up and shook it in his direction.

Without needing any more hints Derrick climbed on the bed and moved behind Dana.

He grabbed the flesh of her ass. "Mmmmmm, now this is nice."

He rested his cock on her back where the split of her ass met her lower back. Dana felt a small drip of desire creep from Derrick's cock. "Come on, I want it now," she commanded.

"Oh, you make me wait and now I am a service station attendant. Well, here's the pump, babe. I guess I'll fill you up." They laughed and Derrick struggled to push his stiff cock down and force it between Dana's legs. It strained upward and Dana's mouth watered, as she knew where he was putting that beast.

Derrick grabbed her hips and Dana reached between her legs and caressed the stiff shaft, pressing the head against the slippery opening of her pussy.

With a hard thrust Derrick sank into Dana's sanctuary. The huge thickness filled Dana and she closed her eyes and felt herself letting go.

"Oh God, ohhhhhhhhhhh."

With a deliberate rhythm he slammed into her. Dana felt his cock swell inside her. She hadn't felt so sexual in such a long time and she didn't want it to stop.

With all her might she tightened her inner walls around Derrick's large cock.

"Damn, you feel so fucking unreal. Ohhh, man. Mmmmmm, I love this."

Derrick couldn't stand it anymore and pounded into her. Over and over he pushed deep within her. The *slap, slap, slap* of their flesh echoed through the bedroom. The headboard hit the wall as Derrick groaned loudly.

"Oh, I'm coming, Derrick. Oh, oh, I'm coming, ahhhhhhh."

With a forceful thrust, Dana's body jerked up and she felt Derrick erupt inside her. Her pussy tensed as she felt it constricting and she came with him. The burn of his hot seed merged with her fluids, leaving her totally content.

Derrick leaned forward and kissed the back of her shoulder.

"You have no idea how long I have wanted to do that."

The feeling of a true sexual experience fulfilled one of her fantasies. Derrick filled the other.

Chapter Six

Are We Having Fun Yet?

Lauren stood by Dana's desk, watching her rifle through her business satchel to find the toy she had ordered.

"AHA!!!! I knew I had it. It fell to the bottom of my satchel. Now quit bugging me, you nympho." Dana laughed and handed the small red bag to Lauren.

"So how do these pleasure balls work?" Lauren asked.

"Shhhhh, keep quiet, silly." Dana was giggling as she whispered to her friend. "You slip them inside and the weights within the balls cause them to vibrate and feel like they are sliding and swelling while they are in your pussy. *I love them.*" Dana's eyes opened wide and she smiled.

Nodding her head as she read the package, Lauren listened to Dana.

The phone rang and Dana picked it up. "Hello? Okay, five minutes . . . Okay, yeah, Lauren's here. Okay, we'll be there."

"Meeting time. I better get my notes and stuff."

Lauren looked up and said, "I need to go get mine too. I'll meet you there."

* * *

Dana sat at the table. She was a little nervous that Lauren would be late. She glanced back up at the clock and tapped her foot.

Lauren rushed into the meeting and stopped, holding on to the tops of chairs as she walked to her seat next to Dana. She had a slight tinge of sweat across her brow even though it was cool in the conference room.

"You had me worried. What happened?" Dana inquired.

Lauren's hand shook and she held the edge of the table for a moment as she sat down. "I went to the bathroom. I was curious, so I put . . . well . . . you know. I put them in." Lauren grabbed the table's edge again, forcing herself to sit still.

"Ohhhhhhh, Dana, I still have them in . . . Ohhhhhh."

Covering her mouth to contain herself from bursting out in laughter, Dana asked, "You're kidding me, right? You are nuts."

"Ohhh, my God, I don't have panties on and I have to hold them in. Ohhhh, mmmmmmm, uhhhhh."

The dim room was filled with all the executives and the slide presentation was causing total drowsiness throughout the room . . . for everyone except Dana and Lauren.

Lauren held Dana's hand and would squeeze it as the balls swirled within her. She needed to get them out but couldn't. Her heart was pounding, her face was flushed and hot, and the balls had just slid to the opening of her pussy and spread the lips. Not thinking, Lauren closed her legs tightly.

The sudden clenching caused the balls to hit together and a vibration shot through her. The ball resting on her clit shuddered. Lauren squeezed Dana's hand again, scaring her, and Dana yelped, "Ouch."

Everyone turned to look and Lauren set her hand on the table and sat upright, straining her chest forward.

"Sorry, poked myself with a pencil." Dana tried to cover her goof-up.

A few men noticed Lauren, her eyes blinking and her nipples so hard they showed through her blouse. Lauren was getting incredibly aroused and wet from the motion and feel of the balls inside her. They reminded her of her wants.

Leaning over to Dana, she whispered into her ear, "If I don't get these out I am going to come right here."

Sitting back up they swayed again and the weighted swirl vibrated inside. Lauren felt her legs opening. As if by instinct, she lowered her hand down. Because of the dim room and people watching the presentation, nobody noticed her pressing on her skirt to push the balls deeper inside.

Stifling a deep, pleasurable moan, Lauren had accidentally slid the balls up to her G-spot. A flash of heat filled her body and she felt her pussy spasm.

She closed her eyes and dragged the tip of her shoe toward her on the carpet. Her toes were curling and her body was now awake and aching. Her tightening and clenching caused the balls to hit together inside and vibrate against her G-spot.

Lauren was now on the brink. Her entire body was alive and the nerve endings were sensitive to even the simplest touch. She licked her lips. She was perspiring from her inner heat.

"Lauren? Are you okay? You look a little flushed," the boss asked.

Dana saw Lauren was a little out of sorts and clutching the table. "We had burritos for lunch. I better help her to the bathroom. Sorry."

She held Lauren's hands and as she stood up, the balls rattled together as she tried to clutch them inside. Her muscles shook and spasmed. Desperate and now beyond help, each step caused waves of pleasure through her soaked pussy. Juices trickled down her thighs and her tightening muscles were sore from clenching.

Dana tried to help, but as she hastened her to move, the vibrations finally got the better of Lauren and she began to orgasm while walking.

Dana held her elbow as Lauren began to giggle and moan.

She was blissful and in an awkward position. Lauren's legs buckled and she leaned her weight on Dana.

Both women started laughing and Lauren moaned again as she felt herself still coming.

As the doors closed the boss looked up and said, "I think we need to stay away from the burritos."

Chapter Seven

Alone Again, Naturally

Dana lay down on her bed. The aching need to feel loved swelled within her again. She was lonely.

The toy parties always made her feel frisky, with everyone talking about sex. She did have a little guilt because she had not tried all of the products she sold. She had heard her friend Jackie talk about how she used a bullet to make her husband's orgasm more intense. She also said it made her come so hard that she almost passed out.

Life was cruel. Even though her life with Ronald had sucked, at least he had been there.

Biting her lip she reached for the phone.

"Hello," a strong man's voice said on the other end.

"You're home, huh?"

"Uh, yes, just got home from work a little while ago."

"That sucks. Are you relaxing?" she asked.

"Yep, have an ice-cold beer in one hand and the remote control in the other. Why do you ask?"

"Well, Derrick, you said if I ever needed anything, to . . . well, just call."

Derrick's voice cracked as he replied, "Well, um, yes, I did say that, didn't I?"

"Derrick . . ."

"Yes?"

"My pussy is really wet. I have been lying here thinking about you and I just keep getting wetter and wetter. Can you talk to me?"

"This isn't fair, Dana. Yes, I will do whatever you want."

"What would you do if you were here with me right now?"

"I'd bathe you in oils. Rub your skin, relaxing you as my hands caress every inch of your sexy body."

"Mmmmmm, and then what?" Dana replied as she began caressing herself, imagining it was Derrick.

"Oh, I'd love to kiss you. Kiss your lips gently, kiss the slope of your neck, kiss your breasts, kiss your nipples." Derrick heard Dana moan as she put the speakerphone on, setting the headset down to free her hands.

"More, I want more," she groaned as she tugged at her nipples.

"Damn, Dana, this is giving me a hard-on," Derrick laughed, telling her the effect it had on him.

"Is your cock getting big, Derrick?"

"Yes, it is. You know how this gets to me."

"Mmmmm, I'd love to suck on your cock right now." The low, deep groan echoed in the phone as Dana slid her hands between her legs.

"Fuck, I just want to eat you out until you beg me to fuck you," Derrick blurted out.

"How would you eat me, Derrick? Tell me."

"I'd use one hand and cup your breast, and hold your pussy open with the other one. I love drawing pictures with my tongue on a pussy. I write words, licking the lips like the canvas and making my tongue the brush."

Dana groaned while her fingers parted her pussy. She flicked at her engorged clit and imagined it was his tongue. "Damn, Derrick, you are making me so hot. Hold your cock in your hand. Tell me what you want to do with it."

"I would push the tip between your pussy lips and make you buck your hips, begging me to force it into you." Derrick tried to remain calm, but this game she played with him made him wild. His body wasn't sure what was going on because in his mind he could see Dana spread wide on the bed, masturbating, and he really wanted to rush over and jump her.

"Ohhh, mmmmm, damn, I can imagine you fucking me, Derrick. You are pumping into me and . . . Ohhhhhhhhh, mmmm, my nipples feel like skyscrapers trying to touch the clouds. They are so stiff . . . Oh my, oh my, I feel it, mmmmm, I can . . . I am almost there, ohhhhhhhh."

"They aren't the only tower that is stiff," Derrick joked back.

"You like the feel of me making love to you?" he asked.

"I don't want you to make love to me, I want to feel you fuck me. Just pure sex. The simple pleasure of just fucking has its good points. Oh God, my clit is throbbing. Mmmmmmm. I am rubbing it now. Mmmmmmm, damn, this feels so goooood. I am coming, I am . . . ahhhhhhmmmmmmmmm. Oh, Derrick, mmmmmm."

Dana felt her blood flooding through her and she was knocking on the door of heaven. "Derrick, I need you to talk to me, please . . . Derrick? Derrick?"

"Thank God for cell phones. I'm at the front door, let me in!"

Click.

Dana didn't even close her robe as she rushed naked to the door. Derrick was knocking lightly, begging to be let into the inferno of lust burning within the walls of Dana's apartment.

She peeked through the peephole, took a deep breath, and opened the door.

She saw Derrick standing there, a protruding hard-on in his sweatpants and sweating as if he had run the whole way.

Leaping into his arms, Dana smothered his mouth with hers and wrapped her legs around his hips.

Staggering into the room, Derrick closed the door with his

foot. He felt the warm wetness from her pussy soaking through his shirt.

"I couldn't wait . . . I had to . . ."

Dana let go of Derrick, slid down his torso to her knees and tore at his sweats. She yanked them down and his stiff cock thrust forward. She wasted no time and almost swallowed it whole.

Derrick groaned as she sucked it in and out of her mouth. Like a tiger feeding in the jungle she tugged and pulled at his cock and wasn't going to be filled until she finished.

Derrick leaned down and ran his fingers through her hair. He was enjoying this pleasure but wanted more.

Grabbing her face, Derrick motioned for her to stand up.

Letting the massive, swelling head pop free from her mouth Dana gasped for air.

Holding her chin with his finger he kissed her, ever so gently. Like a stroke of an artist's brush, he painted her lips with his tongue. From desire burning at an inferno's heat to the gentleness of a candle in the wind, the mood had changed.

"Oh, Derrick, this is so romantic. You wanna?" Dana smiled wickedly.

"Let me think . . . okay!"

Dana reached down and grasped Derrick by the cock and led him down the hallway.

He waddled, sweats around his ankles. As she stopped to open the door to her bedroom Derrick stood behind her, pressing into her. Dana's legs turned to Jell-O. She felt a man wanting her, a good-looking man. Mainly, he was HER man. The heat between them was intense. She stood, one hand on the doorknob, the other holding this man's beautiful cock.

His lips were hot and he pulled her robe from her shoulders and kissed the soft skin of her neck. Derrick could feel Dana gripping his cock and she slowly began stroking the length with her hand.

Dana moaned and the wetness from her passion trickled between her thighs. She wanted Derrick. Every carnal thought she had was about him. On top of her, behind her, just inside her burning ache.

She opened the door and pulled Derrick to her.

Sitting on her bed she looked at Derrick's cock and the drip of anticipation on the tip. Her mouth watered and she wanted to taste him again. Her tongue traced the firm ridge of the head and Derrick moaned. She wanted to savor him. Her lips kissed the head of his throbbing cock. She felt the heat from his blood pulsing to his erogenous zones. Her tongue followed the lines of the veins, drawing a picture of his cock.

Derrick leaned back, almost letting himself fall. Dana was teasing him to the point of torture.

Sliding the length of him between her lips, Dana felt the pulsing of his heart. Her body ached and her pussy was an inferno of lust. She cupped her swollen labia with her hand and took Derrick in and out of her mouth.

This was her fantasy, to take Derrick to the point of ecstasy.

Her fingers became engulfed in her own juices as she slid her index finger between the swollen lips of her pussy. Her eyes fluttered and she looked up at Derrick.

His head hung, his hair fell across his sweating forehead and his mouth drooped open. He was gloriously blissful.

With a hard suck she let him free from the grip of her lips. He popped out and sprung upward. Derrick gasped for air and Dana reached over to her bedside table.

She pulled out a small pink vibrator. Looking up at Derrick's glazed eyes she slid him back between her lips.

The vibrator was for her. It was a steady and reliable friend. It was also the first toy she had ever bought. It easily slid into her pussy and she closed her eyes, continuing to savor Derrick's flavorful cock.

She churned the vibrator in and out of her pussy with the

rhythm of her sucking on Derrick. This was so hot to her that she found herself almost coming instantly, again. She couldn't handle this need. The vibe was filling her, but Derrick was what she wanted.

She slid the vibrator out of her pussy, leaving a void she would soon fill with Derrick's cock. Thinking, she remembered something a woman at a party told her.

She pulled Derrick's cock from her mouth and held the head with her palm. As she licked along the base of his seeping cock she rested her vibrator between his legs, vibrating against his balls.

Derrick's knees weakened and he groaned. "This isn't fucking fair. Damn, I'm about to explode!"

"Mmmmmm, aww, poor baby. You wanna come, baby? You want me to release you?" Dana teased Derrick's weakened state.

"No, I want to have a hard-on like this for a week."

"Oh, okay, I'll stop." Dana let him go and acted like she was going to leave.

Desperately, Derrick yelled, "What the hell are you . . ."

Before he could finish his plea, Dana grabbed his ass in her hands and pulled him into her mouth. With a fury she sucked him in and out between her lips. She drooled, trying to keep the entire length of him in her mouth. Dana could feel him growing thicker by the second. This only made her suck harder.

Derrick set his hands on the back of Dana's head. With a deep groan Derrick felt himself erupting. He threw his head back and exploded into her mouth.

Dana felt the hot seed shoot down her throat, almost gagging her. She found herself not wanting to let his cock free until she had drained him of his essence. She felt the fluids seep from the corner of her mouth as he weakened.

"Mmmmmmmm, now you can go. I'm done with you!" Dana jested.

Chapter Eight

The next morning Dana's alarm woke her. She lay in bed, warm and relaxed. Her pussy was a little sore from the previous night's activities with Derrick.

His large arm lay across her hip and the deep, steady breathing in his sleep rushed past her neck. She didn't want to get up. She could lay in bed for hours just soaking up his scent. Life was a bitch; she had to get up.

Gently she got up, trying not to wake her man. She started to giggle as she attempted to slide out of the bed, and when she got to the edge she fell out with a thud.

Derrick didn't budge. He lay there like a sleeping giant. Dana stood naked, staring at him.

He mumbled something about the San Francisco 49ers, scratched his balls and rolled over. The blankets pulled loose and he was bare-assed across her bed.

Dana's first thought was, breakfast in bed. Her second thought was, *damn, I better get to work or I'll be late.*

Standing in the shower, the warm water soothed her body. She was so mellow and relaxed. The water cascaded down her breasts and along the crevices of her skin. The warmth rinsed her pussy and she could feel the tender muscles almost begging to be massaged.

She soaped up her hands to clean her makeup off because she was in bed all night with it on. The bubbles and smooth foam cleaned her face, and she closed her eyes.

Grabbing the showerhead from the handle she rinsed the soap from her face and washed her body. The pulsating head reminded her of the night before.

With a wicked smile she lowered the showerhead to rinse her pubis.

The warm water pulsed against her skin and Dana bit her lower lip. She was easily aroused by any attention to her pussy. This was how she discovered she was able to have multiple orgasms.

She set the soap down and when her body turned, the water burst against her pussy. Dana moaned, remembering how good she felt last night. The way the water seemed to lap against her pussy reminded her of Derrick's slick tongue as he ate her out. She knew she shouldn't, but her eyes closed and she took herself back to last night.

The water was his tongue. Over and over he stroked her pussy lips. His long, thick fingers pried them apart, exposing the pink flesh within them. Dana's mind worked overtime as she felt herself being washed into her fantasy. Derrick would lick and suck on the lips of her pussy then make a yummy sound between them as if eating a gourmet meal, savoring the taste and juices from it. His tongue sought out her clit instinctively, and with ferocity would savagely suckle and nibble on the stiffened bud.

Her other hand found her clit as the showerhead nuzzled against her. Dana rested her head against the shower wall and lifted her leg up onto the small ledge made for sitting and setting shampoo on.

She was now totally exposed to her probing and the water gushing against her sensitive flesh. In her mind she saw Derrick forcing his long, hard cock in and out of her. Her fingers were his cock and the steady thrusting in and out had her panting with passion.

Her clit was throbbing and with her thumb she stroked against it, sending shock waves of pleasure through her. The constant flow of water washed against her pussy. Dana felt the cusp of her orgasm getting close and her fingers spread her labia apart, letting the jets of water splash against them.

She felt her body letting go, so she dropped the showerhead and frantically rubbed her clit. With a ripple of tension she felt herself come. She moaned and rocked back and forth, with her fingers wobbling inside her pussy. The water from the showerhead shot up like a sprinkler and trickled along Dana's flexing legs. She giggled and blew out a breath and sighed. *Mmmmmmmm, I love showers.*

Dana turned off the water. Resting her head against the wall she stood dripping and almost fell asleep in her comfort and satisfaction.

"Oh shit, I'm gonna be late," she said as she shook herself back to the real world. In record time she got dressed, put her makeup on, did her hair and was ready to bolt out the door.

Looking at the bed as she walked by she saw her Adonis of a man sprawled across her bed. Dana longed to touch his legs, his muscular back, the large arms and firm ass. As if she were standing in a block of concrete, she couldn't move. *I do have a few sick days I could take,* she thought.

No, she had a meeting with the boss and couldn't skip out.

Dana walked over to the side of the bed and leaned over Derrick. She kissed his cheek and rubbed his back, trying to wake him. "Hey, babe, you better get up. It's six forty-five. You said you needed to get to work by eight.

"Five more minutes, just five more minutes," Derrick moaned out like a kid telling his mom.

Dana grabbed his ass and squeezed it. "You better get up and let yourself out. I don't want you blaming me for you being late." Then she kissed his cheek again.

"Okay, I'll get up . . . just five more minutes . . . zzzzz."

Dana walked out, shaking her head, knowing she'd have to call in ten minutes to get Derrick awake.

The meeting wasn't what she had planned. It wasn't her department; it was just her and William, the company CEO. Her relaxed and mellow mood from the night before was now being transformed into an uncomfortable situation and a lecture.

"Now, Dana, you've been with us for, what, six years? You have come a long way and you have done some impeccable work." He stared out his window and continued talking.

"It has come to my attention that you have a little side job in sales."

That bitch, *Sara!*

One day when they were having lunch together, Dana had talked to Sara about her toy sales. Sara seemed so interested and Dana thought she was thinking about buying something. Now she knew she had been milked for information to tattle to the boss. She must have told him. *She always wanted my job,* Dana thought. Angry that her little secret had come out and that her boss was lecturing her on morals, Dana was now thoroughly pissed off.

"Now what you do outside of work isn't any of my business." William turned and faced her, still not meeting her eyes. "But we do have a rather upscale image here, and with you being the senior account executive, you are in charge of some of our bigger accounts."

"But—" Dana tried to defend herself.

William cut her short. "Let me finish. You have the Samuel Church and the City Children's Theatre accounts and I am not sure they would be really happy knowing that their top senior account executive sells . . . well, sex toys on the side. Now, they won't change who they are dealing with. They have made that clear. You have done way too much work on their accounts and they are very happy with your professionalism."

"You mean you called them and asked if they would change reps?" Dana barked back.

"Well, we have their and our images to protect here, Dana."

"What I do with my own time is no business of yours or the company's, William. If you knew half of the things people did on the outside . . ."

William held up his hand. "Don't try to be so defensive. Your job is not to shift focus to others. I am not threatening you or your job. I was just saying that you might want to think about maybe changing your little hobby." William sat back in his black leather chair and loosened his jacket.

"William, it isn't a full-time thing and won't take me away from my job here. It is something I do for me. I don't want to give it up."

"Well, you have to do what you must do. I just think you might want to rethink it a little. We can't have some of our biggest clients worrying about their image. All the politics and other innuendos and comments could damage that." William tried to be all businesslike and not cross the line and threaten her livelihood by using his position to have her change her mind.

Chapter Nine

Joyce's Party

Sitting in the living room, the ladies started talking. Since it was a Pleasure Party, they obviously talked about sex.

"Now if you rub this oil in a circular motion just below his stomach and above where his hair is, you'll find his cock will get very aroused."

"Dana, how did you get into this? "

"To be honest, after I broke up with my boyfriend I was asked to go to some parties and, well, found out a lot about myself." Dana put the oil on the table and sat back in the wicker chair. She reached into her bag and pulled out another toy.

Holding up a fat, black dildo she continued. "Now if men really looked like this I don't think we'd have a need for them other than sex." She looked back at the dildo and kissed the tip. "I like this one myself. I call it *Tonka Tyrone.*"

"Hey, not all of us have a man that will let us open up. Some of us women are afraid to try something like bringing a toy to bed."

Joyce burst into laughter. "Can you imagine the look on Barry's face if I brought that dildo to bed? *Oh my God!!*"

"Well, there are a million things you can try." She reached back into her bag and laid down a twelve-inch-long string of jelly-filled beads.

"What the hell are those?" Tami asked. "They look like pearls on a stick."

"These are anal beads. These are made to enhance the male or female orgasm. You lubricate them, and as the muscles of the anus tighten, you slowly pull them out during the orgasmic spasms."

Looking confused and a little curious, the group looked back at Dana.

Tami perked up and said, "In English, okay?"

"When he comes, you slowly pull these out of his ass. It's supposed to be extremely intense."

"Dear Lord, I hope you wash them afterward. They would smell like shit!" Tami made a disgusted, wrinkled-nose face.

The group started giggling at the thought.

"Well, I think if you talk to your partner they might surprise you. I know some men get off on everything from this to watching a woman masturbate. Call them a research partner."

"You have a research partner, Dana?" Tami asked, winking and wiggling her eyebrows.

Blushing again, Dana thought of Derrick. He was a great research partner and a damn fine fuck-buddy. He also was a great friend. For the first time she thought of him more as a boyfriend and lover than just a friend.

The ladies sat talking about sizes, how long their partners lasted and mainly about themselves. Dana smiled and felt a warm glow from what she was doing.

This was one main reason Dana decided to have these Pleasure Parties. She loved how her little parties could make women open up, talk and not worry so much about their sexuality. Nobody judged them. They were just . . . the girls. She didn't want them to be like she *used* to be.

Dana showed up at Derrick's apartment for dinner. He was outside on the small patio. She saw his head bobbing over the fence. He was cooking something that smelled absolutely wonderful.

"Mmmmmmm, what smells so good?" Dana asked, peeking over the fence.

"You never mind. Come on in, babe, there's some cheese and crackers on the kitchen table. The door's open."

Derrick's apartment was typically male. Unmatched couch and loveseat with old end tables and a horribly scratched coffee table in the living room that looked like it had been used a lot . . . as a footstool. Dana knew which way to go because there was a well-worn path in the shag carpet. There were two beautiful leather La-Z-Boy chairs set side by side in the center of the wall. They looked immaculate.

A painting of a mermaid was hung proudly on the wall behind the chairs. It had her half submerged, nude, lying on rocks with a ship in the distance and a blazing sun tanning her. Long, flowing blonde hair floated in the water. Even though it was a standard male fantasy, it was rather sexy.

"Hey, Derrick, you want a beer?" If there was one thing she knew for sure, it was that the fridge would have beer in it.

"Sure, thanks. The kabobs are almost done." Derrick began grunting and whistling as he cooked. Just like a caveman. All men grunted and basked in the glory of a fresh kill. Even though his fresh kill was on a skewer and the meat was bought at the supermarket.

As she expected, the refrigerator was basically bare except for two twelve-packs of beer, sectioned off. It seemed Derrick and his roommate took sides on everything. There was also some old pizza, various Tupperware dishes full of who-knows-what and a strange-looking vegetable in the back. Dana could swear she saw it move.

She grabbed a beer for Derrick and walked toward the patio door. She stood staring out the back window and saw Derrick cooking over the barbecue . . . shirtless. At first she wasn't sure what she had suddenly become hungry for—the smell of the cooking meat, or the tanned meat in front of her. Tough decision indeed. He wore typical, baggy jean shorts and red tennis shoes.

She felt a little overdressed in a white sleeveless shirt and a black skirt. She kicked her black pumps off instantly and stepped outside to join Derrick. She stood behind him, gazing at the muscles of his back glistening with perspiration from the warm weather and the heat from the barbecue.

With an evil grin she reached up and pressed the icy beer against his back.

"*Ahhhhhhhhhhhh,* damn, that's cold."

Derrick spun around and looked at Dana. "Well, you look great. I feel like a slob. The kabobs are done, I just have to heat up some rice and take a quick shower. Then *dinnertime.*" Derrick smiled wide and took the last kabob off the barbecue.

"Why don't you let me cook the rice and make a salad? Go get cleaned up."

Derrick leaned over to kiss Dana.

She kissed him softly then touched his shoulders. Pushing him away, she giggled. "Go take a shower. You're all sticky. Shoo."

Derrick laughed and patted her on the butt as he walked by her. "Damn, I love your ass."

Dana finished cooking the rice and made the salad, adding in a few of her own touches with some bacon bits and a sprinkle of pepper. She decided to go tell Derrick she was done. She also hoped to get a peek of him naked. Her devilish side began to stir again.

Standing in the hallway, Dana could hear the water spraying against Derrick. It was bad enough that her fantasy about Will and Kathy crept back into her mind. Now she pushed the door open slightly and could see Derrick's silhouette through the translucent glass of the shower.

Now this was temptation and torture. She could see him leaning his head back, rinsing his hair, the faint outline of her favorite part of him protruding outward. Her mouth watered and her pussy woke up.

Gulping, she stuttered, "Ummm, Derrick, uhh, the rice and salad are done. I'll wait in the kitchen."

"Don't leave. I'm done. You can talk to me while I dry off and get ready."

Another tough decision. "Uhhh, okay."

Dana put the seat down on his toilet and sat listening to him. She looked around and saw the small trash can overflowing with debris. Smiling, she remembered the way her mom used to complain about her dad and what a messy guy he was.

"So how was your day, dear?" he asked.

"Oh, you know, same old thing. Work is a drag but at least it's Friday so I don't have to worry about it this weekend."

Derrick reached over to grab a towel and it fell to the floor. "Crap," he muttered.

Dana reached over to pick it up and when she looked up, Derrick's cock was about a foot away from her face and the sudden urge to open her mouth took over. "Uhhhhhh, I think I better go wait out there. I am suddenly hungry for hot dogs."

Dana laughed as she hung Derrick's towel over his cock and started toward the door.

"Hey, I bought some toys for us tonight."

Stunned, Dana stopped and turned around. "What?"

While drying his hair Derrick continued, "Well, sweetheart, you always have something incredible that turns me on. I figure I'd show you something you can talk about at your parties." With a huge grin he turned away from Dana and shook his butt at her.

As Dana headed back out the door, she heard a noise down the hall. She closed the door quickly and turned to Derrick. "Hey, is someone here? I can hear the TV."

Derrick tossed his towel off and grabbed the shorts he had on earlier.

"It's probably Tom, my roommate. I told him I had a date tonight. This guy is a living hemorrhoid. He doesn't care about anyone but himself."

Listening, he heard the TV. He opened the door and stepped into the hallway. Dana was close behind and as they went into the living room, they saw Tom, munching away on two steak kabobs with the remote in the other hand.

"What the fuck are you doing, Tom? I told you I had a date tonight! Hey, asshole, that's our dinner!"

"The game is on, dude, I thought . . ." Tom was obviously a little drunk and Derrick's clenched fists made him slightly uneasy.

"I cooked those for Dana and me tonight. Not for you."

Tom held the stick back toward Derrick. "Here, I just ate part of them. Christ, man, it's just a damn kabob. It was damn good, though. You need to relax a little. Get you some . . . ummm . . ."

"Every time I try to do something you have to fuck it up. I stopped bringing Candie over because you kept hitting on her when she was waiting for me while I was at work. Then you eat everything I buy and drink all my fricking beer with your asshole buddies." Derrick was on his last nerve. His night was messed up because of his roommate's stupidity and total disregard for him.

Tom shook his head and started yelling back. "Hey, this is my place, too. I can do what I want here. You asked to move in after Dave left, remember? You should be thanking me for letting you move in."

"Dammit, I am so tired of your shit. I pay over fifty percent of the rent. Your girlfriend comes over and leaves her shit everywhere and doesn't like me because I kicked her out of my bed that one night when she was drunk. I leave when she comes over because I can't stand her fucking stupid cackle when she laughs. I am just so tired of all . . ." The veins in Derrick's neck began to bulge and pulse with his heart.

"Whatever, Derrick. Jezus, you bitch like a woman."

Tom's snide remark just fueled Derrick. He was extremely pissed off and Dana was afraid he might kill his roommate.

"Sweetheart, let's just go to my place. I don't want this to ruin our date." Dana tried to calm Derrick and get away from the situation.

"Yeah, listen to your lady friend. Go to her place. I want to watch the game in peace and quiet. Hey, aren't you Ronald's old girlfriend? I knew I had seen you before. Hmmmmm, yeah, he told us guys about you." With a smirk across his face, Tom nodded and acted all smug. If he was a friend of Ronald's there was no telling what he might say. "He told me he saw you at a bar a while back with some gorilla, and lap dancing with two girls."

"Mutherfucker, you better watch your step. She's my girl now, so you better be cool. I don't talk shit about the women you bring over." Derrick glared angrily at his friend. The burn from his eyes made Tom a little more on edge. The total lack of respect and his attitude wore down the last fiber of tolerance Derrick had.

Derrick stepped into his room and grabbed a polo shirt and a paper bag he had beside the door.

"You know, Derrick, you don't need to be a dick about this. I mean, you can always take your girlfriend somewhere to fuck. Jeez."

"Oh fuck, you asshole." Dana started toward Tom and a look of terror crossed his face. "I am nobody's whore!"

Derrick grabbed her shoulder and held her back.

"That's it, Tom. You find yourself another roommate. As soon as I find a place I am out of here. Then you can find yourself another person to fuck over. Maybe one of those skanks you find so appealing. No self-respecting woman would tolerate your shit. That's why Vickie left you, fucking asshole. Oh, and the two La-Z-Boys come with me because I paid for them." Derrick wrapped his strong arm around Dana and walked toward the door.

"Hey dude, I'm sorry. You don't need to—" Tom was cut short by Derrick holding his hand out like *The Nanny*'s "Talk to the Hand" sign. He then turned it over and flipped him the bird.

Chapter Ten

Eating at the "Y"

Derrick unlocked his Saturn door for Dana, and as he walked around the front of the car he made a call on his cell phone.

Hopping into the car he said, "Sorry about all that, Dana. That's the way it has been for a while. I'm tired of it. But, I won't let it ruin my plans for tonight. I have to stop by a place downtown. The drive will help me relax."

As they drove, the evening sun had set and a beautiful romantic skyscape glowed bright orange just over the mountains. "What a beautiful night, huh?" Dana asked.

"Yes, you look beautiful tonight. I mean, the sky is beautiful," Derrick joked as he put his hand just above Dana's knee. "You don't mind me referring to you as my girl, do you? Maybe I should have asked first."

"I don't mind at all. In fact, I like it." Dana felt a warm glow over her body. It was either from the fact she felt part of someone's life again or because Derrick's hand had crept up her thigh a little and she was becoming aroused. She placed her hand on his and pulled it toward her lap. Derrick knew what she wanted and rested his warm hand on her inner thigh. The heat from her body radiated from her pussy.

"Mmmmmmm, at least I know what I will eat for dessert."

Derrick winked at Dana as she looked at him and squeezed her legs together on his hand.

"Here we are. I called Dave to make sure it would be ready when we got here. Wait here just a second, dear." He stopped by a very nice Szechwan restaurant and picked up some food. She saw the man by the door and watched as Derrick handed him a fifty-dollar bill and waved goodbye.

He jumped back in the car and she looked into the boxes. There were kabobs, chow mien, some rice, a few egg rolls and a side of steamed vegetables. "Mmmmmm, this smells great!" Dana said while the scent of the food filled the car.

"Dave makes the best stuff. I have known him since college. A little spicy but it tastes fantastic."

"Kinda like you," Dana snapped back.

Dana liked this feeling of being on a date. To go out, even just for dinner. The comfort with each other was there. The familiarity and history was there. The sexual attraction was *definitely* there.

The scent of Chinese food filled the car and Dana leaned into the plush seats. The warmth of the food in the bag began to radiate through her lap. She was now warmed throughout her body, but hungry. Smelling the food didn't help.

Derrick was concentrating on the traffic so Dana took this moment to reach into the bag and grab an egg roll. Dana blew on the steaming end and slid the hot roll between her lips. It was hot and tasted scrumptious.

Derrick looked over to say something and saw Dana close her eyes, her lips encasing the smooth length of the egg roll.

She bit into it and a stream of juice trickled from the corner of her mouth. "Mmmmmmm, this tastes great. It explodes in your mouth and the hot juices just flow down your throat."

A sudden urge swept through Derrick as all the blood from his brain flowed to his cock.

Dana looked at Derrick, then looked at his pants. "Ummm,

sorry. Did you know you missed our turnoff?" She smiled and leaned over to kiss his now blushing cheek. Patting his lap, Dana whispered into his ear, "Later. Relax."

They pulled into her complex and Derrick ran around and grabbed the bags of food. He held them at waist height to hide his now bulging pants.

Dana walked in front of him and opened the door. When they stepped inside, Derrick leaned down and gave Dana a kiss, then smacked her ass.

Curiosity began to get the better of Dana—*what did he have in that silly paper grocery bag*? That and the urge to pounce on Derrick.

Getting a few nice plates from her cabinets, she set them on the table and grabbed some silverware. The food aroma filled the room and Dana had everything set up for a nice dinner. "Let's eat. I'm starving," she said.

"So how's the food? You like it?" Derrick asked as they started eating, watching her glancing toward the paper bag. "Making you think, isn't it?" He knew he had piqued her curiosity.

Derrick got up, walked over to Dana's stereo and turned it on. He fumbled through the radio stations and stopped when he heard a slow groove from Toni Braxton echoing through the speakers.

Walking back to the table, Derrick picked up the bag and held his hand out to Dana.

Drawn into his advances Dana placed her small hand in his.

He leaned forward and kissed the tender skin of her hand. A slight shiver of excitement shot through her. Lifting her up, Derrick leaned further into her and their lips touched. The smooth wetness of their lips met and the sweet wetness of desire crept between her thighs.

Dear God, this man turns me on, she thought.

As his mouth devoured hers, Dana felt her legs weaken. Derrick continued kissing her cheek then the nape of her neck.

Dana's moan acknowledged to Derrick that he was doing the right things.

Running her fingers through his hair, Dana closed her eyes . . . swept into the music . . . swept into the mood . . . swept over by her man. She had never felt so in tune with anyone before. It wasn't just the sex—even though he made her cream inside with his simple touch; she was comfortable. In a way, he freed her. He awoke desires and feelings buried away that until recently she didn't know she had. Her own sexual exploration brought them to her attention. Derrick brought them to a full, blossoming experience.

They stood together, merged in a warm glow. The music began to make them move in tandem. They were dancing in an enclosed world where it was just them, lost in that moment of time.

Derrick felt warm and aroused by Dana's sweet fragrance. Her hair smelled of perfume, her skin that of a rose. She was intoxicating him. There was a difference to their slow dance of seduction. There were feelings being exposed; they were falling in love.

Her eyes closed, her body opened and Dana became lost in the mood. Her hands caressed Derrick's back. The wide spread of his shoulders, the indention of his lower back and the rounded curve of his ass; Dana wanted to feel all of him at once. Her body ached for him.

Derrick held her so tight against him that her breath brushed across his chest. He wanted her to melt into him so he could be closer.

Dana reached between them and ran her fingers up his stomach and to his chest. His body was hot to her touch. She nuzzled into his chest and lifted his shirt up. Her mouth became drawn to his tight nipples and her own desperate need for him to suckle at her breasts made her kiss his. Her wet tongue flicked across the nipple, causing Derrick to moan as he watched her. She switched to the other side and licked across his sensitive skin. She ran her fingers through the small, thin patch of hair on his chest. This was so erotic to her; she felt the tingle of her juices streaming between her thighs.

Derrick held her hips in his hands and ground against her. He was so aroused that Dana could feel his cock harden through his jean shorts.

Her mouth kept circling his nipples and she lowered her hand. She grasped the fullness of his cock and she moaned, cursing the way her pussy melted at the thought of this wondrous flesh buried within her walls.

Dana looked up into Derrick's deep blue eyes and kissed him again. Her grasp tightened around his cock. Her mouth salivated for his taste. His tongue tangled with hers but that wasn't enough. She wanted more.

As she tried to step back Derrick grabbed firmly on to her ass, pulling her closer. "No, not yet."

His words cut into her desire as he gripped her butt, massaging the flesh and making her wet pussy lips rub together. Derrick kissed her again, slipping his tongue between her lips. His hands tugged and pulled at her underwear. The tightening and loosening against her pussy was driving Dana crazy.

She wiggled her panties down her legs and stepped out of them. Not wanting to be the only one free from containment, Dana pulled Derrick's jean shorts from his waist. She had to pull the front out and over his thickened cock. Derrick reached into the back pocket of his shorts and pulled out a condom. The waistband around his ass was the only thing holding his jean shorts up. Pulling his hand free from the pocket, the shorts fell in a clump on the floor.

For a second they stood, almost naked, pondering the moment.

Their desire filled the air, and Dana leapt into Derrick's arms. She wrapped her legs around him and his stiff cock rested, straining, along the wet slit of her opening. Her labia were like a blanket to his throbbing cock. She wanted him to take her *now*.

Derrick wobbled, trying to regain his balance. He glanced over to the kitchen and saw the dinner table. Each step he took made his cock press and rub against Dana's spread lips and clit. Her body was a whirl of feelings. Every inch of his shaft dragged against her clit and the friction was pushing her to the brink.

Derrick sat her on the table. Dana looked down their bodies and saw the swollen head of his cock, inches away from its home. It belonged inside her.

Pushing the head down, Derrick teased at her opening. The juices covered the head as it slid between her labia. The warm wetness beckoned him deeper. But he toyed with her. "Mmmm, that feels nice. You are so hot . . . mmmmm . . . and wet."

"Oh please, I can't stand this, Derrick. I want you so bad."

Derrick licked his fingertip and rested it along the top of her pussy.

Dana leaned back on her hands and urged Derrick to move forward and into her.

Derrick tore the package open and Dana watched as he rolled the condom down the length of his shaft.

"Purple, huh?" Dana smiled.

Derrick tapped the head of his cock against her pussy. He was teasing himself as much as he teased her. Piercing the swollen opening, Derrick sank the head into her wanton pussy.

"Ohhhh yes, mmmm. More," Dana begged.

A wicked smile crossed Derrick's face as he began to move his finger in a circular motion around her clit.

"Mmmmm, oh, don't do th—ohh, don't stop." Dana became increasingly aroused and her passion took over.

As Derrick inched into her, Dana felt herself falling back on the table. Her mind fell into the incredible feelings of her body as

Derrick massaged her clit with his finger and pushed his thickened cock deeper and deeper. Dana saw flashes of blinding light behind her closed eyelids as her nerve endings became supersensitized.

Derrick began massaging her breast through her blouse with his other hand. Her nipples were so hard they poked through the fabric and Derrick's thumb rolled them side to side.

Derrick grabbed the table's edge and forcefully rammed himself home. The abrupt jarring of Dana's body pushed her closer to the brink of orgasm. Derrick's loud groan filled her head as he began pounding inside her.

If they had just finished eating dinner on this table then this was the most scrumptious dessert she had ever had here.

Overwhelmed and close to burning up inside, Dana sat up and grabbed Derrick's shoulders. He was sweating and pounding in and out of her. Dana looked between them and could see her flesh holding on to his cock for dear life as he slid within her heat.

"I want on top," she cried. Derrick tried to pick her up and move her but he lost his balance and sat in the chair with his cock inside her.

The force from his falling back and her own weight pushed Derrick to the entrance of her womb and Dana looked up and came. Her pussy convulsed and she didn't move. All she could do was smile and spasm with his thick cock filling her to the fullest.

"Oh shit, I can feel you coming. Oh shit, this is incredible." Derrick was feeling dizzy and Dana wasted no time.

She lifted and lowered herself onto Derrick's swollen cock like a piston from a motor. Her thighs tightened and loosened as she milked him of his seed.

Derrick leaned back and the wooden chair creaked. Pulling his hands over his eyes he groaned loudly and erupted like a volcano inside her. "Ahhhhhhhhhh . . . Oh man . . ."

Dana licked her dry lips caused from panting. Slowly lowering back down, she wrapped her arms around his neck.

Their heartbeats, in unison, slowed to normal as they sat wrapped around each other. "I don't want to move," Dana mumbled.

"Me neither," said Derrick. "But I think we are stuck anyway because I feel all sticky down there. I think the condom couldn't handle the pressure."

Laughing, Dana leaned back and kissed Derrick again. "I'll go get a towel. You stay there, stud."

"Nawww, it's okay, I need to go to the little boys' room. I'll be back in a few." Derrick waddled, sweats around his ankles, to the paper bag and picked it up. He walked like a duck down the hall.

Dana saw his ass tightening as he shuffled along.

Dana straightened herself up and put the dishes in the sink. She stood, sipping her wine for a second, and caught her breath. She wondered what was taking Derrick so long in the bathroom and walked down the hall quietly.

At the door she listened. The only sounds were the paper bag rustling and Derrick humming the *Mr. Rogers Neighborhood* theme song.

Gently knocking on the door, Dana asked, "Are you okay in there? Did you fall in or what?"

Derrick laughed. "No, I'm almost ready. I'll meet you in the bedroom in a couple of minutes."

Mmmmmm, the bedroom, Dana thought.

She went in and stood before her full-length wall mirror. Unfastening her buttons, Dana stared at the reaction simple thoughts had on her body. Derrick's rough skin against hers, his mouth and tongue entwined with hers. Everything about him affected her.

Unzipping the side of her skirt, it fell to the floor. She opened the top drawer of her dresser and pulled out a sexy, hunter-green nightie. Setting it on top of the dresser, Dana reached back and unhooked her bra. The loosening felt nice and she could breathe easier from the freedom. Her breasts were firm and full. She let her bra fall past her shoulders and then she stood naked in front of her mirror.

She licked her lips, making them glisten from the dim light of the room. Her reflection stared back at her. Seeing herself made her curious as to what Derrick saw. She was of average height, average weight, a little short but not too tiny. Her breasts were a perfect C-cup and other than her rounded ass, she thought she looked pretty good.

Slipping the silky nightgown over her body felt like a breath of fresh air washing over her skin. It barely touched her, except for the protrusion of her erect nipples and the soft slope of her tummy.

Behind her she saw something move and turned to see Derrick in the doorway.

"*Ahhhhhh,* what the hell are you wearing?" Dana held her hand to her chest, scared out of her wits.

"What? You don't like it?" Derrick stood in her bedroom doorway with a purple rubber beanie, a stethoscope and a work belt with various toys in it instead of tools. The elephant underwear with his cock inside the trunk was a nice touch.

"Okay, who are you supposed to be?" Dana hesitantly asked.

"Well, I am your favorite toy, of course! Wanna play?" Derrick winked and smiled wide.

Dana rolled her eyes, bursting into laughter. "Oh God, you are so weird."

"Hey, I am a special toy. I come with attachments!" Derrick looked into his work belt. "See? Vibrators, massage oils, a banana, a camera, whipped cream, a rubber chicken, a microphone, those stress relievers, a flashlight, flavored condoms and a Mr. Potato Head."

"A *what*???" Dana held her sides. She was laughing so much it hurt.

"Mr. Potato Head." Derrick laughed while he talked.

Derrick frowned as he looked at Dana, all red-faced and laughing. "I think there is something wrong with you, dear. You look like you need a physical. You had better lie down."

"Oh, Doctor Derrick. I feel faint. You think I have a temperature?" Dana began to play along with Derrick.

"Mmmmm, well, good thing I have a thermometer. A perfect fit, too."

"I hope it isn't a rectal one."

"Nooo, this one is a total oral one. Now lay down and be a good patient." Derrick walked over to the bed and breathed onto his stethoscope, cleaning it like a doctor would.

Dana crawled over the bed, staring into Derrick's dark eyes.

Her look caused a stir in Derrick. His elephant trunk seemed to grow as Dana sprawled onto her back. Her head rested beside him and the trunk of the elephant pajamas suddenly became fuller.

"Ummm, you need to pull your clothing off, dear." Derrick was a little distracted. His words became jumbled.

Dana reached down and slowly revealed her naked skin under the sheer fabric. The glistening flesh of her pussy made Derrick salivate. Her breasts were flattened and her nipples erect. This was a vision of loveliness. She was so perfect, so stunning, and she was his.

"Ummm, okay, first the finger test." Derrick stood above her head and kneeled down. He slid his hands down her shoulders to her breasts. He cupped them both in his palms and squeezed gently.

"Mmmmm, these feel fine. How are the nipples?" Derrick let his fingers roll over the erect tips and looked upon her face below his. He kissed her closed eyes and then let his tongue ride along the bridge of her nose.

"Your stubble tickles my face," Dana whispered as she giggled.

Derrick began to kiss her lips upside down. Their tongues became meshed together in a slow, savoring dance of seduction. Dana moaned as Derrick's fingers tugged at her nipples. Her legs squeezed together as her arousal grew stronger. She was creaming inside.

Derrick followed the trail of his fingers as he stood back up. His eyes gazed upon her supple breasts and soft, peach-colored skin. His appreciation for women was taking control. Dana was a woman he could become lost in. She possessed him in body and mind.

Leaning down to the bed, he lay next to her. His mouth savored the succulence of her supple breasts.

Dana moaned as he gently nibbled on her nipples and his hands found their home between her legs. Turning her head to the side, she saw Derrick. Actually, she saw an elephant with a thickened trunk.

"Looks like we need a little deeper examination here." Derrick slid lower and pulled the small pink vibrator from his belt. It had a thin cord attached to a microphone on it.

"Now that's something I have never seen before. What does it do, sing a song as it goes in?"

"Actually it hums. You know what I mean." Derrick wiggled his eyebrows as he rubbed the tip along the outer lips of Dana's pussy.

"Mmmmm. Derrick, why are you doing this? This is so cra . . . mmmm . . . zy."

"Because I feel like it. Because I want to share things with you. And because I am a little freaky in bed when I get playful." He turned the vibrator on and the slow droning hum vibrated against Dana's pussy. She closed her eyes and stroked Derrick's shoulder as he slid the toy back and forth along the slippery entrance to her heaven. Dana smiled, feeling so kidlike as he played with her. The tip rested on her clit and she jerked with excitement.

"Aha, I found it. It must have been hiding from me." Derrick's devilish laugh made Dana all warm and feisty.

"Ohhhhhh, yeah. That's the spot. Ohhhhhhh, yes, just like that." Dana's body warmed to the attention. Her clit was now engorged with blood and firm to Derrick's touch.

Dana arched her back as Derrick slid the vibrator into her dripping pussy. The hum silenced as it vibrated within her, then became more pronounced as it was withdrawn.

"Now for my next number, I shall sing to you." Derrick held the microphone he had attached to the vibrator and began to sing.

"Pussycat, pussycat, I love you, yeeessss I doooo . . ." Derrick's voice echoed inside Dana like he was in her body.

"Oh shit, what did you do?" Dana arched her back up against the reverberations of his voice inside her pussy.

"I rewired a vibrator I bought and added a small speaker. This way I can talk to you as I play with you. Didn't I tell you I was your favorite toy?" Derrick smiled proudly as he did his best Darth Vader impression. "Come with me. Cross over to the dark side."

The vibrations made Dana's legs jiggle and she couldn't stop laughing.

"You like that, huh? I had a lot of fun the last week or so goofing off with these toys. The guy at the Radio Shack thought I was nuts asking for this stuff."

Derrick got up and held the microphone in his hand. "MMMMmmmm, yummy. I am sorry to say, on to the next show." Derrick leaned down, kissing Dana's tummy and slid the vibrator out of her. He looked down at her and licked the juices off it.

Dana flinched and bit her bottom lip. "You're gonna get it, you big goofball!"

"I sure hope so!" Derrick winked back at Dana and walked around the bed. His elephant trunk dangled, to Dana's delight, and Derrick set the Mr. Potato Head on the nightstand and grabbed a small black box. He made sure it was aimed at the bed. The small box was a handheld TV monitor. He held it in his hand and plopped down next to Dana.

"Check this out. I made Mr. Potato Head into a little digital camera." Derrick turned the screen so Dana could watch the view of their bodies from Mr. Potato Head's point of view.

Dana lay next to him, stroked his chest and set her leg over his. Her hand caressed the skin of his body and found its way to his elephant trunk. "You know it's a shame to waste all that hard work for nothing. You watch your little TV, dear. I have something to show you."

Dana crawled across Derrick and positioned the Mr. Potato Head so it faced Derrick's lower torso. Her breasts swung just above Derrick's chest and when she moved back to her position at his side, the tender, soft skin of her excited breasts brushed against the hot flesh of his chest.

"Now, you watch your little TV. There's a new show coming on called *The Cock Hunter*."

Derrick looked at his eight-inch, handheld monitor and saw Dana pulling her hair back. She lowered her face between his legs.

Her hair rolled to the side of her head and the loose strands tickled his inner thighs. Kissing the gray cotton fabric of Derrick's new underwear, Dana smiled and couldn't help but think of *Dumbo*. Her tongue followed the lines of the fabric and she felt him grow within the underwear.

Derrick watched as she teased him. The pictures weren't the best quality but it sure beat the hell out of any 3-D movie he had seen. This one came with feelings. Staring at the screen, Derrick's eyes widened as he saw Dana pull his trunk out of his shorts. Her lips were like a blanket to his hardened flesh. He moaned and his eyes fluttered when he watched Dana slide his length into her mouth and down her throat.

Dana was relishing Derrick's cock like a last meal. Her craving for a hot dog was now being fulfilled with a different kind of meat. She loved it. Again, she slid him deep into her mouth until she almost gagged. The swollen head popped free from her lips and she took it back into her throat just to hear Derrick moan with pleasure.

Sucking hard, Dana let Derrick loose from her drooling lips.

"You still watching the show?" she asked, knowing the answer.

"It's hard to concentrate, but yes."

"Mmmm, you're right, it is hard," Dana flirtingly answered.

"Hmmm, let me see here." Dana crawled back up Derrick's body, lay on top of him and reached over to the nightstand. She grabbed the Mr. Potato Head and set it on Derrick's abdomen. She grasped Derrick's left hand and had him hold on to the toy to make sure it didn't fall over. "Can you see okay?" Dana asked.

"Oh yeah, I can see you perfectly. Look how hard you have made me." Derrick added a sarcastic tone to his voice.

Dana sat up and straddled Derrick's legs. The camera focused on the wet flesh over her pussy that hovered over Derrick's extremely hard cock. "Mmmmm, I hope you're watching this."

Dana held Derrick's cock in her hand and kept herself propped up with the other. She let the swollen head of his cock slide between the wet lips of her pussy. Her passionate juices soaked the tip of his cock. Her pussy ached to feel him fill her again. The void he filled before was awaiting his return. Dana lowered herself onto Derrick with a slow, teasing motion.

Derrick groaned, feeling her juices against the base of his cock. Dana sat straight up and rested her weight on his body. Like a sponge, the creamy insides from her arousal wetted his groin. She sat motionless, enjoying the sensations of him within her. *A perfect fit,* she thought.

In a slow grooving rhythm, Dana began to roll her hips back and forth, back and forth, letting the stiffness of his cock spread her tight walls apart. Her eyes were closed and her mind was a whirlwind of lust. Pressing her palm against his chest, Dana let her other hand find a place between her legs.

"My God, this is fucking incredible. I see your pussy holding my cock as you pull up." Derrick groaned. "Damn, you are so beautiful."

"Oh, Derrick." Dana began to stroke her finger against the hood of her clit, overcome with her desperate need to let go.

Her fingers became wet and slippery from touching her pussy. Reaching up, she wiped her juices across Derrick's lips.

"Mmmmm, you taste good."

"Derrick, I want you to let me do something I haven't done before, okay?" Dana rolled her hips, becoming intensely wet and incredibly turned on.

"Anything, babe, you know that."

Dana lay flat against his body. Letting her breasts rest on his upper tummy, she released him from her pussy. Rolling off him, Dana got on all fours and lowered her breasts to the bed. "I want it this way," she said, looking at Derrick.

"Oh, okay, no problem."

Setting the Mr. Potato Head on the nightstand, Derrick moved behind her, rested a hand on each hip and knelt to let his slippery cock enter her swollen pussy again. With a firm steady thrust he sank fully inside her again.

Dana moaned with pleasure and put her hand between her legs to feel her clit again. She violently rubbed it, causing her body to quiver.

Derrick leaned back and let the tip of his cock leave her pussy. Leaning forward he was about to enter Dana again when she held the tip in her fingers and pushed it higher up, to her anus.

Not sure what to do, Derrick lowered himself again. Dana again pushed the tip higher.

"Are you sure?" Derrick asked.

"Yes, I want it."

The slippery tip of his penis pressed between the round cheeks of her ass and Derrick gently leaned against Dana's sweet body.

She could feel the pressure build as her fear and her need fought for control of her body. A sudden pain shot through her legs as Derrick's cock pierced the virgin opening of her anus. Dana clenched her eyes tightly. She wanted this, and she leaned back against Derrick. The walls were being opened wider from the firmness of his cock entering her. Dana felt her pussy flowing with juices and the now tense muscles relaxed as Derrick slid fully into her ass.

Pushing her body up, she reached back and tried to grab Derrick's torso to have him continue.

With a slow methodic tempo, Derrick began to slide in and out. The tightness ached and burned but something in her made her become almost animalistic and dark. She was experimenting with her own boundaries and the rush of adrenaline empowered her. Dana became lustful and passionate.

"Come on, baby, fuck me. Come on. I want to feel you harder, harder."

Her words spurred Derrick's own primal cravings and he started smacking Dana's ass as he pushed himself back and forth.

Not able to hold herself up, Dana fell to the bed and reached her hand to her pussy again. She felt the juices flow down her thighs and her finger poked in and out of her swollen pussy as Derrick fucked her ass.

"Oh God, damn, you are so tight I can't take this much more," Derrick yelled with desperation. Dana wanted to finish this journey with a climax. Her mind saw flashes of light from the pain and the hard pounding of their bodies. Clenching her inner wall muscles tightly around his cock, Dana sensed herself on the cusp of another orgasm and wanted Derrick to come with her.

"I'm almost there, baby. Come inside me. Let me feel you,

Derrick. Come inside me. I'm almost . . . oh my God . . . oooooo." Dana was on the edge, and with a hard thrust, Derrick erupted within her. A bright flash of pain shot through Dana and she came. Her fingers were doused with her juices as she flowed inside.

Derrick groaned loudly and spewed his seed within her. His cock throbbed and spasmed. When he pulled it out, the dribble of his loins leaked from the tip. He was spent.

Dana lowered herself flat onto the bed. Her ass was sore, but she was contented and warm.

Derrick flopped beside her and breathed a deep breath. "I had only done that once before. It was nothing like that. My God, Dana, you make me act so different . . . so free. I could grow to really like this feeling."

Dana lay, quiet and smiling at what Derrick had said. She was happy. She was content, and mostly, she was secure with Derrick. There were no games, except for his little toy fetish, and he wasn't afraid or scared to explore her—and himself—sexually.

The room was quiet and Dana sighed a deep, comforting breath. "Derrick?"

"Yeah?"

Dana hesitated then rolled to face Derrick. She looked into his eyes. Her feelings lay naked and exposed, as did her body. "You know how you said you wanted to get out of your place with Tom?"

"As soon as I can. It sucks, babe. You see how it is." Derrick fell to his back, pulled his arms up and linked his fingers behind his head and yawned.

"Well, um, I was thinking. Um, you know how I told you about my work and how I may have to change jobs?"

"Yes, I remember you telling me, Dana, just say it. What's on your mind?"

"Would you like to move in here with me? I mean, you already stay here all night when you come over." Dana twisted her fingers in the thin patch of hair on his chest, hoping he'd agree.

"Hmmmmm, I would like the thought of waking up next to you every morning. Of course, it would help me get everything straightened out." Derrick scratched his head and rolled onto his side.

"On one condition. I won't budge on this either. You know I am building a house over by the lake, don't you?" he asked.

"No, you didn't tell me that." Dana was surprised. Imagine, a nice lake house with Derrick all shirtless and . . . she had to concentrate.

"When I finish you have to come stay a few weeks with me and let me pamper and spoil the hell out of you. I have been working on it for about a year on weekends. I just need to get a few friends to help me move the wood flooring and sheetrock in and I'll have it done in a few months."

"Oh God, Derrick, it sounds great. If you need someone to help you move the big stuff I have a friend that might be able to help." Dana now thought of her and Kris lying on the deck, watching their beefcakes working outside and their muscles flexing and . . . concentrate, Dana, concentrate.

"You have to let me pay for half of the bills, too. I don't want you taking care of everything. You've seen me eat. Can you imagine the food bill?" Derrick smiled with a devilish grin.

Dana smiled. "Well, you are a big eater. But I guess I could live with your conditions, even though I don't want to. I'd understand that you don't want to seem like you are taking advantage of a poor innocent lady. You know, a 'Sugar Momma' and you're my sex slave."

"That does have a nice ring to it, huh?" Derrick held out his hand in a gesture to secure the deal.

"A handshake? You must be kidding. I'll need something much more substantial than a handshake." Dana giggled and rolled on top of Derrick.

For a single moment, everything seemed almost perfect. Everything was the way it should be. Nothing could make Dana happier. Derrick stared into her eyes and ran his fingers through her hair. He pulled her close and kissed her ever so gently. Like petals of a flower against skin, he was so tender. Dana realized she was wrong.

Now, kissing this man, the moment was perfect.

Chapter Eleven

Stephanie's Party

Dana sat after her presentation at the party, confused and a little upset. The ladies all seemed to be having fun goofing off with their door prizes.

"Dana? What's wrong?" Christina asked, sitting down next to her.

"What? Oh sorry. I'm fine, just thinking."

"Well, this was a great party. I was happy Stephanie invited me. I always miss out on the stuff with the girls." Christina was a pretty blonde. She talked very little during the party.

Dana noticed she had bought some of the Stay Hard oils and a really nice Pyrex dildo. The dildo alone was a hundred and thirty bucks and made this her first thousand-dollar party.

"If you need an ear I am free to listen. I know I'm a stranger but sometimes it helps."

"Well," Dana started. "My boss at my full-time job doesn't think I should do these parties anymore. He's afraid it will hurt the company '*image*' if some clients find out. I think it sucks."

"You are in advertising, aren't you? You mentioned that in your presentation."

"Yes, I mean, I shouldn't say anything but I am a senior account executive at Smith and Anderson." Dana was leery of bitching about work, but Christina seemed to be so nice and listened to her as she complained. It actually was helping her to talk about it. "My boss is a nice guy but he works all the time and is so anal about everything. I personally think he needs a good dose of some *hot sex*." She laughed, thinking about what she was saying.

Christina listened, then piped in, "Really? I have heard of that company. I don't think it is any of their business what you do on your own time. It's not like you are a prostitute or doing something illegal. You are, ummmm, how do you say it? Spreading the message. Maybe that should be spreading the good vibrations." Christina smiled and saw Dana's mood brightening, so decided to ask her about a few products.

"Hey, fuck that place, I need to ask you about these toys!" Christina was giddy and bouncing in her seat.

"Okay, what would you like to know?"

Looking at some of the other ladies Christina slyly pulled out her small bottle of Stay Hard cream. "How does this work?"

Wiggling her eyebrows, Dana said, "Great." She continued, "This desensitizes his penis a little so he will last longer during intercourse. In other words, he can fuck longer." Smiling, she watched Christina blush.

Christina looked at the bottle, then looked up at Dana.

Dana sensed her wanting to know more. "Here, I have a small sample of it. Let me see your hand." Dana put a small amount on Christina's fingertip and some on hers. She rubbed her fingertips together and Christina followed form. "See how it feels silky and smooth? In a few seconds you'll feel how it will start to tingle and get a bit numb."

Smiling, Christina nodded with a goofy grin on her face. "This feels weird. Does he still feel, ummm, I mean, when he's inside, does it feel different?"

"He will feel the same to you when you are having sex. It will just make him last longer because he will be a little desensitized. It can affect you a little too, but trust me, you'll love it!"

Dana saw Stephanie motioning for her to come over to talk to a few of the other ladies.

"Christina, I'd love to talk more but Stephanie is asking me to come over to her. Here you read this write-up on the Stay Hard lube? I'll be back in a bit." Dana got up and walked over to the small group of ladies next to Stephanie.

"Okay, Dana. You tell them about the glow thing. You know *the glow* thing." She winked and nudged Dana's shoulder.

"Ohhhhhhh, *that* thing. This ought to be fun. All right, ladies, this will help any man see in the dark and make sure he finds the right hole." Dana was giggling while she dug through her bag.

"Stephanie, turn off the lights."

The room became dark. The flicker of candlelight from the kitchen was the only illumination. Dana pulled out a glow-in-the-dark dildo. Like a lightning rod, it glowed bright. She then grabbed some condoms, a glow-in-the-dark sleeve and glow-in-the-dark pleasure balls.

"Now, this is a good friend to have during a power outage." Dana held the dildo in her hand. "It also works as a light saber or you can use it as a rolling pin."

The ladies all laughed. Dana handed them a blue and red one. They sipped their wine and took turns holding the toy and playing like Darth Vader.

Dana felt proud about what she was doing. The party ended and she said goodbye to the new acquaintances she had made. Christina gave her and Stephanie a hug and waved goodbye. With three more bookings she wondered if she should pass them on to another consultant.

"She's a nice woman. I liked her," Dana told Stephanie as they packed up.

"Yeah, but her husband is an asshole. He treats her like shit. If he knew she came here he'd flip." Stephanie turned as the phone rang. She picked it up and started laughing and talking to her husband.

Dana waved and let herself out as Stephanie started telling her husband about the party.

Working Hard

Starbucks was busy as usual and Dana stood waiting for her Caramel Frappachino. While leaning against the counter she read the want ads. She hadn't read through them with a purpose in quite a while.

Someone thumped Dana on the shoulder. "Hey, bitch, give me the damn paper."

Confused and now grumpy because she hadn't had her coffee, Dana turned around putting on her meanest "don't fuck with me" face.

"Oh my God. How have you been, Kris?"

"Oh, give me a hug, we shared a helluva lot more than most women." Kris gave Dana a big hug and they just happened to call their names at the same time for their order.

"You wanna sit down and talk?" Kris asked before she ripped the lid off her mocha and took a big swig. "Ohhhhhh, almost as good as sex . . . almost. So why are you looking at the want ads?"

"Well, my job isn't too happy with me. They sort of asked me to stop doing some things I like doing."

Kris looked at Dana, then looked around, then looked back at her. "Hey, Dana? This is me here, you know . . . Kris. What's wrong?"

Dana sighed. Kris was right. "My boss asked me to stop having the Pleasure Parties. He thinks it might hurt the company image if some of our clients find out. It's stupid."

"And what you do on your own time after hours is their business because . . ." Kris shook her head. "How anal can you get? If the so-called clients knew what most of the management did after hours they'd shit. Sorry, it just upsets me a little. You want me to have Adam go over there and rough him up?" Kris grinned.

"How is Adam? "

"Mmmmm, yummy. Oh, you mean how is he doing. He's doing great. Working his ass off but I give him a rubdown with some of those oils I bought from you. It's a tough job rubbing that big muscular chest but I suffer through it."

Dana remembered that wide, tanned, muscular chest vividly. "What a sacrifice you put up with, tsk, tsk."

"What about you? How're things in the singles scene?" Kris sipped her coffee and leaned back in the chair.

"Remember that guy I told you about? The one you told me to *go for it* with?" Dana blushed, knowing her happiness began to bubble over.

"I think his name was Derrick or Dave, I think it was Derrick." Kris tried to remember.

"Yes, Derrick, he and I are together now. Now don't tell Adam and don't take this personally but Adam has moved down to number two on the best sex chart for me."

"Well, you little slut! You mean you two hooked up? That's great. We'll all four have to go out sometime. If he's into football, he and Adam will hit it off just fine. Adam won't say anything, Dana. He's a gentleman and never talks. I love that about him."

Dana blushed again, and as her confidence with Derrick grew so did her realization that she wasn't going to let her work dictate her life. She liked her job but sitting there talking to Kris reminded her of why she started her little side job in the first place. Now, instead of seeing the effects she had on others, she saw the effect she had on herself.

She was a strong, sexy, confident woman with a man that understood and cared deeply for her. She had made her decision and if her work didn't like it, she would go somewhere else.

After finishing their coffee, Dana gave Kris a big hug again and swapped phone numbers with her.

"You give Adam a hug for me, okay?" Dana winked to Kris and waved.

Loud enough for everyone to hear Kris blurted out, "I'll give Adam a blowjob for you. That'll make him happier!"

Dana turned twelve shades of red, scurried out the side door and then burst into laughter.

It was time for her meeting with the boss, and she decided to go a bit early. Things would be fine. She now had Derrick moving in, she had a great job and the Pleasure Parties were her fun, but she couldn't throw everything away because of it. Her boss would have to make a choice.

Christina was frantically rubbing her swollen clit while her husband fucked her like a wild animal on his desk. "Shit, I am going to have to buy a case of this from Dana, your cock is so hard. Oh baby, mmmmmm, ohhh."

Christina's face was straining as she felt herself letting go. "Oh yeah, baby, oh yeah, fuck me harder, oh yeah, like that. Oh my God, I'm coming, baby, I'm coming, I . . . ahhhhh, mmmmm."

Her husband grabbed her hips and the steady slapping sound from his stomach striking her ass filled the room.

Christina's pussy convulsed and she felt the tingling effect of the Stay Hard oil on her clit.

"Oh damn, mmmm, I can't hold it anymore, mmmm. You feel so fricking good. I can feel you inside, mmmm, it's been so long." Her husband's voice moaned as his back arched and he drove his cock in to its fullness.

"Mmmmmm, damn, that stuff works fucking great. Come on, baby, come on." Christina now had a wide smile and her eyes were closed tightly as she felt her lover about to explode.

With a loud groan and one final thrust, Christina felt her husband erupt inside her. His cock spewed his hot seed over and over. She wallowed in the bliss of satisfying her man. For too long they had been just husband and wife. She had missed her lover.

As she collapsed on her back, she heard her husband laugh as he staggered backward and awkwardly tried to compose himself. His face was flushed. Christina pulled her pantyhose up and brushed the front of her dress.

"I'll see you at home later, dear. You better tidy up. You have meetings today. Thanks for lunch." Christina patted her husband on the crotch, making him flinch, and kissed him on the cheek as she strolled out of his office.

Dana walked down the hall toward William's office. She was rereading her resignation letter to herself again, making sure she got her point across if he forced her hand.

Turning the corner, she slammed right into another woman walking in the other direction. Stunned, she knelt down to pick up her paper and looked up to see Christina. Still wobbly from butting her head, Christina looked at Dana with a raised eyebrow and an unhappy scowl.

"Sorry, Christina, what the hell are you doing here?"

Christina's frown turned to a smile and she said, "I was here seeing my husband. Sweetie, that cream *really* works *great*!"

"Christina? Ummmm, your dress is tucked into your nylons in the back." Dana snickered.

Christina rolled her eyes back and turned bright red. "I am such a blonde sometimes." She straightened herself out and turned back to look at Dana. "Where are you going?"

"Well, I am putting in my notice. Remember I told you that my boss was threatening me with my . . . ummm, my job and . . . and Christina, who is your husband?"

Smiling, Christina answered back, "William is my husband. I couldn't say anything because most of the ladies there know Will and don't know who I am. I apologize. But you'll be happy I am his wife."

Christina gave her a hug and waved goodbye, snickering under her breath. Dana was a little worried but didn't really care as she watched Christina pulling her underwear from her butt.

Dana went to William's office and knocked on the door. It creaked on its hinges and Dana pushed the door open wide. William had his back to the door and was fumbling with his zipper.

"Ahem, um, William, I am here for our meeting." Dana was torn between turning away, or standing and watching.

"Ummm, yes Dana, umm, yes, the meeting." William finally turned around, straightening his tie. His shirt was buttoned wrong and his zipper wasn't pulled all the way up. He tried to hide the bulge in his pants by closing his sports jacket. It was to no avail because the bulge made the folds of the jacket open.

Dana sat down and tried not to laugh. She waited until William adjusted himself and finally began to speak. "William, I have been giving this a lot of thought. I love my job here and think I have earned a lot of respect from coworkers as well as management. But I can't be blind to the fact that you threatened my livelihood because I happen to have a hobby selling lingerie and pleasure products to women."

William sat there listening to Dana very intently. His silence, however, was beginning to bother Dana. She wasn't sure what he was thinking.

"William, I just don't think my work should be interfering with my life outside. It doesn't affect the company and basically it is none of your damn business what I do after hours. So I am giving you my notice. As soon as I train someone to replace me I'm leaving." She handed William her resignation letter.

For a moment, there was a deafening silence. Then William sat forward in his chair and looked at Dana.

"Dana, I was wrong. I can't accept your resignation. You are too important to this company. I mistook my position and worries and thought it would affect this company. To be blunt, it isn't any of my damn business, like you say. I hope you accept my apology and stay here. The clients love your professionalism and your bright spirit. I wish we had more of that here." William held her letter in his hand and motioned for her to take it back.

For a moment Dana sat, contemplating what to do. She sighed, took the letter and tore it in half. Tossing it into the trash she knew what she really wanted to do was stay.

"William, be honest. What changed your mind?"

"It was a few things actually, Dana. For one, you were right in what you said. Also, I don't like to mess with a good thing. We are doing well as a company and having you leave would mess things up, and you are up for a promotion in three months. I don't think we could find a qualified replacement. Dana, I don't want you to leave. Nobody does. It was a bad decision for me to act like it was a problem for the company. And . . ." William paused and looked around the room as if worried he would be heard.

"And Christina talked to me and told me how much fun she had the other night. If these 'parties' you have cause that kind of reaction I see nothing wrong with them. In fact, I encourage them!" William winked and he and Dana started to laugh.

William stood up and reached his hand out. Dana stood up and shook it. They smiled back at each other and Dana turned to leave.

"Um, William? I couldn't help but notice your, ummm, your fly is down."

"I have to tell you, this damn cream stuff you sold my wife is incredible. Can I get a bulk discount?"

They both burst into laughter and Dana replied, "I'm sure we can work something out later. Thank you, William."

Chapter Twelve

Party On, Derrick
Party On, Dana

The loud crash of the champagne bottle was followed by applause. The small group of friends was gathered at Derrick's "newly finished" cabin by the lake. It had taken longer than expected, but from the huge redwood deck that overlooked the lake to the gazebo with a bench swing surrounded by blooming roses, it was perfect.

"Oh, man. The place is beautiful but my back is fucking killing me." Kris bent backward as if stretching out her sore muscles.

"Shouldn't you be resting? I mean, you are six months pregnant. But you can't tell by looking at you," Dana added, trying to make Kris feel better. She was miserable.

Dana and Kris stood sipping at their drinks. Dana had a little champagne and Kris had sparkling cider.

"No offense, but this stuff tastes like shit! I would kill for a kamikaze. Or a daiquiri, or a Sex on the Beach." Kris was a little grumpy.

"You poor thing. After you guys have the baby you'll have to bring Adam back up here for a sex weekend." Dana rubbed Kris on the back while standing with her. "I mean, he helped Derrick so much with the floor and the decking. Without his help Derrick wouldn't have gotten the place done for a year."

"Well, it's your fault I'm pregnant."

"Mine? How?" Dana asked.

"Adam saw how you and Derrick were so happy. He got all mushy and wanted us to get engaged and all that. I was going to ask you to share Derrick with me but Adam got serious so I just couldn't. I mean, he is yummy. I am so happy for you, Dana. Really I am. I'm just moody and horny."

"Well, you know we have the guest room. You two can always, well, you know."

Kris looked at Dana with a desperate stare. "We can't have sex until after the baby is born. Adam is so big the doctor doesn't want his weight on me, or the extra pressure from sex. It fucking sucks. I have given him so many blowjobs my lips have calluses."

Derrick and Adam stood looking over the stained wooden railing they had built just two weeks earlier.

"Hey, I told you they'd get their asses kicked in New York." Adam finished his comment then downed his beer.

"Adam, I appreciate all you did for me. Dude, without you this place wouldn't be half as far along. That deal you hooked me up with for the brickwork, man. I owe you."

"Derrick, you don't owe me shit. I didn't have too many guys that I could just hang with that weren't hitting on Kris. You have been really cool and Dana is a wonderful, wonderful woman. She has been great for Kris and she offered to help with watching the baby and stuff." Adam reached over to the cooler and grabbed another bottle of beer and tossed one to Derrick.

"Adam, Dana told me about you guys that night after the party. She wanted everything in the open with us. I know it was before she and I got together so it's cool. She said I am better in bed, though."

Adam spewed his beer as he started to laugh. "You asshole."

Dana and Kris stood by the table with the food on it and Kris was constantly picking at the celery and carrots, dipping them in the ranch dressing. She had more dressing than vegetables as the dressing dripped down onto her belly.

Christina tripped coming out of the French doors and was giggling. Behind her William tried his best not to laugh.

Dana looked at Christina, who was laughing and all goofy.

Kris stared at Dana, then motioned with her fingers, like a cock in a hole, and nodded her head in their direction.

"Hey, where were you guys? Ummm, Christina . . . ummmm . . . your skirt is on backwards." Dana grinned, knowing what they were doing.

"Another blonde moment." Christina was trying to adjust her clothes and William walked by and gave her ass a healthy squeeze.

"I'm going over to see what the guys are doing. Hopefully they are talking about the playoffs. I need some sucker to take a bet."

William kissed Christina on the forehead and held his hand out to Dana. "Great party, Dana. I am really happy everything has worked out so well. The company had that merger and our stocks went through the roof. And I have to say, you have been an inspiration to Christina and I. Things are like when we first got married."

William looked down at his little belly and looked back up at the girls. "Well, like before with a few extra pounds. Derrick has built a beautiful house here."

Dana blushed and replied, "Remember what he said. You two can come up here whenever you feel the need to get away. Just don't forget to bring a second set of sheets." Dana laughed as William smirked, then rolled his eyes. He walked toward the guys, who were looking over the railing.

The three women stood, watching their men talking loudly and acting all manly.

It was a nice moment. There was a small group of friends at the housewarming. Just friends. The day was beautiful. The afternoon breeze crossed the lake and cooled the sun's rays.

"Damn, this dressing is giving me gas!" Kris broke the silence with one of her typical comments.

The party wore down and one by one the guests left.

Kris and Adam left first because she had a horrendous hormonal attack and told Adam she needed Chinese food *right now*!

Christina picked up an order of strawberry-flavored lube and wanted to try it out later that night. All Dana saw was William sitting in his Jaguar and Christina's head lowering into his lap while he pulled out of the driveway.

The few other friends from Dana's work and Derrick's contracting associates filtered out.

Derrick took Dana's hand as the last guest's rear taillights dimmed away from the cabin. "Now we can have a proper housewarming. Let's try every room in the house."

As they walked up the wooden staircase to the bedroom loft, Dana paused.

"Did you bring your tool belt?" Her fiendish smirk widened across her face.

"Yep, and Mr. and Mrs. Potato Head too."